Three Kisses a Day

"Simply make sure that I am kissed three times before the day is out, and you are safe."

The devil was in Hawkeswell's eyes as he teased Verity. Only it was the devil that also suggested he was not only teasing.

"Three, then," she agreed. "So we catch up." She quickly stepped toward him, rose on her toes, and planted a quick kiss on his lips. She tried to peck him again, but he angled back, out of reach.

"That is one," he said. "Two to go."

He appeared to be having a fine joke at her expense. She held herself straight and tall and prepared for the other two.

To her shock, he took her face in his hands. The hold was gentle enough, but very intimate. The sensation of his warm palms against her cheeks startled her. "We did not agree that you could touch me like this. You are just supposed to—"

"Hush," he muttered, his lips hovering near hers, but not exactly kissing her. "When I kiss a woman, I do it properly."

Properly meant he watched while his thumb caressed her lips in a manner that made them sensitive and tingling. It meant nipping her lip, creating a jolt to her body much like an arrow of sensation spiraling downward. It meant a stunning closeness that made her too alert and too aware of him. When his lips finally touched hers, her breath caught.

She did not step back at once. Being held like this, she was not sure she even could. But the kiss provoked something inside her that caused her to forget momentarily that she wanted to get away.

Still cradling her face in his hands, he looked down at her, those blue eyes watching, watching, and darkly pleased with whatever he saw. "That is two."

Jove titles by Madeline Hunter

RAVISHING IN RED
PROVOCATIVE IN PEARLS

Provocative
in Pearls

MADELINE HUNTER

JOVE BOOKS, NEW YORK

THE BERKLEY PUBLISHING GROUP
Published by the Penguin Group
Penguin Group (USA) Inc.
375 Hudson Street, New York, New York 10014, USA
Penguin Group (Canada), 90 Eglinton Avenue East, Suite 700, Toronto, Ontario M4P 2Y3, Canada
(a division of Pearson Penguin Canada Inc.)
Penguin Books Ltd., 80 Strand, London WC2R 0RL, England
Penguin Group Ireland, 25 St. Stephen's Green, Dublin 2, Ireland (a division of Penguin Books Ltd.)
Penguin Group (Australia), 250 Camberwell Road, Camberwell, Victoria 3124, Australia
(a division of Pearson Australia Group Pty. Ltd.)
Penguin Books India Pvt. Ltd., 11 Community Centre, Panchsheel Park, New Delhi—110 017, India
Penguin Group (NZ), 67 Apollo Drive, Rosedale, North Shore 0632, New Zealand
(a division of Pearson New Zealand Ltd.)
Penguin Books (South Africa) (Pty.) Ltd., 24 Sturdee Avenue, Rosebank, Johannesburg 2196,
South Africa

Penguin Books Ltd., Registered Offices: 80 Strand, London WC2R 0RL, England

PROVOCATIVE IN PEARLS

A Jove Book / published by arrangement with the author

ISBN-13: 978-1-61664-031-6

JOVE®
Jove Books are published by The Berkley Publishing Group,
a division of Penguin Group (USA) Inc.,
375 Hudson Street, New York, New York 10014.
JOVE® is a registered trademark of Penguin Group (USA) Inc.
The "J" design is a trademark of Penguin Group (USA) Inc.

PRINTED IN THE UNITED STATES OF AMERICA

Provocative in Pearls

Chapter One

A good friend lets one spill bile, even if he finds it boring. So it was that Grayson, Earl of Hawkeswell, took advantage of Sebastian Summerhays's friendship while they were both trapped in Summerhays's carriage this bright August morning.

"I curse the day my cousin introduced me to the bastard." He heard his voice snarl with anger. He had sworn to himself, *sworn*, that he would not do this, but here he was fuming like a chimney at the idiocy of life and pouring woe into Summerhays's ear.

"Thompson was not at all willing to cooperate?" Summerhays asked.

"Hell, no. But, her trustee has agreed to join me in pressing for a new inquest, and with the help of Providence and the courts, I will be free of this complicated disaster by year's end."

"It makes no sense to interfere with the inquest. The man is not rational if he tries that."

"He wants the connection. Or rather, his wife does. She is mining it for all it is worth while she can, hoping the new ties hold once the connection itself is severed. He is also comfortable with the way things stand. He has control of that company, which is what he wanted. If we end this impasse, he risks losing that."

"It is good for you to be going down to the country, then. You can use some peace."

Summerhays smiled like the good, understanding friend that he was. There was something of the physician's sympathy in his expression, as if he worried for the health of the man he placated.

Hawkeswell saw his umbrage the way Summerhays must, and his anger turned to bitter amusement. "I am a comical figure, am I not? Such are the punishments for selling oneself in marriage for some silver, I suppose."

"Such matches are made all the time. You are the victim of an odd circumstance; that is all."

"Let us hope the circumstances change soon. I am in dun territory up to my eyebrows and have sold what I can. It will be porridge this winter, I think."

The talk turned to other things, but part of Hawkeswell's mind remained fixed on the marital conundrum that had plagued him for two years. Verity had drowned in the Thames, but her body had never been found. How she got there on her wedding day, why she left his estate at all, remained a mystery. There were those who wanted to blame him.

His old reputation for a bad temper fed that speculation, but any fool could see it was not in his interest for Verity to disappear that day. An unconsummated marriage was an ambiguous marriage, as her trustee had so clearly explained when he refused to hand over her income from her trust. The Church would have to decide if there had been a marriage at all if she were ever declared dead. In the meantime . . .

In the meantime, her husband, or maybe not her husband, could wait. He could not remarry while she officially was still alive. The money that led him to the altar was out of reach, however. He was in limbo.

That powerlessness goaded him. He resented being a pawn of fate. Worse, this could go on for years.

"I appreciate your company, Summerhays. You are too good to tell me I am tedious. It was generous of you to suggest I accompany you out of town before taking to horse for Surrey."

"You are not tedious. You are on the horns of a dilemma and I regret that I have no solution. Since you will not allow me to lend—"

"I do not want one more debt, least of all to a friend. I have no expectations of being able to repay what is gone already."

"Of course. However, if it does come down to porridge, perhaps you will accept my offer for the sake of your cousin and aunt."

"I cannot accept." Except he could, of course. If it got that bad, he probably would. It was one thing to suffer this himself, but even worse to watch it affect those for whom he was responsible. He carried considerable guilt already, not only for his aunt and cousin, but also for the good people who lived on his entailed lands and who deserved more care and generosity than he could afford.

"Did you tell your wife that you were coming down a day early?" he asked. Summerhays had married in the spring, and his wife visited her friends in Middlesex with some frequency. Her stays this summer were often extended, to avoid the heat in town.

"I cleared my affairs so late yesterday that there was no point. I will surprise her. Audrianna will not mind."

Hawkeswell admired the security with which his friend said that. Generally women did mind when husbands interfered with their plans. If Summerhays were another kind of man, and his wife another kind of woman, showing up unexpectedly, a day early, at a house party in the country could lead to some awkward explanations.

The coach rolled down the main lane of the village of Cumberworth, with his black gelding trotting along on its tether. He would have to visit his aunt once he reached Surrey, he supposed, and tell her that he would soon have to let her town house go. It would not be a pleasant meeting.

Even worse would be the consultations with his steward, who would again advise enclosures of the common ground on the estate. Hawkeswell had long resisted following the modern practices on that. He had sought to avoid the hardships that enclosures would bring to the families whose lives depended on that land.

People who had not seen the roofs over their heads maintained properly by their landlord should not now be deprived yet again, and in worse ways. His finances had become dire, however, and unless they improved soon, everyone would suffer anyway.

The coach took a turn outside the town. A half mile along, it carefully made another turn onto a private lane. A sign marked the property: THE RAREST BLOOMS.

The coachman stopped where the trees fell away in front of a pleasant stone house surrounded by a handsome perennial garden of free, rustic design. Summerhays opened the coach door. "You must come and meet the ladies. Audrianna will want to see you."

"I will take my horse and be off. It is you she will be happy to see."

"The horse needs to rest. I insist you come with me. Mrs. Joyes will give you some refreshment before you begin your ride, and you can see the back garden. It is among the finest in Middlesex."

Since the duties waiting in Surrey did not encourage haste, Hawkeswell fell into step beside his friend and they walked to the door. A thin woman opened it and curtsied when she saw Summerhays.

"Lady Sebastian was not expecting you today, sir. She is not packed, and is in the garden."

"That is fine, Hill. I will not mind waiting. I can find my own way to the garden, if you have other duties."

Hill curtsied again, but walked with them through the house. They passed a sitting room and a cozy, small library, crowded with stuffed chairs. Hill left them when they entered another, more informal sitting room in the back.

"Come with me," Summerhays said. He guided the way down a corridor that gave into a large greenhouse. "Mrs. Joyes and the ladies have a business here, called The Rarest Blooms. You have seen their artistry at my wedding, and at many parties last season. This is where they work their magic."

The greenhouse was impressive, and large. Citrus trees and ferns, plants and vines, filled it with greenery and scents. High windows had been opened and a cross breeze fluttered leaves and petals.

They strolled to the back, where a grape vine laden with

clusters of fruit hung over some iron chairs and a stone table.

Hawkeswell looked out through the wall of glass. Distorting waves in the rectangular panes made the scene beyond more a watercolor wash than a Renaissance oil, as colors paled and blended and blurred. Even so, one could identify four women out there, at what appeared to be an arbor near a brick wall on the far side of the property.

Summerhays opened a door and the images clarified. It was a rose arbor covered with white blooms. Audrianna sat on a bench under the arbor, beside the pale, perfect Mrs. Joyes of the dark gray eyes. Hawkeswell had met Daphne Joyes at Summerhays's wedding.

Two other women sat on the grass, facing the bench. One was a blonde with elaborately dressed hair. The other wore a simple straw bonnet, and its deep brim obscured her profile.

Mrs. Joyes noticed the gentlemen emerging from the greenhouse. She raised her arm in greeting.

The two women on the ground swung their heads to see whom Mrs. Joyes hailed. Then that bonnet turned back and the woman wearing it gave her attention to Audrianna.

An odd sensation vibrated in Hawkeswell, like a plucked string of a soundless instrument. That patch of grass was shaded, and that bonnet made deeper shadows. And yet . . .

He peered hard at that bonnet, so still now. It did not turn again, even as Audrianna and Mrs. Joyes called for Summerhays to join them. The tilt of the head, however, made that string pluck again.

He walked toward them with Summerhays, along sand paths that meandered amid thousands of flowers.

"Who are the others?" he asked. "The ones sitting on the ground."

"The blonde is Miss Celia Pennifold. The other is Miss Elizabeth Smith. Lizzie, they call her."

"You have met them before?"

"Oh, yes. I am well acquainted with all the rarest blooms."

Hawkeswell exhaled deeply. Of course Summerhays would have met them all. The alarm in his instincts was uncalled for.

"Well, not Lizzie, now that you mention it. I had never realized it before, but while I have seen her in the garden and through the greenhouse glass or even passing by in that bonnet, I do not think that we have ever been introduced."

They approached the ladies. The bonnet's crown remained resolutely turned to them. No one else seemed to notice that, or consider it rude, in the chaotic exchange of greetings and introductions that followed.

No one seemed to realize that Lizzie had never been introduced to Audrianna's husband, either, just as Summerhays himself had not. But an earl had entered the garden for the first time, and that head's immobility could not last forever in the courtesies that followed. Eventually Audrianna began the official introduction to Lizzie.

The bonnet rose as Lizzie stood. Blood pounded in Hawkeswell's head as that lithe body, hidden beneath its shaft of simple blue muslin, turned. Head bowed modestly and deep brim shadowing her face, Lizzie curtsied.

The pounding eased. No, he had been wrong. And yet his memories of the particulars were so vague. So shockingly vague. But, no, his mind had played a trick with him; that was all.

"I will go ask Hill to bring out refreshments," Lizzie said quietly. Very quietly. Like a whisper.

She curtsied again, and walked away. The circle of women and the buzz of talk did not much notice her leave.

The tilt of that head again. The manner of walking. The pounding began again, savagely.

"Stop."

Everyone froze at his command and stared at him. Except Lizzie. She kept walking and did not look back. Her gait altered, though. She looked ready to bolt.

He strode after her and grabbed her arm.

"Lord Hawkeswell—*really*," Mrs. Joyes scolded, her expression one of stunned surprise. She looked with distressed curiosity at Summerhays.

"Hawkeswell—" Summerhays began.

He raised a hand to silence Summerhays. He stared at the delicate nose visible beyond the bonnet's brimmed profile. "Look at me, please. Now. I demand it."

She did not look at him, but after a long pause she did turn toward him. She shook his grasp off her arm and faced him. Long, thick dark lashes almost touched her snow-white cheek.

Something shivered through her. Anger? Fear? He had never before felt someone's spirit react as he did in that moment.

Those lashes rose. It was not the face that told him for certain. Not its oval shape or her dark hair or her rose of a mouth. Rather it was the resignation and sorrow and hint of rebellion in her blue eyes.

"*Damnation*, Verity. It *is* you."

Chapter Two

"If she is not down here in two minutes, I am going up there. I swear that I will tear this house down with my bare hands if I have to and—"

"Calm yourself, sir. I am sure there has been a misunderstanding."

"Calm myself? *Calm myself?* My missing wife, assumed dead for two years, has been living the sweet country life here, mere miles from London, knowing full well the world was looking for her, and you say I should *calm myself*? Let me remind you, Mrs. Joyes, that your role in this borders on criminal and that—"

"I will not listen to threats, Lord Hawkeswell. When you have composed yourself enough to have a civil discussion, send word to me. In the meantime, I will be at the top of the stairs, with my pistol, should you think to be brutish." Mrs. Joyes floated her ethereal, pale elegance out of the sitting room.

Summerhays had been poking in cabinets. "Ah, here is

some port. Stop that infernal pacing and get that temper of yours under control, Hawkeswell. You are in danger of being an unforgivable ass."

He could not stop pacing. Or looking at the ceiling toward where *that woman* had taken refuge. "If ever a man in the history of the world had an excuse to be an ass, Summerhays, it is I. She has made a fine one out of me, anyway, so I lose little in playing the part."

. "No glass. This will have to do." He held a delicate teacup in one hand and poured the port. "Now, drink this and count to fifty. Like old times, when you got like this."

"I will look idiotic drinking out of that— Oh, what the hell." He grabbed the cup and downed its contents. It didn't help much at all.

"Now, count."

"I'll be damned if—"

"Count. Or I will end up having to thrash sense into you, and it has been many years since your temper forced that on me. One, two, three . . ."

Gritting his teeth, Hawkeswell counted. And paced. The red drained out of his head but the anger hardly dimmed. "I don't believe that Mrs. Joyes did not know who she was. Or that your wife did not."

"If you dare to imply again that my wife lied in saying she was ignorant, I will not finish with you until you need a wagon to bring you back to town," Summerhays said dangerously.

"Don't forget, as you remember old times, that I give as well as I get, or better." Hawkeswell bit back his fury and paced out his count. "What the bloody hell is this place?" he asked when he got to thirty. "Who takes in a stranger and does not even ask her history? It is insane. Mad."

"It is a rule here, not to ask. Apparently Mrs. Joyes has cause to know there are often good reasons why women deny their histories and leave their pasts behind completely."

"I can't imagine why."

"Can't you?"

Hawkeswell stopped pacing and glared at Summerhays. "If you imply that she had reason to be afraid of me, I swear that I will call you out. Bloody hell, she barely knew me."

"That alone might make some women fearful, I expect."

"You are talking nonsense now."

Summerhays shrugged. "You are only at forty-five."

"I am fine now."

"Let us keep it neat."

Hawkeswell stomped five more steps. "There. Now I am all becalmed. Go tell Mrs. Joyes that I *demand to speak to my wife, damn it.*"

Summerhays folded his arms and inspected him carefully. "Another fifty, I think."

Lizzie sat on her bed, listening to the bellows of indignation coming from below. She would have to go down there soon. She could be forgiven, she thought, for taking a few minutes to prepare herself, and to accommodate herself to the notion of prison before the gaol door actually closed.

She had been a sentimental fool. She should have left as soon as Audrianna agreed to marry Lord Sebastian last spring. Or at least last week, after her twenty-first birthday passed. She had known that she had a war to fight once she came of age. Now she might not be able to fire a single shot.

Hawkeswell would have found her eventually when she returned to the world. There would have been no way to avoid that. However, she had planned to be among people who knew her and who would help, and she would have been prepared for him. Now dallying in this house had brought catastrophe, and she might find herself imprisoned by that marriage after all this effort to avoid it.

She stopped castigating herself. It had not been mere sentiment that made her put off her departure. She had not really been a fool. Love had kept her here, more love than she had known in years. She could be excused for surrendering to the lure of spending one final week with her dear friends, all of them together one last time. The news that Audrianna would visit had come the very day she planned to say good-bye, and it had been enough to vanquish her weak resolve and growing fear.

Stomping shook the house. Another curse penetrated the floorboards. Hawkeswell was in fine form.

That was to be expected of any man making such an unexpected discovery, but she had always suspected he had more of that male fury than most. She had surmised at once that they would not suit each other when they first met. They never would now, that was certain. He was in league with Bertram in all of this, of course. And she had humiliated him by running away and not dying for real.

A delicate rap on her door sought her attention. She did not want to face her friends any more than she wanted to face the man spilling curses below, but neither could be avoided. She bid them enter.

They came in wearing expressions much as she expected. Audrianna was wide-eyed with astonishment beneath her fashionably dressed chestnut hair, but then, she was too good to imagine a woman daring such a thing. Celia, who probably could imagine women doing any manner of things, appeared merely very curious. And Daphne—well, Daphne was exquisite and pale and composed, as always, and did not seem very surprised at all.

Daphne sat beside her on the bed. Celia sat on the other side. Audrianna stood in front of her.

"Lizzie—" Audrianna began. She caught herself as the name emerged, and flushed.

"I have thought of myself as Lizzie for two years. I suppose that you should call me Verity now, however. I expect I had better get used to it again."

Audrianna's face fell, as if she had clung to the belief that this was all a mistake.

"Then he is correct," Daphne said. Her tone indicated that she had rather hoped it was a mistake too. "There has been no error. You are the missing bride of Hawkeswell."

"Did you never guess, Daphne?" Verity asked.

"No. Perhaps I have been blind. That tragedy seemed far away and in another world. Never once did I think the young woman I came upon near the river that day was the girl who had gone missing."

"I guessed. Or rather, I wondered," Celia said. "Once or twice, it crossed my mind."

Audrianna gawked at pretty, blond Celia. Celia in turn took Verity's hand and patted it. "But then I would say to myself, no, it can't be. That girl is dead for certain. Lizzie can't be that girl unless she has lost her memory. A woman does not run away on her wedding day to live in frugality and obscurity. Especially if she is an heiress, and her new husband is an earl."

No one said anything. There was a rule in this house.

One did not pry. One did not demand explanations. It was why she had been able to stay here. Now, she knew, explanations were very much on everyone's mind.

"Why?" Audrianna blurted.

"I am sure there was a good reason," Daphne said, coming to her defense.

Verity rose from the bed. She went to her looking glass and eyed the damage the bonnet had done to her hair. Should she set herself to rights before going below and facing Hawkeswell? It would be courteous. Only she feared the gesture would put her at more of a disadvantage.

She had to smile at her calculations. She suspected every woman was at a disadvantage with Hawkeswell, and that he took the imbalance for granted. Not only his title tipped the scales. He was a handsome man, tall, lean, and broad shouldered, almost godlike in his physical person. Even without his ruggedly chiseled face, those blue eyes would leave most women stammering all by themselves.

It had been those eyes that told her she had been found when he entered the garden. In her quick glance, that was all she had seen, and she had known him at once. Even from across a garden on a sunny day you could not miss noticing eyes the color of sapphires.

"I did not choose that marriage." She set about straightening the dark topknot of hair that had gone askew. Celia came over, pushed her hands away, and dealt with it better. "My cousin Bertram coerced me. He tried to force me, but I would not agree to it. Finally he tricked me. I discovered right after the ceremony how it was done, how a promise made to me, to obtain my consent, had been a lie."

"What kind of promise would make you take such an irrevocable step?" Daphne asked.

Two years of discretion had formed a habit, and she hesitated telling them. She did not want to bring any more trouble to Daphne. However, she also feared that they now reassessed her character, and wondered if the promise had been some small, silly thing.

"Near my home, there is a woman whom I love like a mother. Bertram threatened to have her son transported, or worse, for his political views. My cousin has influence in the county, and friends with even more influence. I do not doubt he could harm that woman and her son if he chose. Right after the wedding, I was told that Bertram had indeed harmed the son, and through the son the mother."

An echo of the series of shocks she had experienced that day sent tremors through her now again. Some of the same rebellious anger leaked into her blood in reaction too, however.

Celia stepped away. Now the looking glass displayed dark hair transformed by an artist, and a young woman with fearful blue eyes struggling to maintain her poise.

Verity faced her dumbfounded friends. "Should I have stayed? Just accepted my fate? I had been badly used. My consent had been obtained through the worst trickery, and I believe Lord Hawkeswell was in on the entire plot. Worse, the deception affected far more than my marital status. I was so angry that I could barely think. I decided that I would not let them do that to me. I would not allow their plan of deceit make me mere chattel. So I ran away."

Audrianna pressed both her palms to her cheeks. Her green eyes misted. "Sebastian was supposed to come tomorrow, not today. You would have avoided him, if he had held to the plan, wouldn't you? He told me below that he was at your wedding, and would recognize you, so you managed never to meet him, nor he you. He had not realized that until today, how cleverly you always slipped away." She gazed over, still astonished. "I had not realized it either. I am so sorry that my presence here, that my visit and now his untimely arrival, has brought this about. I should have—"

"I will forever be grateful that you made this visit," Verity said, embracing her. "This past week, with all of us together again, has been one of the finest in my life. I will never forget it."

"What are you going to do?" Celia asked.

Verity removed the long apron that covered her simple blue dress. "I am going to go below, and hope that the stranger I married is not too angry to hear what I say."

Chapter Three

Audrianna appeared at the sitting room's door and gestured for her husband. Summerhays went to her and they held a private, whispered conversation.

Audrianna then left, and Summerhays returned. "Verity is coming down. I beg you to hear her out. She may have a very good reason for everything."

Hawkeswell could think of several reasons, and there was nothing good about any of them. "I promise to listen to all she says."

Summerhays did not appear confident that the storm was over. However, the ladies must have concluded it was safe enough because light footfalls could be heard on the stairs. Verity descended into view. The apron was gone. The simple, unadorned blue dress should have made her look very common, but she carried herself with a grace and confidence that would put some duchesses to shame.

She stopped at the threshold to the sitting room. Summerhays excused himself.

"Please close the door as you go," Hawkeswell said.

Summerhays looked to Verity for agreement. She nodded.

It was the first good look Hawkeswell had of his wife in two years. He noted again how few of the particulars survived in his memory. The details of her appearance had quickly faded to mere impressions, along with those of her character.

Lovely, he had thought when he met her, and meek. Young and innocent too. Except for the first, these were not the qualities he sought in women, but then he had never sought a wife before and, of course, different requirements were in order.

She did not look especially meek now. Lovely still, yes. More than before. A little maturity favored her. The hair was just as dark, the face just as white, the eyes just as blue, but a subtle definition enhanced her softness. Her expression struck him as boldly confident for someone caught at what she had done. That prodded his temper, and he concentrated on not reacting to the pokes.

"I ask that you not blame Daphne or any of the others for harboring me. They did not know who I was. I would like your promise that you will do nothing to bring trouble to them."

"My interest is in your behavior, not that of your friends. However, that is a conversation better held later, after we return home."

"I may have no choice except to leave with you, but I will not go willingly."

She did not hesitate to throw down that gauntlet, even if her manner remained mild and quiet. She left him no choice but to reason and cajole, which hardly seemed fair since he was blameless. The alternative would be to use force and be the brute Mrs. Joyes had intimated he might be.

Even his anger could not justify that. Nor would Summerhays agree to help carry her out. Verity had sized up the limitations this situation put on him, and was prepared to exploit them. Which meant she was not meek after all. At least not anymore.

He gestured to a settee. "Won't you sit? If we are going to talk about this here and now, you may as well be comfortable."

She accepted the invitation, but did not sit on the settee. Instead she perched on an armless wooden chair.

"You let us all think that tragedy befell you, Verity. Did you never consider that your acts caused others to grieve?"

"I am very sure that my cousin and his wife did not grieve. As for you— Did you mourn for me, Lord Hawkeswell? Our association was brief and formal, and it was not a love match."

He felt himself flushing. No, he had not mourned. The cool skill with which she put him at a disadvantage increased the pokes at his temper.

"I may not have grieved, Verity, but I did worry. A good deal."

"I am sorry for that. I thought that I would be accepted as deceased after a few months, as the evidence that I fell in the Thames mounted. I never thought two years would pass and still, legally speaking, I was only missing."

"You speak of that evidence with amazing confidence. You planted it, I assume?"

"Oh, yes. I did not want you or Bertram looking for me, so I thought that it would be best if I were thought dead for a while."

Yes, I did it. Deliberately. So sorry it put you through hell.

"There are some people who I think did grieve, however," she said, finally displaying some remorse. "I regret the pain I may have given them."

"A flaw in your plan, then."

"Yes. That is my one consolation in your untimely discovery of me. I can make certain that they know the truth quickly now."

He paced the length of the chamber, deciding how to approach the many questions crowding his head. He felt her gaze on him, and sensed an odd mixture of caution and pique in her. The latter did nothing to calm his own mood.

"Are you attempting to find the proper words to inquire about the state of my virtue, Lord Hawkeswell? I expected that to be foremost in your mind."

Her frankness astonished him. "It is one of many questions that I have, Verity."

"Allow me to put that concern to rest. There has been no grand affair, or even an ordinary one. I am still a virgin."

He was glad to hear it, as far as the answer went. Her virginity hardly put the fullness of the matter to rest. There could still be another man involved. It was the most logical explanation, but all of that could wait for another day.

"And you, Lord Hawkeswell? As long as we are on the topic— What has been the state of your virtue during my absence?"

She astonished him again. Mockery sparked in her eyes at his stunned reaction.

"I read all the papers and scandal sheets," she said. "My proximity to London allowed me to obtain news from all over the country, and keep apprised of the doings of the ton. I think that if we compare virtues, you will agree that you have little right to speculate further about mine."

How in bloody hell had he ended up on the low ground here? "I thought *you* were dead. You knew *I* was not."

Her lids lowered. "No court declared me dead, so I was only missing. I know all about your love affairs, is all I am saying. I do not mind, but I hope that you are not such a hypocrite as to question my word on this matter, or to pursue it any further."

He fought to conquer the profound irritation that she had already bested him twice now in a skirmish where she should not even hold a weapon.

Exasperation won out. He crossed his arms and pinned her in place with a glare he felt all the way to the back of his own head. "Are you going to tell me why you did it? I think that I have a right to know."

Her cool calm seemed to crack. Her blue eyes glinted beneath those feathery lashes. There was nothing contrite in her expression, and precious little fear. However, she stood, as if she concluded that his stance required that she respond from a less submissive height.

"I left because I was not needed anymore for your and my cousin's grand plan. Everyone has had what they wanted for these two years, because the wedding ceremony took care of that. You obtained the money you sought, and Bertram continued to control my father's business, and Nancy has had the social connection she craved. The marriage settlement was all any of you cared about. It did not matter whether I actually lived the marriage during this time."

Her smug satisfaction almost undid him. "It did not work out as you assume it did, I assure you. The law in such situations is much more complex than you guessed."

That startled her enough that her damned poise wobbled. *Good.*

"What do you mean?"

"The settlement has not been settled, as it were. It remains in limbo." *As do I, damn it.*

"Are you saying that you have received *nothing*? No access to the funds held in reserve by that trust? Not even the income from these two years?"

"I have not received one damned pence."

Worry drew her expression. "Your discovery of me has been even more unfortunate than I guessed. If you have been denied even the least of my settlement all this time, I fear that you will never agree to be sensible."

"I am being most sensible. Also very patient. Most other husbands would be reacting very differently."

She tensed, as if it had been a threat, even though he did not intend one. She looked as though she braced herself for a blow, which insulted him and annoyed him even more.

"I meant that it is unlikely that you will listen to my very sensible plan for what to do now," she said carefully.

"The only possible thing to do now is return to London, let the world see you are alive, and make some attempt to put your capricious adventure behind us as we embark, finally, on this union."

"I was *not* capricious. Furthermore, you are incorrect. That is not the only possible thing to do."

"I cannot think of a single other choice."

She was the one who paced now, as if she were a trapped animal. Back and forth in front of him she moved, frowning with distress.

"You can petition for an annulment. It is possible to obtain one. We never even had a wedding night, and I am told—"

"Why would I seek an annulment?"

She stopped walking right in front of him. She no longer played the mild, quiet wife, but revealed herself as an adversary. Emotion tightened her expression and tensed her posture.

"Because *I never wanted this marriage*," she said. "And you do not care either way."

"Of course I care. I consented. I signed the papers. I said the vows. *Just like you*."

"You mean that you care about *the money*. I will find a way to give it to you anyway. The life this marriage demands of me is not the one I was supposed to have."

"I cannot believe that you are suggesting such an absurd idea, Verity. The Church does not give annulments on a woman's whim."

"I did not escape that day to indulge a passing whim."

"Then why? We began with that question, and we now return to it."

She squared her shoulders and looked him right in the eyes. "I did not freely consent."

That took him aback. The Church *did* give annulments for that reason.

"A chamber full of people heard you consent. A witness to your consent is in this house."

"I discovered that my consent had been obtained ignobly and deceitfully."

"Not by me."

"If you say so."

Her distrust infected the air along with her distress and rebellion. The mix did not bode well for the future.

He forced a new calm. He sought to both reassure and soothe her. "I do say so. When did you learn about this deception?"

"Right after the wedding breakfast."

"Tell me what happened."

She examined him as if she debated whether he was

worth the effort. "I resisted the match. In the end, I said the vows only to help a family that I know and love, from my home. Bertram threatened them with great harm if I did not agree to the marriage."

She told the story frankly, and not with a lot of conviction that her husband gave a damn whatever she said. Or perhaps she did not give a damn what he thought of it. He could not tell which way her mind went on that.

"In other words, you set aside your objections for these people, to protect them from Bertram."

She nodded. "Then, right after the wedding breakfast, Nancy spoke to me. Privately. She told me that Bertram had already violated our agreement. That he had done that which he had promised not to do if I married you."

"I am sorry that you believe you were hoodwinked by your cousin Bertram. In the end, however, the wedding did take place, Verity. It is unlikely that your claims now to being unwilling will get a hearing. You have no proof. If such claims were accepted readily, it would be too simple a way out of marriages because people would lie. It is time to accept that the marriage will stand."

"We do not know for certain my claim would not get a fair hearing. You don't want to find out. You do not want to risk losing the money."

They were back to money. He could hardly object. It had been the basis of the marriage, after all. "It is how matches are made. Your anger is perhaps understandable, but with time you will find some happiness, if you allow yourself to do so. Now, we need to arrange our return to London."

Her little fists clenched at her sides and her eyes blazed. "You have not heard anything I have said."

"I have listened carefully to every word. They change

nothing. You are my wife in the law, and that cannot be undone."

"Only because you will not agree to help me try."

"No, I will not."

"And if I do not agree to return to London?"

"Please, do not do this. Do not make me force you to come with me. Even if you find a way to prevent it now, eventually you will have to. You know this. I have rights as your husband. It is just how it is."

"I was not raised by a man who thought that way—*it is just how it is.* I do not think that way either. This more than anything says that we do not suit each other. "

"Two years ago we agreed that we did suit each other. One is not allowed to change one's mind. Nor have I changed mine."

"You and I agreed to *nothing.* Why, this is the first private conversation that we have ever had. If you had demanded the chance to know me back then, you would have learned how we did not suit, and the reasons why I resisted the offer in the first place."

His temper had frayed badly, but he held on to it despite her infuriating stubbornness.

"You have made it explicitly clear that you assume this marriage will be a type of hell, Verity. I can only say in response that you had better find a way to survive the flames, because what is done is done, and you are now discovered, and there is no undoing it. I have heard you out and I understand your views all too well. Nonetheless, I will send to Cumberworth for a hired carriage, and we will return to London forthwith."

Her chin rose and her eyes sparkled with anger. "I will not go willingly. This marriage was never supposed to happen. *You* were never supposed to happen."

"As if I give a damn about that," he snapped. "You had best pack what you want, or you will go with the clothes on your back."

She eyed him from head to toe, taking his measure. Discouragement tinged her determination, but did not defeat it.

"I expect that you have the strength to force me into that carriage when it comes. So be it. In the meantime, I will retire to the places in this home where I have enjoyed a rare peace, and await your forcible exercise of your rights."

Chapter Four

The new hybrid pelargonium looked a little peaked. A line of yellow edged two of its leaves.

"It has had too much sun. You must promise me to move it back in the afternoons until late September," Verity said to Celia. "New hybrids are such unknowns in these things."

"I will remember to tell Daphne."

They continued their stroll down the aisle between the tables that held a variety of potted plants and Verity's horticultural experiments.

It was either luck or fate's plan that it had been Daphne who came upon her that day, and who eventually offered a home with this greenhouse attached. Although she had always enjoyed flowers, she had not gardened until arriving here. Now she did so with a passion, and was happiest either outside or in here, checking her plants and watching the miracle of growth day by day.

"Lord Sebastian was trying to convince Hawkeswell to

avoid acting in haste when I passed the front sitting room," Celia said.

"I doubt that Lord Sebastian will have much success. Nor, if it comes to it, will he stand against Hawkeswell on my behalf. I am about to lose any freedom I hoped to have, and I may never see this home again."

"You will convince Hawkeswell to let you come visit us, as Audrianna did with Sebastian."

"Hawkeswell is an earl, and one who is proud of his privileges and heritage. He married down, but he will not allow me to keep what I know, because it will reflect on him. You taught me these things about the highborn, Celia, so do not put a pretty face on it now to make me feel better. You and I both know that man will not allow me to visit you, or anyone else from my past."

Even worse for these dear friendships, she suspected, was that her time in this house had been an insult to him, and would now embarrass him badly. He blamed Daphne for harboring her, even though Daphne was ignorant.

She wondered what Lord Hawkeswell would say or think if he knew about that initial meeting along the Thames between Daphne and herself.

The day had turned cool by the time the wagon on which she had begged a ride from Surrey had crossed the bridge. She had ridden long enough for her shock to pass and her anger to abate, and she had formed a simple plan. She would snag bits of her veil and dress in the brush along the river, and trust the authorities would take both as evidence of her death. That would keep anyone from searching too hard for her.

She had made quick work of both, and was gazing into the river when a gig began to pass. A lovely woman, perhaps twenty-five years old and pale as moonlight, drove it. The gig stopped for some reason.

Perhaps Daphne had sensed the discouragement that washed her after that veil's ends sank in the water. How simple, really, to escape all guilt and duty and indignity by drifting down after them.

She had known so little happiness after her father died, and felt so little love. Had she grown up that way, she might have suffered it better, but her childhood had been so happy that the contrast only made the last few years harder to bear.

Bertram's treachery had been the final insult in many, the last abuse after years of it. She did not remember him being so cruel when she was younger, and her father would not have named him guardian if he had revealed himself to be so. Perhaps Nancy had changed him, or encouraged the darkness in his character that would have been better battled if he'd married a different woman.

Nancy had social ambitions, and now Bertram did too. And she, Verity, had been the perfect means to attain what they sought. Dangle an heiress to a huge fortune around London, and eventually an impoverished lord will rise to the bait. In swallowing it he has to swallow his pride too, but if the meal is tasty enough in either beauty or wealth, he can stomach it if he must.

She was supposed to be happy it had been Hawkeswell that they had landed. They expected her to be so dazzled that she would ignore how this marriage would interfere with her own plans, and in the life she was supposed to have.

How often had Nancy scolded her on that? *He could be old and fat and smell of death,* she would scream. *Only a fool would reject a man who looks like him. A woman can barely think when she looks in those eyes. You are a stupid ingrate not to appreciate how well we have done for you.*

At ten years her senior, he was not at all old. He did have wonderful eyes, but they were not for her alone. Any woman would do, she could tell. She had merely been the passable-enough commoner of suspiciously high fortune, obtained by craft and trade, who would solve his financial problems.

"At least he is handsome. That is one consolation, I suppose," Celia said, as if reading her thoughts. "The ladies do like him, so he is probably not unskilled in bed, if it helps to know that."

"I doubt he is much inclined to employ a lot of skill with me now. Regrettably, he is not angry enough to want to be rid of me either." She bent to smell a freesia. She never tired of their scent. "I had rather hoped he would be. Foolish, I suppose."

Celia rarely appeared surprised by the ways of the world, but she did now. "Were you expecting him to want to divorce you? Does he have cause?"

"I was not brave enough to give him cause. Now I rather wish I had been. No, I was hoping he would prove very amenable to supporting my petition for an annulment, when I told him I had been unwilling. I have reached my majority, you see. So if I can get free, I no longer have to go back to my cousin's authority. I will be independent."

"I expect he refused because it would be very public and embarrassing. As bad as a divorce. Worse for him, actually."

"I think he was more concerned about the money. I miscalculated there. I thought that Hawkeswell received the funds in my trust that had accumulated while I was a minor. It was a very large fortune sitting there, waiting for me to marry or reach the age of twenty-one. With that in his purse, I believed that keeping me bound to him would have less appeal. Unfortunately, he says he has received nothing thus far."

"If the marriage were annulled, he may have had to pay it back if he had received it. He still might, even if he gets it now," Celia said. "It would be a rare man who agreed to such a thing."

"I told him that I would make sure he received the money anyway. I intended to explain how I would do that. However, we never progressed that far in the conversation."

If she could explain that more plainly, however, he might see things differently. The notion that all was not lost raised her spirits a little, but not enough to eliminate the way her nerves affected her, and made her stomach sour and sick.

They passed a group of large pots on the floor holding neatly clipped myrtle. "I have been mourning that you will be leaving us, but I think you intended to leave soon anyway," Celia said. "You were merely hiding here until you turned twenty-one, weren't you?"

Verity stopped walking and took both of Celia's hands in hers. She squeezed them. "We are all here temporarily, are we not? Yes, I intended to leave very soon. I pray that you and Daphne would have understood."

"Of course we would have understood. But where were you going to go?"

"North. I planned to go home, far from London and Hawkeswell, and petition for an annulment from there. I want to live among the people of my youth, Celia, and try to save my father's legacy. I would like to use my fortune the way it should be used, and not to prop up an impoverished aristocrat's privilege. And I need to discover just what Bertram did to harm the people I love most, and whether I can rectify his cruelty." She blinked back tears. "Perhaps it has all been only a child's dream, but it has sustained me for two years."

Celia leaned forward and kissed her cheek. "I understand, my dear Lizzie. Everyone here has secrets and dreams, but we never guessed yours were so big. I do not doubt that you laid great and important plans for yourself while you hid and waited and worked quietly with these flowers. However, you may have to change them now."

"I fear that you are correct. Yet, I think that I may still convince him that being done with me is his best choice."

"He married for money. Settle that well with him, and you may yet have all you want."

Verity hoped so. However, even if Hawkeswell would not release her, she could at least move in the world again, in ways denied her while she hid these two years. She could try to have success in some of those plans. She tried to take consolation in that, but her heart still carried thick dread.

"I think that you should tell Daphne that this lemon tree graft has not succeeded, Celia. It was worth our experiment, but we have not seen the strength needed to continue with it." She moved to an orange tree. "Hold out your apron and let me pick some. We can bring them to Mrs. Hill and she can use them in the dinner sauce."

She plucked three oranges.

"I expect that hired carriage will be here soon," Celia said softly. "Will you really make him carry you out?"

Anticipation of that carriage had cast a pall over their time together. There had been much of the mood of a death watch in this stroll through the greenhouse. "Making him force me out may be too much drama for little purpose, other than to make a point that I trust I have already made."

"I fear if you do it, Daphne will train her pistol on him. She is most distressed. She thinks that you are afraid of him, and have cause to be. She has seen that before, you see."

Hearing about Daphne's instincts made Verity's subtle nausea churn more intensely. She also wondered if there might be cause to fear Hawkeswell and his temper, although he had kept it in check during their private meeting today. "I will leave with him peacefully. I do not want trouble for Daphne. I will go and tell her that."

Celia turned her head to the house, and its windows that were visible through the greenhouse's glass. "You can tell her now. She is coming, with Audrianna."

Daphne and Audrianna soon entered the greenhouse. They walked with purpose toward Verity.

"Lizzie, you must hear our plan," Audrianna announced. "Sebastian thinks Hawkeswell will be agreeable, if you are too."

Verity poked her little auger around the base of the potted citrus trees, to aerate their soil.

She heard the door open at the end of the corridor that connected the greenhouse to the back sitting room. Then boot steps. Hawkeswell had come to propose the plan that had been concocted by her friends.

It did not represent salvation, but only a period of purgatory to give her time to accept her fate. It was the best anyone could do, so of course she had agreed. She hoped to modify the terms just a bit, however.

The boots stopped nearby and she had to acknowledge him. Wonderful eyes, as all the women noticed. Had those eyes been dull or shallow, the color would not mesmerize, but they reflected so much instead. Intelligence and confidence and, on better days, humor, and perhaps some of the skill to which Celia alluded. There also showed a touch of the arrogance that was natural to a man of his birth and appearance.

She was a normal woman, and not immune to those eyes and that face. He had intimidated her two years ago when, almost broken by Bertram's treatment, she had all but cowered in this earl's presence.

Such as she did not marry such as he. Not because she was not worthy, and not because she had already chosen a different kind of man and a different future. Any chance of happiness would be doomed because they had known two different worlds, two different Englands, and had almost no points in common and no similar sympathies.

The only thing about him that had been familiar to her had been the mastery in his manner. Her father had been like that. But her father had not been such a big man, and so his mastery did not carry the implications of physical power that this earl's did. Her intuitions about that power had not been good, and his presence had made her want to shrink . . . recede . . . disappear.

She had taken an odd sort of comfort in his face, however. Handsome, to be sure, but not pretty. Not smooth and almost feminine like some elegant lords. It was a thoroughly masculine handsomeness, the kind that might be seen over a forge or in a stable. The strong bones came together with a perfection that seemed more accidental than carefully bred, and the insinuation of disdain was not there the way it could be in other, softer faces.

"Summerhays and Audrianna have suggested that we go to Essex with them," he said. "Their idea is that some time there might help you become comfortable with the future, and with me."

"That is kind of them. Also of you, if you have accepted the plan."

"I am not without sympathy to the shock that you have had in being discovered. If a few days in Essex will ease your distress, we can wait on returning to London."

He was being most solicitous. She was not sure that was a good thing. If he was too kind, it would all be harder.

"I will be grateful for this sojourn before being resurrected, Lord Hawkeswell. The public curiosity will not be pleasant, and I do not mind putting it off. I wonder if I can make a request about this house visit, however. Since it will be brief, perhaps you will indulge me for these few days."

Suspicion entered his eyes, and a bit of pique. No doubt he thought he had already agreed to indulge her more than required. "How so?"

"Since this has indeed been unexpected, I would appreciate it if we would put off any wedding night until the visit is over. Perhaps we can use this time to learn what we have in each other, so . . ." She shrugged, and hoped he understood women as well as Celia claimed.

"You play a shrewd hand, considering that you have no cards. I do not mind delaying those rights for a few days as you ask. After waiting two years, it is a small matter. If you think that you are going to convince me to seek an annulment, however, that will not happen."

How like a man to think he could foresee the future. To think he knew now how he would feel in four days on such an important matter. Once he knew her better, and once he heard her proposal about the money, he would surely be of a different mind.

"I also ask that you not inform anyone about finding me until we leave Essex," she said. "If we can put off all the gossip for these few days, I can better prepare myself for it."

"I will agree to both your requests if you also agree to several things," he said. "First, you must promise not to run away and disappear again tonight."

That was easy to accept. There would be no point in running away with him so close on her trail. Besides, she had things to do, and she could not do them if she went into hiding again. She had been planning on leaving The Rarest Blooms, but not to disappear from the world stage.

He stepped closer and looked down at her. His proximity emphasized his strength and her disadvantage in ways that she felt viscerally.

"I require that you accept one other term in this bargain, Verity. I will not expect my marital rights if you willingly accept three kisses a day."

He surprised her. It would be much better if they did not do that.

"What kind of kisses?"

"Whatever kind you will permit."

"Very brief ones, then."

"Other than the kisses themselves, I will expect nothing more."

"They must be private. I do not want to kiss in front of Audrianna." They would not want witnesses to be quizzed on whether these kisses implied more than they did. It would be hard enough obtaining an annulment if they spent time together in the same house, even as guests.

"I promise that they will be private." He smiled a little when he said it, as if he understood why she wanted that. She thought that was a good sign. It was the first smile of the day too. She had to admit that he had a nice smile, one that brought lights to his eyes and made his face much friendlier.

"If they will be private and brief, I will agree to three kisses. I do not know why you want them so soon, and every day, however."

"Perhaps because you are lovely, and because you are my wife." Still that vague smile, and eyes now veiled with appreciative consideration.

So that was how it was going to be. While she won him over to the idea of not fighting an annulment, he would try to win her over to the idea of her inevitable fate in his bed.

"Then we are decided," she said. "When does Lord Sebastian think to leave for Essex? Today? If so, I should pack my belongings. It will not take long."

"Tomorrow. He and I will go to an inn in Cumberworth tonight, and bring his carriage in the morning."

One more night, then, with her dear friends. It promised to be full of nostalgia.

She nodded her acceptance, and went back to piercing the soil around a lemon tree with her auger. He did not leave as she expected, but stood there, two feet away, watching her.

"Verity, I will have one of those kisses now."

She straightened and faced him. "We are not yet in Essex."

"I did not say they would wait for Essex. You can spare one today, I am sure. This has not been a reunion designed to put me in good humor, and you are smart enough to know that I did not have to agree to this plan, and could have much more than a kiss if I chose."

There it was again, that frank statement of his rights and her lack of power. A shiver of an old fear flexed through her before she could stop it. It would probably always be thus. A woman should at least be truly willing, and have an honest understanding, before she was put completely under a man's authority and subjected to the whims of his humor.

She suppressed both the fear and the rebellion that usually accompanied it now. He had given her no real cause to react this way. It had not been a reunion to please a man, or a discovery that flattered this one. Yet he had been more amenable to this house visit than he had to be.

"You are correct. One kiss today is the least I can do to thank you for the restraint you have promised to show."

He found that slightly amusing, but perhaps not in a good way. He moved very close to her and, with firm fingers, tilted her chin up. The contact felt strange, and a little dangerous. She was not accustomed to being touched by a man, skin on skin, even in this simple way.

He gazed so deeply that she grew uncomfortable. She closed her eyes, braced herself, and prepared to step back after the briefest touch of their lips.

"Have you ever been kissed before?" he asked.

"Years ago, when I was a young girl." A vague snip of memory drifted into her head. She saw Michael Bowman's crooked smile before that first kiss. A deep sorrow twisted her heart.

"How many years ago?"

"Six, I think. Why do you ask?"

"There is the possibility that you did not run from me, so much as run to another man."

The suggestion alarmed her. "There is no man here, as you can see."

"That you are here, and there is no man, does not mean you did not leave because of one."

He did not give her a chance to respond. He tilted his head and touched his lips to hers.

She had no specific memory of the physical parts of that girlish first kiss, other than it had made her want to giggle. Certainly it did not prepare her for the oddness of this intimacy, and the way he suddenly dominated her senses. There was firmness in his mouth despite the velvet pads of his lips, and control in that hand beneath her chin even as it held her gently.

She became aware of how little space separated their bodies, and how his scent encompassed her along with something else that came from him, something invisible but almost tangible. There was too much of his presence in that kiss, and much of it came from within rather than from his physical existence.

She did not suffer it long. She allowed little more than a mere brushing that created an odd tingle, and a slight pressure that she resisted. She stepped back quickly, freeing herself from that careful hand.

He looked at her with deep consideration for a moment, then turned away.

"Until tomorrow, then, dear wife."

Chapter Five

"It is fitting that it is raining today," Hawkeswell muttered. "Appropriate, somehow."

"Are you angry that Audrianna asked Verity to share her chamber at the inn last night?" Summerhays said. "Surely you did not intend to—"

"No, I did not *intend to*. Bad enough that I am an actor in a farce. I don't want to have the inhabitants of a public inn as the audience."

His horse paced beside Summerhays's, and both followed behind Summerhays's carriage. Inside it, tidy and dry, Verity and Audrianna no doubt plotted how to manage him.

With elegant artfulness, the ladies had ensured that they would be alone together on most of this journey, and their husbands would ride alongside. A day and a half had now passed since setting out for Essex, with Verity able to avoid speaking to him or being in his presence for more than a few minutes.

Dinner last night had been the exception. Audrianna and Summerhays had carried the conversation. Verity had studied her food, the walls, the floor, and her friends. Hawkeswell had studied her, and the way the candlelight flattered her snowy skin and delicate features.

"Your bad humor is understandable," Summerhays offered in that infuriating, soothing voice he had adopted ever since Verity had been discovered. "All the same, I hope that you will attempt to swallow your feelings of insult and make the best of this time. It could make all the difference if it goes well."

Hawkeswell peered through the veil of rain dripping off his hat's brim. "I am not in a bad humor as a result of perceived insult. I am in a bad humor because *I am wet.*"

"Of course."

"And what do you mean, 'make the best of this time'? And that other nonsense about a difference?"

"I just thought that if you used that charm of yours and stopped scowling, when you did intend to . . . Well, it might be less unpleasant."

"Damn you, are you giving me advice on how to handle a woman? My wife, no less?"

Summerhays sighed. "Damn you in turn, Hawkeswell. From what I have heard, she barely knows you. You never courted her properly, according to Audrianna. I agree that she has behaved badly, but unless you want a home full of anger and bitterness, you might consider employing a bit of flattery instead of looking so dangerous."

The rain had begun easing. Hawkeswell took off his hat, gave it a good shake, and replaced it on his head. "I am looking dangerous?"

"All the ladies seemed to think so. Audrianna thought you appeared wolfish last night at dinner."

"That was because I was hungry."

"Mrs. Joyes was inclined to refuse to allow Verity to leave yesterday morning, and had her pistol cleaned and ready. Had Verity balked at all, I fear we would have had a dreadful scene. I am afraid that you did not impress Mrs. Joyes favorably."

"That grieves me. Mrs. Joyes's good opinion is so important to me."

"Now you are being sarcastic. That is your bad humor showing again."

"Summerhays, I do not worry overmuch about the views of a woman who harbored my wife incognito for two years, and who threatened to shoot me. I find Mrs. Joyes a suspicious person in general. However, I will try not to scowl, or look dangerous. I will smile like an idiot while my wife and yours devise ways to attach puppet strings to me, as they are sure to try."

"That is not fair. Audrianna is not devising anything."

"You really are in love, aren't you? I can see that you will be worthless as an ally. The enemy camp owns you now, and will use you to their own good. I am on my own."

Summerhays did not like that. "I speak as your friend, and not a member of any enemy camp, even if you are too vexed by current circumstances to realize it. You have seduced countless women in your day, Hawkeswell. It would be wise for you to seduce one more."

He did not need another man's advice about his current circumstances. He had already decided his course of action last night, while he watched Verity flush under his gaze and while he felt his body tighten as he observed how lovely she appeared in the candlelight.

He hardly needed Summerhays to point out that seduction was the easiest, fastest, happiest, and most thorough solution to the entire situation.

"It is a very fine property, Audrianna." Verity peered out the carriage window as the manor house at Airymont came into view on a rise of land in the distance. "I can smell the sea on the breeze."

"The coast is not far away. We will make some outings there if you like." Audrianna tied on her bonnet and prepared for their arrival. Outside, one could hear the rhythm of the coach's horses, and the other two horses following.

Verity thought that she could identify which set of hooves belonged to Hawkeswell's steed. They were probably the ones that fell hard, with an emphasis that did not compromise much with the ground. The man astride that horse had not displayed much inclination to compromise since leaving Middlesex either.

He had been mostly silent at dinner last night, watching her with pensive consideration that charged the air with a mood that made her nervous and flustered. His attention had discomfited her, and might have given her concern if she did not assume that he would be honorable about his promises.

"This estate belongs to my husband's brother," Audrianna said as the carriage moved closer and the true size of the house loomed larger. "Perhaps, when he returns from Bohemia, if that physician is successful in curing his paralysis, he can enjoy country life again. If he must continue to live as an invalid, however, he is better in town, where at least he can have company more frequently."

Verity thought it unlikely that the Marquess of Wittonbury would ever return to England, let alone live here again. She knew that Audrianna doubted it too. His departure had been under a cloud of scandal that would have been more damaging if he had not sacrificed so much in the war. But Audrianna always hoped for the best, and for the return of the brother-in-law with whom she had forged a special bond.

The coach stopped in a large courtyard flanked by two embracing wings. A servant helped Audrianna out. Verity followed just as their husbands swung off their mounts.

The day had turned hot and sultry once the rain passed, and everyone expressed relief upon entering Airymont's reception hall. Its inlaid marble floor and relatively spare furnishing made it a cool sanctuary. Refreshments were brought while servants carried luggage away.

"There is a yacht over at Southend-on-Sea," Lord Sebastian said. "We can go sailing tomorrow if the weather is fair."

Hawkeswell brightened at the suggestion. The two men discussed the yacht, the coast, and what sport might be had. Verity sipped her punch and allowed her presence to recede.

She had learned how to do that after Bertram became her guardian and came to live in the house she once shared with her father. She had discovered that if she withdrew into herself until others became muted to her awareness, she in turn became muted to theirs.

This had been useful the last two years in Daphne's house too. Since she was not required to be any particular place at any particular time, she had also been able to make herself scarce when necessary. When Lord Sebastian visited, for example.

However, in avoiding him she had also avoided seeing

Audrianna in her new life as his wife. She had not been to their wedding, and had never seen Audrianna's new home in London. The full meaning of her friend's good fortune had thus escaped her until now, as she sat on a fatly cushioned chair in a reception hall that was larger than most cottages, glancing up at a ceiling soaring thirty feet above her head, while her humble shoes rested on a floor composed of four different-colored marbles.

Audrianna did not seem intimidated by these surroundings. Lord Sebastian and Lord Hawkeswell lounged comfortably, as if they expected nothing less of their abodes. She, on the other hand, had never before seen such effortless luxury, even though she was an heiress and her father had amassed a fortune of note.

Some invisible, inaudible signal caught Audrianna's attention and she stood. "The housekeeper will show you to your chambers now. There is a small lake not far from the back of the house, through the garden. Shall we all join together there at five o'clock, and dine alfresco?"

Lord Sebastian thought that an excellent idea. He congratulated his wife on her cleverness while the housekeeper led Verity and Hawkeswell away.

Two stories above, the woman handed Hawkeswell over to a manservant waiting at high double doors, and escorted Verity to similar ones thirty feet away. Verity looked over at the proximity of Hawkeswell's chamber just as he did the same with hers. Then his doors opened and he disappeared within.

"I hope that this apartment will find favor with you, Lady Hawkeswell," the housekeeper said, opening the doors to reveal a large chamber awash in fashionable green hues. "It has good air in the summer, and shade in the afternoon. Please let me know if it does not suit you." The three windows had already been opened fully, so that good air could enter.

It was the first time anyone had called her "Lady Hawkeswell." She almost turned her head to see the important woman whom the housekeeper addressed. Instead she went to the window and looked out. Positioned at the end of a back wing, it faced east.

The scent of the sea seemed stronger up here. A good sturdy tree grew right outside, but to the left she could spy part of the flower gardens. Beyond a shrubbery at the back she glimpsed the blue of the lake that Audrianna had mentioned.

"It will suit me very well," she said, since it appeared the housekeeper was waiting for approval.

Audrianna entered then, along with a young woman. The new servant was introduced as Susan, who would serve as her lady's maid. Susan began unpacking under the housekeeper's keen eye. They both showed no reaction on seeing how little Verity had brought, and how plain and lacking in embellishment it all was.

It did not take long to settle her. They left her with water for washing.

Audrianna fingered two stacks of letters and papers on the bed. "These must be the letters that you told me about in the carriage. The ones Lizzie Smith received when she queried the archbishop's men and those proctors about annulments. What are these newspaper cuttings?"

"I have been saving notices and such that address the area around my home." Verity opened a drawer and slipped the letters inside. "I suppose I should hide them. With Hawkeswell's chambers so close, he may wander in."

"I could hardly put him in the other wing, Verity. He may guess that you have confided to me about this bargain you struck, but it would be better not to make it blatant that you did."

"He has given his word. He is not without honor. I do not think it matters which chamber he uses." She believed that in her mind, but his proximity would do her nerves no good.

"I suppose if his honor appears to be wobbling, you can have one of your headaches." She smiled conspiratorially.

"I truly do suffer from them in the spring season, Audrianna. I did not lie about that." Her face warmed. "Not as often as I claimed last spring, when I needed to avoid Lord Sebastian, of course. Do you and the others hate me for lying to you? It was not a big lie, and I had little choice, but a lie is a lie, of course."

Audrianna took her hand and encouraged her to sit on the bed with her. "It was a small deception. I am glad that you told me, however, and also confided about this bargain you have struck with the earl. Daphne, Celia, and I were honored that you shared all the rest with us that last night in Cumberworth too. I will do what I can to help you with your plan, because I do not believe any woman should be forced into a marriage."

Audrianna spoke hopefully, but another emotion showed in her eyes.

"You do not think it will work, do you? You think that this marriage will stand," Verity said.

"I think that he is an earl, and that it will stand or not according to his preference. Celia and Daphne told you that too, and they are far more worldly than I am."

Celia and Daphne had indeed said as much, and it had discouraged her. She had spent two years planning how she would resurrect herself and petition for freedom. It would have been hard, and possibly not successful, but she would have had a fighting chance at least.

Now she feared she had very little chance to even get a hearing, because Hawkeswell could stop her at the outset if he controlled her movements. Unless, as her friends said, she won him over to the idea too.

She had these few days in Essex to achieve that. One week at most, with no danger of a consummation of the marriage. Those letters in the drawer indicated an annulment could be granted even with one, if the evidence were clear, but that lack of consummation would help. Furthermore, lack of children was almost essential.

Celia had suggested that Hawkeswell's preference would hinge on the money. Verity had been contemplating that for two days now.

"No matter what happens with Hawkeswell, now I can at least set about discovering just how Bertram carried out his threats, despite the bargain he deceitfully struck with me. Now that I am of age, Bertram can no longer touch me, whether I am married to Hawkeswell or not."

"And if you do learn the truth of it? What then?"

"I will make amends to that family as best I can, and seek to rectify any injustice done because of me."

She would have to do much more than that, of course. If the worst had happened to Michael Bowman, she would have to change the plans she had made for her life after she procured that annulment.

She wondered whether Hawkeswell might be sympathetic if she explained matters more fully. Not the part about Michael, of course, but the rest of it. Surely he would understand that the life she needed to live would be nigh impossible if she remained here in the south and if she were Lady Hawkeswell.

Perhaps if she revealed her dreams and her heart, he would realize just how much they did not suit each other. Maybe he would decide being rid of her was a good idea after all.

Audrianna scooted off the bed. "I will leave you to rest, and see you at dinner. The servants will escort you to the lake if you fear getting lost."

"I can see it from my window, so I am sure that I will find my way."

No sooner had the door closed behind Audrianna than Verity went to the secretaire in a corner of the sitting room that flanked her bedchamber. She sat down amid the varied green hues decorating the room, to compose the first letter to the world of her childhood that she had written in two years.

H awkeswell surveyed his apartment while the valet did his duty with the baggage. It was a comfortable set of rooms, but then, he expected no less of one of Wittonbury's properties. He judged the carpet to be from Brussels and the silk at the windows from India. The furniture was old enough to possess a nice patina, but new enough to indicate the property had been redecorated not many years ago.

He could not help but compare it with his own property, or what was left of it. Not a thing had changed at his country seat in more than a generation, except for the Titian that had mysteriously gone missing after one of his father's gambling disasters.

Fortunately, his grandfather had bought well, with a good eye that equaled his extravagance. Except for some worn upholstery and drapes, the house did not look too bad because quality always holds up to time. Still, it all begged for maintenance too often deferred, and for remodeling to bring it into the current century in both appearance and conveniences.

The valet hummed while he pressed in the dressing room. Hawkeswell listened for other sounds, from the apartment next to his own. He had half expected Audrianna to put Verity and him at opposite sides of the house. Perhaps Audrianna had not been plotting with Verity on managing him after all.

He left the valet to his duties, and strolled out to the corridor and down to Verity's door. He knocked and waited a good while before the latch turned. She appeared startled to see him.

"Have you been made comfortable?" he asked. "Are your chambers adequate?"

"More than adequate, and I will be very comfortable, thank you."

Silence fell. She half hid behind the door, refusing to open it entirely.

"Aren't you going to invite me in?" he asked.

"I was just about to write a letter, and—"

"I do not have to ask, Verity. I do not have to knock."

She bit her lower lip, then pushed the door wide. "Won't you please enter?"

The main chamber seemed comfortable enough. Not quite as large as his own, it held some chairs and a large bed draped in silk the color of green apples. He went to the windows. His own had better prospects. A large tree that he had noticed grew right outside one of hers. A bird at its top chirped melodically.

"This tree is too conveniently placed. I suspect you know how to climb trees, for all your practiced etiquette."

She smiled, and almost laughed. He wished she would do so. He had never heard her laugh, he was very sure.

"I was once a good tree climber, but I was a child then." She rose on her toes, and peered past him, out at the one in question. "I would say that is a four-minute tree for someone in practice. I, on the other hand, would probably fall and break my neck. Did you come here to judge its convenience?"

"I came to make sure you are pleased with the accommodations, and to say that I am going to take a turn in the garden. Join me."

She glanced over her shoulder, to a secretaire visible in the attached sitting room. "As I said, I was going to write a letter."

"I think that you will enjoy the garden more. You do like them, don't you? Gardens?"

She flushed. "Yes, I do like them. The letter, however—"

"Can be written tonight." He strolled to the door, stood aside, and gestured into the hall with his arm, by way of both invitation and command.

Whether she accepted the first he did not know. Her expression, however, indicated that she recognized the latter. She joined him.

Verity stepped down the stone stairs, into the garden that stretched beyond the house's veranda. Hawkeswell took her hand and guided her, to ensure she did not trip. She could hardly object to the familiarity implied by that touch, but it did disconcert her.

She had been careless in forging their agreement about this house party. She should have found a way to make him accept that while they were here, they would act as if they were not wed at all, with all that meant, and not merely delaying the physical consummation.

If she had been more thorough in her requirements, he would not now be acting as if he was a husband who could demand her time and attention, and enter her chambers whenever he chose, and take her hand at will.

He had made it clear that he assumed he could do all those things. She suspected that he had arrived at her door, and invited her to accompany him to the garden, specifically to make the point.

It was a lovely property, however. This house was not used much, but the gardeners maintained these acres meticulously. The veranda descended to a large courtyard garden flanked by two back wings. Along with the two in front, it turned the house into a gigantic *H*.

The ground sloped gradually away from the house; then the garden spilled out of the courtyard and spread wide, so one could see vast stretches of late-summer flowers. At the far end, at least five hundred yards away, a shrubbery in turn gave way to a screen of trees that marked a transition to wilder plantings, and to the little lake that Audrianna had mentioned.

"Does it meet with your approval?" Hawkeswell asked.

"It is more formal than I prefer, but a superior example of its type."

"Then you were probably more pleased by what has been done to Wittonbury's garden at the family's townhome." He caught himself, and smiled wryly. "Except that you have never seen it, have you? You would not have wanted to visit Audrianna there, and risk her husband recognizing you."

"No, I have never visited her there." She instinctively

paused by a late gladiola and flicked a dead head off one of its tall stalks.

"You were very clever in keeping your secret, I will grant you that. It is a wonder that the ladies rallied around you, rather than feeling deceived."

"You do not understand the acceptance we all give each other, and the rules by which we live. None of us dwells on the past so it works fairly for all."

"That house is a damned peculiar place. There are rules, you say now. Like a convent, or an abbey or school?"

"Much like those. Deliberately so. For example, as independent adults, we do not require explanations from each other regarding what we do and where we go. We do not pry into each other's personal affairs. Also, we all contribute to the house's finances, as we are able. Audrianna gave music lessons, and Celia has a small income. I work in the greenhouse and garden."

"More peculiar yet. It would be necessary for everyone to have secrets, I suppose. You would accept the vagueness in the others because you would want them to accept it about you."

"It is not secrets that allow it to succeed, but mutual sympathies and the good it creates. I do not think anyone there has many secrets, anyway, except me."

"I suspect you are wrong about that. For example, did it never occur to you that perhaps Mrs. Joyes did not demand an accounting of your life because she did not want to give one of her own?"

She stopped walking and looked at him. "What do you mean?"

He shrugged. "Only that she has a very handsome property for the widow of an army captain, which is the history Summerhays gave me. In not demanding an explanation of your movements and history, she also protected her own privacy."

"You are insinuating something scandalous, I think."

"I am musing aloud; that is all. Do not pretend to be shocked. You may not have asked, but you had to have wondered."

"You are implying, not just musing or wondering. I will not have it. Daphne is like my sister, and all goodness. You just want to think badly of her because you blame her for taking me in."

"Quite possibly, and that is not fair. My apologies."

He gave in awfully fast. She doubted he really thought himself in the wrong. He was just appeasing her, so that she would like him more.

They had reached the back of the flower gardens. Shrubs, trees, and wilderness lay ahead. "If you will excuse me, I will return to my chambers now, to rest before we gather for supper."

"And to write your letter?"

"Perhaps."

"With whom are you so impatient to correspond? Since you demanded I keep your resurrection a secret while we are here, I am surprised that you intend to inform someone on your own so quickly."

"I am writing to Katy Bowman. She is the mother of the family whom Bertram threatened. She was my father's housekeeper for years, and like a mother to me too."

"It must be she whom you fear grieved for you. I can see how you would want to correct that sad error."

He prodded at her guilt. She carried quite a bit of it on this point. Since Katy could not read, the letter would have to be read to her. The vicar would do that. Maybe he would also let Katy dictate a response.

Verity hoped so. It would be wonderful if a letter would come that said Nancy had lied, and Bertram had done nothing to Katy's son Michael, that Michael still plied his skills at the forge the way her father had taught him. She dared not count on that, but she could pray for it.

"I will take my leave, Lord Hawkeswell, and see you this evening."

She turned to walk back through the garden, but he took her hand and stopped her.

"Not yet, Verity. I will have a kiss first. Several, in fact."

"Several! It is supposed to be three kisses at three different times, not all three at once."

"You left that clause out of our contract. How careless of you."

He gently tugged. She found herself tripping toward a cluster of tall rhododendrons. She really did not want to go behind those shrubs. She tried to dig in her heels, but even his gentle pull proved stronger than her best resistance.

"You are not being fair," she objected.

"Be glad I demanded only three kisses a day, and not many more. As it happens, I am not claiming any of today's kisses, let alone all at once. I am claiming the ones you still owe me from yesterday."

"We did not agree that you could save them up, and catch up on Tuesday if you forgot to use them on Monday."

"We never said I could not."

"I am saying it now. Why, if that were the rule, you could go half a week and I would have to suffer twelve or fifteen all in one day."

"What a pleasant thought. However, it will be easy for

you to avoid such a fate. Simply make sure that I am kissed three times before the day is out, and you are safe."

The devil was in his eyes as he teased her. Only it was the devil that also suggested he was not only teasing.

How had the perfectly sensible agreement to three small kisses led to such a disadvantage? One where it might be wise to kiss *him* instead of him kissing *her*?

"Three, then," she agreed. "So we catch up." She quickly stepped toward him, rose on her toes, and planted a quick kiss on his lips. She tried to peck him again, but he angled back, out of reach.

"That is one," he said. "Two to go."

He appeared to be having a fine joke at her expense. She held herself straight and tall and prepared for the other two.

To her shock, he took her face in his hands. The hold was gentle enough, but very intimate. The sensation of his warm palms against her cheeks startled her. "We did not agree that you could touch me like this. You are just supposed to—"

"Hush," he muttered, his lips hovering near hers, but not exactly kissing her. "When I kiss a woman, I do it properly."

Properly meant he watched while his thumb caressed her lips in a manner that made them sensitive and tingling. It meant nipping her lip, creating a jolt to her body much like an arrow of sensation spiraling downward. It meant a stunning closeness that made her too alert and too aware of him. When his lips finally touched hers, her breath caught.

She did not step back at once. Being held like this, she was not sure she even could. But the kiss provoked something inside her that caused her to forget momentarily that she wanted to get away.

Still cradling her face in his hands, he looked down at her, those blue eyes watching, watching, and darkly pleased with whatever he saw. "That is two."

"That is enough!"

He shook his head, then kissed her again.

The kiss, his closeness, the giddy tickling sensations, all distracted her. She had no idea that kisses could be so long and involved and . . . busy. A series of delightful little changes and movements, to her cheeks and jaw, to her lips again, nips and varying pressure and even his tongue playing devilishly in sensitive, tiny ways. This kiss was very different from the ones she had shared with Michael when she was a girl. Far more dangerous, and she responded differently too.

Her fascination dismayed her even while she dallied more than was wise. Finally, however, she realized she had permitted a kiss that could be considered several if one were strict, and that he would never give her proper credit on the account.

The memory of Michael helped break the spell. There was no understanding between her and Michael. He might not even be alive now, and even if he was, he knew nothing of her plans. And yet . . . She lifted Hawkeswell's hands from her and took a very long stride backward.

"I think that was more than three in total. You have used up some of tomorrow's."

"At most I have used up half of one of today's."

"It was too long."

"It is for you to decide that, not me. If you do not choose to end the kiss, do not expect me to do it for you."

Flushing badly, she turned and strode away. She would have to remember to end things very quickly in the future. She had been surprised today; that was all.

These kisses were different from what she thought of kisses being when she agreed to this part of their bargain. Now that she knew his intentions, she would be on her guard.

Chapter Six

The early-evening light bathed the placid lake with golden sparkles. It broke through the branches and leaves of the tree under which they all sat, creating dappled, moving patterns on the linens and plates and the ladies' hair.

Hawkeswell found himself looking at Verity too often, even though he pretended not to. Those kisses this afternoon had been very sweet, and her reactions had charmed him.

If she were not his wife, he might feel a little guilty for taking advantage of her. Since she belonged to him, he did not have to question the rightness of it, and could enjoy his surprise in the discovery that she was about as ignorant of kisses as was possible.

Which meant that she had not been kissed much before, or at all, in the recent past. That did not totally eliminate the possibility that she had run away with the hope and intention of being with another man. She still might have been in love with someone else. She still might be, and might have proposed this annulment nonsense for that reason.

He noted her poise, and the careful perfection of her manners. There was something of the recent graduate of the school of etiquette in the way she handled herself at this table. She paused before speaking to himself or Sebastian, as if she carefully edited what she planned to say to make sure it sounded like a lady's speech.

"I am glad that you like your chambers," Audrianna said to Verity. "That is one of my favorite rooms in the house. The colors and good light remind me of a spring garden."

"There is a fine tree outside the window," Hawkeswell said. "I think she wants to climb it. A four-minute tree, she called it. That sounds like an expert to me."

"Then you must leave your window open someday, and climb in," Audrianna said.

"Did she never climb trees in Cumberworth?"

"I never saw it. However, we have a tall apple tree at the back of the property, and the fruit at the top did not go to waste."

"You must have had an active childhood, Lady Hawkeswell," Lord Sebastian said.

A stillness touched both women upon hearing the address. Audrianna glanced at her husband. Sebastian pretended not to see. Hawkeswell was glad for the small evidence that he might have an ally after all.

"I lived with my father in his house near his mill, and played in the fields beyond. He did not notice that I was growing up for many years, so I enjoyed a childhood longer than some other girls."

"And when he did realize it?" Sebastian asked.

"He did what any father with a motherless girl would do. He brought in a governess." She made a little face of distaste, and appeared like that girl for a moment.

"And the drills began, no doubt," Hawkeswell said.

"In triple force, to make up for lost time," Verity admitted. "She took her charge very seriously to educate me. She lectured daily on how the better world behaves and the social consequences of sin."

"I could have saved your father a lot of money," Audrianna said. "There are books to be bought for less than a shilling that explain all that. You remember those books, don't you, Sebastian? The ones your mother gave to me?"

Sebastian looked to heaven with resignation, hoping for deliverance from reminders of his mother's insults. Audrianna laughed. Verity did too, finally, for the first time in three days.

Her eyes sparkled. A little dimple formed on one cheek. It was a very feminine laugh, but not silly and high-pitched. Soft, and a pretty sound.

"Anyway," she said, relaxing into her story, "I was not the best student. I confess that I gave her a bit of trouble at times. If I found the lessons too horrible, I would sneak off to Katy's house where I could still be a child again for an hour or so."

"You may have hated the lessons, but you learned them well," Audrianna said. "Even Celia assumed that you were born a lady, and she is not easily fooled."

"I suspect that she was not fooled by me at all," Verity said. "She noticed, I believe, that I was reciting school lessons, and not speaking the beliefs and knowledge of my own world."

Hawkeswell did not miss how Verity slipped that in.

Once again, she was reminding him that they "did not suit each other," as she put it. It caused him to wonder if she feared always being thought the unsuitable wife, by society and himself.

That would be unpleasant for her. Even now, sitting with Sebastian and himself, it must be trying to rehearse every word and action before speaking or moving.

"Have you written your letter to Katy?" he asked. "She was Mr. Thompson's housekeeper for many years," he explained to Sebastian and Audrianna.

"It is almost finished. I would like it posted tomorrow, Audrianna."

"Certainly. Is there anyone else to whom you should write?"

Verity pondered that. "Mr. Travis, to be sure. There are things I would like to know, that I have worried about, and he would answer my questions honestly. I should wait, however, until I know exactly what my situation is."

Your situation is that you are married. This little slip was the most obvious indication that she thought she could still cause that situation to change. He would have to explain to her, very firmly, that she wasted her time on that idea.

"Who is Mr. Travis?" Audrianna asked.

"He is the real manager of the ironworks. He is also the only man my father trusted with the complete secret of the metal boring lathe that he invented. He is surely still there. Bertram cannot get rid of him."

"That is a dangerous risk to take," Sebastian said. "What if something happens to Mr. Travis? That entire part of the business will cease."

Verity accepted some tea from a servant. "I said that he was the only *man* whom my father trusted. While that governess drilled on etiquette, my father was drilling me on something else. I know the secret too."

Hawkeswell sealed the letter to his aunt. It explained simply that he had been delayed and would not be down to Surrey for at least a week or more. The one beside it on the writing table, to his cousin Colleen, was not any more forthcoming.

Deceiving his aunt about the recent discovery of Verity did not bother him. Colleen was another matter. She had been instrumental in arranging the marriage, and possibly the most distraught when Verity disappeared. She had indeed mourned, for the girl she had come to think of as her new sister. But then, Colleen had some practice in mourning, and perhaps it just came naturally to her now.

He pulled out a clean sheet of paper and considered how to write the next letter. He had promised to inform no one of Verity's discovery while they were in Essex, but he had concluded at dinner that he still needed to communicate with her trustee, Mr. Thornapple.

Thornapple and he did not have the best history. Last spring it had become apparent that someone had hired an investigator to look into Verity's disappearance. Hawkeswell had assumed Bertram was behind it, only to learn it was the trustee. Since that runner had asked insinuating questions about the missing bride's new husband, the only conclusion was that Thornapple suspected the worst.

He composed his words carefully, and presented his inquiries to Thornapple as merely more of the same, and the result of renewed curiosity about Verity's settlement now that there was a chance a new inquest would be held.

Her reference to Mr. Travis had been startling. It had

been a mistake, perhaps, to take Bertram Thompson's word that he, Bertram, managed that business, and to agree that he should be left to do so with a free hand after Verity married. Now it appeared that not only did Bertram not truly manage the mill, on a day-to-day basis, but he did not even know the details of the invention that made the mill so profitable. Only Mr. Travis did. And Verity.

Hawkeswell completed his letter, sealed it, and set it aside. He lay on the bed. The cool night breeze flowed over him, heavy with the scent of the sea. It was sinful to waste such a pleasant night by sleeping.

Not that he expected to sleep easily. First he would have to listen to his baser instincts remind him that a lovely young woman, to whom he had a legal right, lay in another bed not far away. Then he would have to conquer the physical response to that notion, and terminate the speculations it provoked.

If he believed her to be as unmoved as she tried to pretend, the possibilities would not be so compelling. He knew women too well to be fooled, however, and it was very hard to keep his promise when Verity's eyes and sighs reflected an arousal that she insisted on denying.

The reasons for that denial had been explained, but he suspected there was more. More to her reasons for hoping he would still agree to seek an annulment—and he was sure that was her game here. More to her reasons for running away in the first place. Maybe more reasons for not wanting this marriage to begin with.

His letter to her trustee would clarify some things about that business her father established and grew. They were details that may have been explained two years ago, but that had escaped him because he had not listened well enough.

That had been pride's doing. He would be glad to receive her significant income from the mill, and elated to get the large amount amassed while she was underage, but he had not really wanted to know anything about the mill itself. Now, he suspected, it was time to find out what he had neglected to learn then.

A sound penetrated his thoughts. It came in the window, as a shuffling sound not far away outside. It sounded as though an animal was on the building. Curious, he rose and went to the window.

His eyes adjusted to the night. The sound came again, from that tree that grew close to Verity's window. He peered hard, and made out a dark form stretched between the high branches closest to the building and the sill of her chamber window.

The form moved with a swinging motion, and disconnected from the building. A tiny gasp of joy whispered on the breeze.

He could hardly be surprised. He had challenged her to climb down that tree. Or tempted her, with allusions to potential freedom.

A four-minute tree, she had called it.

She had never actually climbed the big apple tree at the back of Daphne's garden. The narrow skirts of her dresses did not permit it. However, with the aid of a ladder she would manage to perch on a low branch, and use a rake's handle to knock down the higher ripe fruit.

It had been years, then, since she had done this, but the skill came back. The way she had tied the wide swath of her undressing gown's fabric high in the middle between her legs, then around her thighs and knees too, allowed her to be fairly nimble. The garment served her purpose of testing herself and the tree tonight. The next time, when she left for good, she would need to find something less ridiculous to wear.

She swung onto the tree and an old, latent, girlish thrill bubbled through her. One felt like a bird when high in a tree. It was very different from looking out a window. It also felt secretive and private. The branches formed a little home that no one else could enter.

She settled herself on a thick branch and looked up. There was not much moon, but the stars were very bright. She loved the way the leaves fluttered against her view of the sky, and the lovely patterns they made.

She deeply inhaled sea air and the promise of freedom. She had not expected the latter to affect her so much, but she was fairly drunk on it.

The potential of being alive in the world made her heady. She felt the cautious, retiring nature that she had assumed after her father died drying, splitting, wanting to be shed like a skin that no longer fit. Sitting in this tree, she tasted again her childhood joy of life.

She unaccountably wanted to laugh. A smile stretched her face for no reason. She acknowledged the Verity Thompson of long ago, reawakening now these last few days. That Verity was something of a stranger after these years, unsure of herself still, because in the time she was asleep, she had also grown up.

Images of Michael came to her, more vividly than they had in months. She saw him as a child and a boy, and as a youth stealing that first kiss. She saw his crooked smile through the years, and its absence the last time they had met, when she had stolen to Katy's house only to find him full of anger at the world.

He was not at all like Hawkeswell. She knew Michael as well as she knew herself, and Hawkeswell would forever be part mystery. Maybe it was the mystery that caused her to react to his kisses the way she did. She could not imagine Michael making her feel that way. She would not want him to.

She closed her eyes, and pictured Michael again, and tried to summon something of that excitement anyway. It would probably be good to have a little at least, if he agreed to marry her. Of course, before that could happen she had to find out if he was even alive, and where he was, and whether she could undo whatever Bertram had done. Still, if all that happened, and they lived in that house together, would there be thrills in their marriage bed, or friendship and comfort?

She opened her eyes again and looked out to the garden, and knew the answer. Not a bad answer. Probably a better one. Fires could be enthralling, but they were destructive too. They consumed that which gave them power until they died from lack of fuel.

She checked the ties that created her odd pantaloons, then began her descent. It took longer than four minutes. It was a tall tree. She was out of practice and a lot bigger than when she did this as a girl. Next time it should go more quickly. She would throw down her valise, scamper down the tree, and run. She was good at running.

Finally, her leg dangled down, seeking the trunk, so she could brace herself while she lowered herself from the bottom branch to the ground.

Her foot hit the solid support and she began to lower herself. Then the trunk grew claws and grabbed her foot, shocking her.

With her weight still on her last branch, she looked

down. Even in the dark she saw sapphire pools gazing up, and the white of a shirt above the hands grasping her foot.

"You misjudged. You were going to fall," Hawkeswell said.

"I was going to jump," she lied. She *had* misjudged, but the fall would not have been far or serious.

He set her foot on his shoulder, then reached up, closed his hands on her waist, and swung her down. "You are fortunate that I happened by just in time." He angled his head to see her costume. "You have very pretty legs. I was awed by the sight of one hanging above me. Are those pantaloons that you have on, or drawers?"

She bent to untie her undressing gown so her lower legs would not stick out so scandalously. "Neither. Thank you for your help. You can continue your stroll now."

"I am in no hurry."

One of her knots would not come undone. She continued working on it with increasing frustration. "You really should go. I did not expect anyone to see me, and I am not dressed appropriately."

"I am your husband, Verity. If I saw you completely naked, it would still be appropriate."

She froze, bent over her leg, with her fingers in mid-pluck at the knot. A most peculiar sensation flowed down her, a teasing stimulation much like she felt during those last kisses.

She straightened, with her undressing gown released on one side but still bound to her other thigh and knee. She doubted that the deep shadows under the tree hid how foolish she looked. "I must go now. The knot is snarled and I need to go to my chamber and—"

"You went to great trouble to get out. It would be a pity to return so soon. Here, come with me." He took her hand

and led her into the moonlight, much the way he had dragged her behind those rhododendrons.

He dropped down on one knee and lifted her leg to prop her foot on the other. The skin of her uncovered leg glowed like white flowers do at night, making her leg very visible from knee to slipper. He bent his head closely to work at the knot.

"Please do not trouble yourself. I can do this upstairs." She did not like the sensation of his hands so near her body. His head and face were dangerously close to her too.

"I insist. It is good for you to see how useful husbands can be sometimes."

She suffered it. He seemed to take a very long time, but then, the knot had been badly snagged. She counted out the heavy pulses of time while she looked down on that dark head.

Finally she felt the fabric fall loosely around her thigh and knee. He did not move, however. He did not let her foot return to the ground or allow the undressing gown to cover that which was bare.

He looked up at her, and caressed up her leg to her knee, his palm sliding slowly. His other hand covered her foot so she could not remove it. He was a big man, and even while kneeling his face was not all that far from hers. She could see his expression well enough to know that this accidental meeting had been unfortunate for her, and for his promise.

She felt his masculinity in the air, invading her. She had no idea how to thwart that power. Her feminine instincts not only shouted warnings but also reacted to the things about this man that would excite any woman. She worried that he might act on the thoughts evident in his hard expression, but also waited for him to do so with a shocking anticipation.

Instead he released her foot, and stood. "If you intend to climb trees, we will have to obtain proper garments for you. Although that undressing gown is very pretty, and you look lovely in the night."

He strolled around her, to get a better look at her dishabille. She in turn noted his. No cravat or coats. He wore only trousers and boots and that white shirt that opened at the collar. She resisted turning defensively as he paced behind her. She felt his vague touch on the long tail into which she had tied her hair after Susan brushed it out.

He tucked her arm to his own, like an escort. "Come with me."

She knew that she should not go with him. She was sure that doing so would be unwise. But she really had no choice, because he did not leave the decision to her.

"Were you testing the tree, to see if you could escape if you ever decided to?"

Hawkeswell was almost sure of the answer, but not positive, so he asked it. Some conversation would also distract him from the speculations about the night and their isolation and the possibilities that suddenly wanted to make an argument for being not only attainable, but desired by her as well as him.

That was his blood talking, urging the bad judgment that so often got men into trouble. Even if she comprehended the mood surrounding them both, and he was not sure that she did, she would deny it. Why she would had become a significant question today. Enough that he was wondering for the first time if he had been unforgivably careless two years ago, with her future and his own.

"I think that you should look to your own honor, and not try to direct mine," she said.

The white of her skin was very visible, down to the ruffled edge of her undressing gown. The skin of her leg had been just as clear in its delicate, feminine curves. So had the scent of her, and the faint musky odor that said his proximity stirred both her fears and her sexuality.

"You remind me of my honor only to avoid my question. You have no reason to doubt it. I may have wanted to caress much more than your leg back there, but I did not, did I?"

She tensed at his boldness, but she did not miss a step. Her delicate profile remained facing him as she looked to the garden path they trod. He resisted the urge to stop her and embrace her and make her look at him.

"When we spoke in Cumberworth, you said that if I had made an effort to know you better, I would have understood why you resisted the marriage," he said. "Since we are supposed to use these days to become more familiar, perhaps you will explain it now."

Her undressing gown was full and shapeless and festooned with layers and little bits of lace. Its fabric hit his leg while she walked. The body within it did not, however. She was very careful about that, which took some effort on her part.

"We both know I will never be accepted. Not truly. It is not my world. You know that I am correct on this. The title, and that world, were alluring, but when I was honest with myself, I admitted the reality would never match the dream."

In other words, she had concluded he brought her nothing, since his place in society was the only currency he contributed to the bargain.

Her cool dismissal of his status was not a view to which he was accustomed. Yet even as his ire gathered, he guessed that she was humoring him, and giving him an answer that would cost her nothing and make sense to him.

"I do not believe that a few rocks on the road as you traveled in society would matter that much to you. Other women might require that total acceptance, but I do not think you would. I think there was more to it."

"Much more. The most important part. The part that my cousin deliberately violated in forcing this marriage, and perhaps the reason he did so."

Now they were down to it. "What was that?"

"It was not my father's wish for me to marry such as you. He intended my husband to be a man who could take his legacy and my inheritance and continue building his dream and his company."

"I have never met a man like your father who did not want his children to raise themselves up. He probably would have been delighted to have you made a countess."

"If you had known him, you would realize how humorous that is. He taught me that the guillotine had been a suitable end for those aristocrats in France, and we could use a few such machines here. He would have never bequeathed me the majority share of his company if he thought I would marry a man who disdained industry, and who was devoted to nothing but pleasure."

It was well-known that Verity's father had not been any upholder of tradition. A man who devises a new method of machining iron could be excused for believing the old ways in everything could use some new inventions.

Joshua Thompson had hardly been known as a radical,

however, let alone one of the revolutionaries who called for the abolition of the nobility. Either he had saved those views for those closest to him, or Verity was exaggerating for her own ends.

"You do not know me well either, Verity. Furthermore, you speak a common and inaccurate prejudice. A man of my station cannot be devoted only to pleasure, and is not respected if he is. I have duties in Parliament that are a form of industry in themselves, and I am responsible for managing the land bequeathed to me, to the betterment of the many lives it supports." He lightened his tone, so his response would not sound like a scold. "However, I will admit you are partly right. We aristocrats have enjoyed various pleasures for generations, and with practice have become expert in indulging in them."

"I do not know why you asked about this, if you are only going to treat my reasons as an excuse for lectures and clever wordplay."

"My answer was an effort to be polite. Actually, I am trying not to mind too much that you just implied that you would rather see my head cut off than be married to me. The notion raises the devil in me, for some reason."

He thought a good response from a wife would be her reassurance that of course she would not like to see his head cut off.

"I am being honest," she said instead. "You asked why, and I am telling you why. You were never supposed to happen. This is not the life I am supposed to have." She stopped walking and managed to extricate her hand and arm. "I have a proposal. Now that you know something of me and my mind, I think that you will agree that it is in your interests to accept it."

"Let us hear it, then."

"I am of age now. If I am free, that business is mine to shepherd and enhance. Bertram wanted me married to a man who would take no interest, you see, so he could be in control even without the majority share. But if I am free—"

"Surely you cannot think to manage it yourself."

"I want to exercise the rights of ownership that are mine by legacy. One of those rights would be to do whatever I choose with the income and profits. My proposal is this: If you petition to be free of me, and I of you, and we succeed, I will give you half of whatever that income will be. Forever. By contract, so if I ever marry, even my husband could not undo it."

Her voice carried earnest sincerity. He wanted to laugh, not so much at her naïveté about the world in concocting this plan, but at his own amazement that she would go through so much trouble and cost to get rid of him.

"Verity, if I do not seek to be free of you, I will get *all* the income. It is unseemly to talk about this, but since you are determined to—"

"Your tone is that of a patient elder speaking to a child, Lord Hawkeswell, but it is you who are the child if you believe that Bertram will *ever* give you a fair accounting of my share's value. Trust me, you will do better with my plan than with his apportionment of your rights." She stepped closer and peered through the night at his face. "And God forbid I should die in truth, I would put your share in my testament so it continues for you and your heirs. As I said, it will be yours *forever.*"

She had it all planned out, he realized. She had spent these two years calculating what she would do when she came out of hiding. Marriage, at least to him, was not part of the plan. That much was obvious.

"I am not interested in your proposal, Verity."

But he was not totally uninterested either, and his brief hesitation before responding probably told her that. They most likely did not suit, except in the sensuality that he thought might be common ground once it was explored. Bertram probably *would* fix the accounts to steal part of the income too.

He had married for money, after all, and her proposal probably guaranteed more in the long run.

He needed to contemplate this, and accommodate the realization that she had just revealed a shrewd mind that her mild manner and lovely face obscured.

He also needed to think it over when the vision of her looking like a moon goddess in the night was not encouraging his blood to disregard any suggestion that he might not take her soon.

She knew that he was eyeing the lure she had cast. She sensed his interest, and she smiled. He was sure that he saw the stars enter her eyes.

The next thing he knew she was right in front of him. Her hands went to his shoulders and she rose on her toes. In quick succession she planted three kisses on his lips, each one lasting an instant. She startled him so much that he did not grab for her until she had already turned on her heel and begun to run back to the house.

"Think about my offer," she called over her shoulder as she fled. "Also, we are even on the kisses now, my lord, and can start afresh tomorrow."

She lifted the billows of her undressing gown's fabric and darted through the night, her long tail of hair flying and her white legs flashing in the dark.

Chapter Seven

"Did you have a good night, Verity?"

Audrianna's welcome the next morning when Verity entered the breakfast room seemed a little peculiar. It was not the words that were odd, but the tone that Audrianna used.

"A very good night, thank you." She sat across from Audrianna and accepted the coffee offered by a servant.

Audrianna just smiled. She folded her hands upon the table's top and smiled again.

"What is vexing you?" Verity finally asked.

"Nothing. Nothing." Audrianna's hand went to her chestnut hair, feeling absently for errant locks even though her lady's maid had dressed her hair perfectly. She glanced over. "Well, not nothing. It is only—after all that time explaining to me in the carriage why this marriage cannot stand, I expected you to show a little more fortitude when Hawkeswell turned his charm on you. Not that I am criticizing you, please understand. The earl is a handsome man—that cannot be denied—but really, if you were so distressed, I thought you would at least give Hawkeswell a good run first, before ceding the race." She smiled. "That is all."

"I have not ceded any race. Why would you assume that I had?"

"You haven't? I must apologize, then. It is only that you were seen last night. In the garden. Together. In dishabille. Both of you." She smiled weakly. "Together, as I said. It is just assumed that—" She shrugged.

"Who saw us? Who assumes this?"

"Sebastian. My maid. Who knows who else? Almost every bedchamber can view the distant garden, and a white shirt and pale undressing gown would be visible out there even with little moonlight—" She shrugged again.

"We were only talking about our unfortunate situation. You must tell your husband and maid that they misunderstood. I need you to be most firm with all of them, Audrianna. I cannot have the servants, and Lord Sebastian of all people, assuming more has transpired than has."

"Certainly. I confess that I found their reports odd, since I know your plan."

"I am still very determined on my plan. In fact, I have cause to think that I may have convinced him of my views. I believe we could be very close to a right understanding on the entire matter."

Audrianna raised her eyebrows. "Indeed? You astonish me, Verity. I do not think you should have to live this marriage after what you told me about your cousin's deception, but I did not have much hope that you would ever get Hawkeswell to agree. Especially when, during that dinner at that inn, I became convinced that he intended to do his own persuading, in his own way."

"He has seen the light, I believe. Since there has been no consummation, we may triumph in the church courts if he joins my petition."

Audrianna's expression flexed between optimistic and skeptical. Verity did not need her good friend to explain how the odds were against her, so she turned the conversation to the environs around Airymont.

"Southend-on-Sea is charming, although visitors from London can crowd it in August. Perhaps we can tour it after we sail today," Audrianna said in describing the closest village on the coast.

"I would rather not go sailing. Would it be too rude if I declined?"

"Surely you are not afraid of being seen now? If you wear your bonnet, I doubt that you would be recognized, anyway, even in the unlikely event that someone who knew you was in Southend."

"It is not fear of recognition, and I look forward to visiting the seaside. I would prefer not to spend the entire day with Lord Hawkeswell. I also find the sea frightening. The idea of being on a small vessel, at the mercy of all that water, distresses me. Could I not travel to the coast with you, and visit the village for a few hours while you sail?"

Audrianna reached over and patted her hand. "Of course you can decline to sail. We will use your fear of the sea as the reason."

"I will go, then, and prepare, and jot a quick letter to Daphne and Celia while I wait for us to depart." She stood. "You will be very firm with your husband and your maid about what they saw outside last night, won't you? It is very important, Audrianna."

"Of course, Verity. However—it might be wise, since

you are determined on your plan, to avoid being alone with him when you are half-undressed. No matter what promise he made to you about this sojourn, he is a man."

"You are very sure that you will not join us, Lady Hawkeswell?" Lord Sebastian made the offer again while servants carried on board the necessities for several hours at sea.

The yacht was at least fifty feet long with sturdy masts and several sails. Lord Hawkeswell and Lord Sebastian had already removed their frock coats to prepare to play sailors, but two servants would be the ones to climb those masts if necessary.

"I will be happier with my feet planted on dry land," Verity said. Audrianna was settling herself in a chair under an awning. Her broad-brimmed hat and parasol would further protect her from the sun.

Hawkeswell worked at some fishing lines. "There is really nothing to fear," he said. "I am a good swimmer, and the sea is peaceful today. If anything happened, I would get you to shore safely."

"I am sure that your skill is unsurpassed, Lord Hawkeswell, but so is my cowardice. My father drowned in little more than a swollen stream and the sea's power truly frightens me. I will occupy myself in the village and await your return. Audrianna gave me a list of places of interest to visit, so I am sure that I will not be bored."

Hawkeswell put down the fishing lines and came over to her. "Take this." He pressed some pound notes into her hand. "It is not wise to be off on your own without the means to hire help if you need it."

She glanced down at the notes. There were perhaps fifteen pounds in all. "I really cannot—"

"Think of it as pin money. Buy a new bonnet if any shop sells them. However, I want your word that you will not use it to hire a carriage for the purpose of running away. I would follow and find you within a day, so there is little point in it."

She had not expected this suspicion on his part. She looked at the pound notes.

"Your hesitation gives me pause, Verity. I am thinking that I should join you while you tour the village, to ensure you do not disappear again."

"I have no intention of disappearing again. Nor would you be a good companion today if I am keeping you from your sport." She looked him in the eyes. "You have my word that I will not use this money to hire a carriage for the purpose of running away."

Apparently satisfied that he had guessed her game and ended it before it began, he joined Sebastian in getting the yacht ready.

After all was in order, they cast off. Verity headed for the village. She stopped once she saw the yacht well out on the water, then opened her reticule to put the pound notes inside.

They fell alongside some others, and rested atop the soft, rolled chemise that hid her gold chain and other meager valuables. She looked in that reticule and whispered an unladylike curse.

She *had* intended to hire a carriage and be well gone before that yacht returned. There was a chance she had convinced Hawkeswell last night to accept her proposal, but she could hardly count on it. If she could get away, the sensible course was to do so.

She had even left a note in her chamber at Airymont, explaining it all to Audrianna. Hawkeswell was devilish to hand her the money that would make her escape much easier and simpler than bartering that gold chain, but also force her to promise not to escape at all.

Taking some solace in admitting that her plan of escape had been only half-baked, and reminding herself that Hawkeswell might very well accept last night's offer, she resigned herself to passing the hours onshore as she had promised.

Southend-on-Sea was a fishing village that had grown to accommodate those visitors from London whom Audrianna had mentioned. A long, broad terrace faced the water, raised from the beach on a little cliff. Expensive bonnets and very fine boots mingled on the walkway with the simple garments of the local people. Hotels and guesthouses lined the terrace, facing the sea at the western end.

After visiting the little church with its tidy, attractive garden and ancient gravestones, and the famous Royal Hotel, she strolled down the lane of better shops. Then she set her steps eastward, toward the old neighborhoods and the fishing boats.

None of the Londoners ventured here, and the common folk went about their business as if nothing had changed in generations, which it most likely had not.

A few boats had already returned, and women hawked the catch at a market that clogged the lane. The smell of fish—briny and salty and unmistakable—filled the air. The glances cast her way were not due to her garments, which were plain enough to attract no attention. Rather this was like Oldbury, the village back home near the ironworks. Everyone knew everyone else and a stranger was notable.

She paused to admire the wares at one fishwife's cart.

The woman, red-haired and bronze faced, eyed her in turn. "You looking for that girl? She was right outside the village, where the cliff gets higher. Just sitting there. She is there still, I guess."

"I am looking for no one. I am only taking a turn through the village."

"Not many visitors take a turn on this lane. She is not from here and seemed lost. I thought someone would come looking for her; that is all."

Verity did not know how anyone could get lost in this village, with its one lane along the sea and one more a block back. However, this girl may be very young.

She pushed through the women crowding the fish-wives, and looked along the shore. The cliff walk rose higher on the eastern end of the village. She thought she saw someone up there, and decided to go and check. If a child had become lost, it would not do to leave her there alone.

As she approached she realized the girl was not a child at all. Although she sat on the cliff's edge, with her legs dangling in a childish way, she was at least fully grown. She wore a bonnet much like Verity's own, with a deep brim and little adornment.

Curious now, Verity pretended to be seeking a good prospect of the coastline and village. She paused near the girl, who neither moved nor acknowledged her.

She noted that the girl wore a very nice muslin dress, with lilac sprigs on its white fabric and lavender sleeves. A fair amount of soil showed on it, however. No, this girl was not from this village, and most likely not from these parts at all.

"Forgive me for being forward, but the villagers think that you are lost. Can I be of assistance?" Verity said.

The head did not move. After a spell, however, a voice too mature for a girl, let alone a child, replied. "I am not lost. I know where I am."

So much for doing a good deed. Verity began to walk away, but she looked back. Something about the young woman's stillness and voice plucked at her worry.

Had Daphne had that same intuition when she stopped her gig on the road beside the river? Had she seen a young woman too absorbed in her contemplations, clearly not where she was supposed to be?

She returned. "The sea fills one with awe, doesn't it? I find it frightening."

"I do not find it frightening at all. It looks soft to me. Cleansing."

"You are braver than I. There is not much beach down there at this spot, and this cliff is uncomfortably high. One false step— Do you know how to swim? I never learned."

No answer this time.

"Are you down from London?" she asked, trying again.

"I am from the north."

"Do you have family here that you are visiting?"

"No. I begged passage on a fishing boat. The men who work it live here. So I am here too now."

"They take passengers? I had no idea."

"For coin, some will."

Verity looked down on those boats. She had promised not to hire a carriage to run away. She had said nothing about a boat.

It would mean conquering her fear of all that water. She gazed out at its vastness, then down where waves broke relentlessly. Perhaps if the boat stayed close to shore . . .

The young woman really did not want to converse. She wished Verity would go away, it was clear. Verity wanted to believe it would be fine to do so, and go have a conversation with some of the fishermen instead.

She gazed at the woman's back. This was really not her business. Yet leaving her alone, unprotected, did not seem right. Every instinct said the woman was indeed lost, in the worst way, and needed help.

She glanced at the boats again, and sighed. Later, perhaps, there would still be time. If not, maybe another day she would have another chance, if she still needed one.

She turned her full attention back to the lost woman. What had Daphne done that day, to extend help and friendship? She certainly had not demanded explanations and reasons for why Verity stood alone in a fine dress at the edge of the river. She had not scolded or warned. Instead she had guessed the one thing that would garner attention from someone left to her own devices. Food. She had merely invited a stranger home for dinner.

"I am going to find something to eat. I intend to look in this area of the village, and not near the yachts and guest-houses. Would you like to join me? I have enough money to buy two meals."

The head turned. Dark eyes finally looked at her. Whatever choices this young woman had been debating, hunger now set them aside. "That is kind of you. I have not eaten in over a day."

"Then let us go and find a good wife who will sell us some bread at least."

The woman stood and dusted off her skirt. Her shoe dislodged a rock. It tumbled down the cliff, startling her. The churning surf quickly submerged it.

"My name is Verity," she said as they walked back to the village. "What may I call you?"

A pause. A familiar hesitation that told Verity far more than any words.

"You may call me Katherine."

T he fish could not wait to be caught on Summerhays's hooks. They all but jumped into the yacht at his command. Already the large barrel brought for the catch was filling, and soon there would be enough to feed the entire household at Airymont.

Hawkeswell had caught no fish at all. It was symbolic of something, no doubt. A big damned metaphor of nothing good. His inactivity left him with plenty of time to debate Verity's grand proposal about all that money, however.

She had been very shrewd. In one day she had outlined all the reasons they would not be happy in this union, itemized his worthlessness, and described her resentments of the way it had come about.

After failing to win him over with these gentle persuasions, she had now resorted to a bribe. And a very handsome bribe it was.

It had struck him as vaguely dishonorable on hearing it. Insulting, as if she assumed he could be bought. Now he admitted that he was making a point that was far too fine. He had married for her fortune, hadn't he? He *could* be bought—and in fact had already been, in some sense. She merely offered to compensate him for his disappointment in the financial area, should they apply for and receive an annulment.

Looked at that way, it was not so much an insulting bribe as it was a consolation.

Whatever it was, he would not lie to obtain it. However, if Verity's story were true about being forced into the marriage, a good case could be made for an annulment.

He eyed Audrianna, sitting under her awning reading a book. He set down his pole against the yacht's side and sidled over to her.

"Do not just leave it like that," Summerhays scolded while he braced his strength against the fight of yet another fish. "If your lure is taken, the equipment will go overboard."

"If the line goes taut, you can grab the pole. I am done with watching the churning sea and listening to nothing besides your self-congratulations. I want some conversation."

Audrianna set aside her book when he settled into a chair beside hers. "The fish do not bite for you, Lord Hawkeswell?"

"I think that they find my lures bitter."

"It is hard to know what will attract a fish. Not all rise to the same bait. I expect that some even see the hook and suspect the consequences of taking a nibble."

"Just my luck to have only suspicious fish responding to my lures, then."

"With time I am sure that a fish that thinks the meal is worth the cost will swim by."

He glanced back to Summerhays, who was hauling in another huge fish while one of the servants waited with a big net. "Let us speak directly, Lady Sebastian. I am curious about only one fish, and she is already hooked and landed. As you know, I think, she wants to flop out of the barrel and back into the sea."

Audrianna's eyes glistened with humor, but her expression was sympathetic. "I am sure that you find that surprising. I certainly do."

"Then you do not agree with her plan?"

"Oh, I agree with it. If she was coerced and tricked, she should not have to accept that scoundrel's deception. I am surprised that our Lizzie is proving to be made of such determination, however. She was always the mildest among us. The quiet one. Daphne is a glistening waterfall and Celia is a rushing stream. Lizzie was a still lake."

"Perhaps a deep one, however."

"Deeper than any of us guessed, it appears."

"Do you believe her? That she was coerced?"

Audrianna's eyes narrowed while she looked out to sea and considered the question. "She displays a good deal of anger when she speaks of it, so, yes, I believe her. She blames herself too, I think. She said things as we journeyed here that lead me to say that. She forgets, perhaps, how young she was when her cousin became her guardian. Now, with maturity, she looks back and castigates herself for not being stronger, and more clever and suspicious of his promise, and less meek. I also know that she worries about that poor family, and blames herself for the trouble that her friendship brought to them."

"There is no reason to blame herself."

"Women tend to do that, Lord Hawkeswell. Blame themselves. The world allows it. Expects it. Daphne says there are women who are beaten by their husbands and who then blame themselves for it. That is hard to believe, isn't it?"

She did not speak of Verity with that reference, he was very sure. This was not an allusion to his temper, or a suggestion that Verity had cause to fear him. And yet,

Audrianna's comment, coming in this conversation, raised
a possibility that he had not thought of before. The notion
raised the devil in him.

"Her cousin Bertram coerced her, she says. Do you
know, Lady Sebastian, how he did that?"

"She does not say. I broached the question. We had a
lot of time in that carriage. She changed the subject."

Which alone might well say it all. He barely checked
the fury that began splitting his head. If that scoundrel had
hurt her, he would tear Bertram apart limb by limb.

"I speak out of turn now, Lord Hawkeswell. I know
her mind and intentions and I cannot disagree with her.
However—" She hesitated, thinking better of whatever
she was going to say. "However, I think that there may be
one point of essential misunderstanding on her part. Only
you would know, of course."

"What is that?"

"Whatever happened, she believes you knew about it,
and permitted it. She said that first day that you were in
on the plot."

He stood and walked away, to the rail of the yacht, so
Audrianna would not see how appalled he was. No matter
how Bertram had coerced her, there had been no plot. In fact,
Bertram had not even indicated that the proposal had been
turned down.

*She is young and fearful the way young women can be.
We will take her home, and give her time to consider your
generous offer, Lord Hawkeswell. Perhaps you will offer
again in a month or so, and she will know her mind better.*

What had Verity been saying the last few days, however? *If you knew me better, you would have understood
why I resisted the marriage.* She did assume he knew the
resistance had been there. But if *she* knew *him* better, she

would know that he could never have agreed to be a party to such a thing.

Had conceit made him blind? He did not want to think so. He tried to remember the particulars of those months, of how she demurred at first and later accepted. He had never guessed that she had been forced and tricked. Not that it was likely that she would believe that now.

He returned to Audrianna. "Thank you, Lady Sebastian, for speaking out of turn. Now, your husband is not yet done with emptying the sea of fish, but I am done with watching him. I will ask that the yacht take me in to shore. Then you and he can enjoy the rest of the day together alone on the waves."

Chapter Eight

"Thank you," Katherine said after dabbing the cloth to her mouth. "It was delicious."

It had not really been delicious. The chicken stew's broth had been thin and the cook stinted on seasoning. It had been filling, however, and a hungry person's tastes are not too particular.

Verity and Katherine sat in a simple house on a cross street from the main lane. Verity had gone back to the fishwife who'd pointed her toward Katherine and asked where a meal might be bought. They had been directed to this widow's kitchen and the pot of stew that simmered here every day.

The little house's scabby paint displayed the effects of the salt in the air. The table and chairs that they used were rustic, but there was a nice prospect of the sea from this kitchen window with its blue shutters, and there was a cool light now that the sun had crested.

Katherine had not spoken much. Verity studied her.

Gentry, she decided. Born at least as high as Daphne and Audrianna. This young woman had been bred to the etiquette she now demonstrated as she ate. She had not learned it the way Verity had.

"You have been very kind," Katherine said. "I should take my leave now." She stood to do so.

"Where will you go?"

Katherine looked down. Verity guessed that she remained silent because she had no answer.

Unfortunately, this was not exactly the same as with Daphne and herself. Having fed Katherine, she could not now offer a bed, and act in the morning as if the visitor belonged in the house and was not expected to depart anytime soon. It had been a fortnight before Daphne officially extended the offer of permanent residence, but Verity had known it would come from that first dawn at The Rarest Blooms.

"Do you have any money?" she asked.

"Not money. I do have some things that I can sell, though."

Jewels, hopefully.

Verity guessed Katherine to be in her young twenties. A matron, most likely.

"Please sit." She lowered her voice, so the widow knitting in the next room might not hear. "I have a friend. She does not live near here, unfortunately. However, I think that you could stay with her for a while. Until you know where you are going, that is."

Katherine appeared skeptical, but hopeful too. "She will want—I cannot risk—"

"She will not ask, as I have not. Except I have one question now, and I beg you to be honest in answering it. She is like a sister to me, and I dare not put her in harm's way." She lowered her voice even more. "Have you done something bad? Are you running from a crime?"

Katherine shook her head, and tears filled her brown eyes. "I am not a criminal. I am not bad, or stupid and worthless, or even disobedient."

It was a fuller and more revealing answer than Verity expected, and it tore her heart. Suddenly she was a girl again, a stranger in her own home, trying to hide from the notice of two people who resented her existence and made their displeasure known through insults and cruelty.

She reached over and grasped Katherine's hand to encourage composure. "No, you are none of those things, although someone has said you are, again and again, I think. If I am correct, it is good that you left."

Her attempt at comfort had the opposite effect. Emotion distorted Katherine's face. Then she broke with a heart-rending wail, and buried her face in her hands and wept.

Verity embraced her while the anguish poured out. The widow peered in the room curiously and Verity shooed her away. She did nothing to try to ease Katherine's tears, and could not stop the way they called forth her own until she wept too.

Memories assaulted her. Not images, but sensations, and bone-deep feelings of fear and the ugly anticipation of punishment. When she heard rebellious fury within Katherine's weeping, she understood that too. It was a good sign, and necessary. When the anger no longer came, it meant you were broken forever.

That fury heralded the end. Katherine rested in Verity's arms after the worst had passed, spent and sobbing. Eventually she extricated herself, and wiped her tear-stained face.

Verity looked in her eyes and Katherine looked straight

back. A familiarity passed between them, a knowing deeper than most people ever have of another person.

Verity's mind went to work. Of course she had to help Katherine now. She had no idea how much it cost to send someone by stagecoach to Cumberworth, or whether Southend-on-Sea even had a coaching inn. There would be food to buy on the way, and beds to pay for, and—

"Come with me, Katherine. We have much to do."

Where the devil was she? Hawkeswell had checked every shop. He had visited the large hotels and the little church and any other place of interest in this village. He peered down the long terrace, to where the buildings became bleached and rustic. Might she have gone there? He supposed he should check and see.

He strode east, annoyed that Verity was proving so hard to find, half convinced that she had baldly lied and indeed hired a carriage to run away. Having made his decision, he wanted to tell her before common sense defeated altruism. Already financial considerations had begun pressing into his mind again, after a blissful few days of thinking they were all resolved.

That hell would probably return now. Her trustee was sure to sit on her entire fortune until any petition for annulment ran its course. That could take years. The notion of dwelling in limbo again did nothing for his humor, no matter what his resolve.

He kept his eyes out for a woman in a pale yellow dress and simple straw bonnet. All the same he was practically on top of her before he realized it. Her appearance startled him, but only because she was not alone. Another young woman about her age, with dark hair and very dark eyes, walked alongside. They conversed about something so earnestly that Verity did not even notice that he blocked their path.

When she finally did, she startled badly, like a child caught stealing sweetmeats. "Lord Hawkeswell! Is the sailing done so soon?"

"I had them put me ashore. I have been looking for you."

"Oh! I was just strolling. . . ." She gestured vaguely behind her.

He looked pointedly at her companion. The other young woman kept her gaze to the ground. Verity glanced back and forth between them. "Lord Hawkeswell, this is my friend Katherine . . . Johnson. Katherine, this is the Earl of Hawkeswell."

Katherine gaped. Something other than awe widened her eyes. "I am honored, my lord. I will take my leave now, so that—"

"You will do no such thing. Miss Johnson has unaccountably become separated from her party, Lord Hawkeswell, and they appear to have left without her. I was going to help her obtain transport home. Perhaps you would aid us."

"Of course. I am sure that we can hire a carriage or at least a gig, Miss Johnson."

"She will need to go some distance. However, a gig could take you to a staging inn, Miss Johnson, and you could purchase transport from there to your home." Verity smiled brightly. "That would work, would it not, Lord Hawkeswell?"

"Certainly. I will see to it."

"You are very kind, sir," Miss Johnson said.

"There is a shop selling sundries down the lane a bit,

on the left," Verity said. "We will wait there while you procure the gig, Lord Hawkeswell."

He bowed, and set off to find the gig as ordered. Verity had gotten rid of him fast enough; that was certain. Little did she know that she only delayed learning that she had won.

Katherine tucked some of the necessities they had bought into her lilac reticule, along with some pound notes, while Verity tucked the rest into her own.

"I cannot thank you enough. You have a good heart."

"I am glad to help. We can do nothing about your garments. You will have to travel without a change. At least with that soap you can wash some things at night." Verity pulled Katherine away, to a section of the merchant's counter that had some privacy. "Now, I must write quickly, because Lord Hawkeswell will return soon. It does not take an earl long to find gigs, I think."

She dipped the pen in the ink. She had begged both, and the paper, from the merchant in exchange for a few pence.

She jotted a few lines to Daphne, asking her to give Katherine a bed for a night or so. It would be up to Daphne to decide if the hospitality extended beyond that.

She folded the note and gave it to Katherine. "Do you remember what I told you, about how to find The Rarest Blooms once you reach Cumberworth?"

Katherine nodded. Verity took a deep breath and called up whatever strength and nerve she could muster. "I am going to leave you here for Lord Hawkeswell to find, Katherine. He will put you in that gig, and you will be on your way. I, however, have something that I must do now, and I cannot wait with you."

Katherine frowned. "I do not understand."

"Give him the message that I will meet him here shortly. He will treat you like the fine gentleman he is, so do not worry about his reaction to my absence."

Katherine appeared skeptical, and frightened. Verity grasped her wrist. "You will acquit yourself splendidly on this journey. You found your way here alone. You will find your way to Cumberworth. Godspeed, Katherine. We will meet again someday, I am sure."

After putting Katherine in the gig, Hawkeswell waited ten minutes for Verity to return. When she did not, he knew she never would.

He strode down the lane, glancing in shops, knowing she would not be in any of them. She had bolted. She had bold-faced lied in giving her promise, and found her own transport while he was arranging that gig for Miss Johnson. He had warned her that he would follow and find her, but in truth he had no idea where she was going.

He found himself on the edge of the old section of the village. He went down to the beach, to see how far out Summerhays's yacht was, and whether he could hail it.

As he squinted at the bright water, a fishing boat made its way into the shallow cove. It moved along the edge of his view, finally drawing his attention.

He stared at that boat. It was coming in to shore, not leaving with any young woman on board, but it reminded him that not only roads connected this village to the world.

He had been an idiot. He had elicited a promise that she would not hire a carriage, but on the coast she would not need to. She might indeed be afraid of the sea, but she was displaying a determination that could overcome that if necessary.

His head snapped to the left, to where other fishing boats had clustered. He strode along the beach toward them.

"Can you not go faster?" Verity asked desperately.

"He is coming with the water now, Madam. You wouldn't want to be without it. We be looking at six hours easy, maybe more, before we are onshore again."

Her stomach clenched at the notion of being at the mercy of the sea that long. Still, she tapped her foot impatiently while the fisherman's son rolled a keg to the boat, and hoisted it on board. She had never guessed it took so long to get a little boat under way.

"We be all set," the man said. He extended a hand. "You jump on board now, and we can cast off."

She got into the boat clumsily, but finally the man and his son started throwing off lines. Fear at being caught turned to elation at getting away. She kept her back to the sea so that bigger fear would not ruin the joy.

The last rope loosened. She watched the buildings get incrementally smaller as they drifted away and more water surrounded them. Just as she was having disconcerting images of a huge wave rising up and swallowing her, she noticed a man striding toward them on the beach.

Hawkeswell.

"Hurry," she urged. "An extra pound if you get this boat away right now."

The son began unfurling a sail.

They were maybe a hundred yards out when Hawkeswell noticed them. He stormed onto the weathered, short dock and stood there, glaring. She felt his fury roll toward her over the water.

He yelled for the boat to return.

"Who be that?" the son asked.

His father shrugged. "A gentleman, it appears. Do you know him, Madam?"

"He is some distance away and it is hard to see in the sun. I would pay him no mind, my good man. Once we are out of the estuary, remember that I want to go north."

Hawkeswell gestured hard for the boat to return. She trusted he would give up soon.

"What's he sayin' now?" the son asked.

His father cupped his ear. "Hard to tell. Sounds like . . . ab-abduction." He jolted alert. "I think he is accusing us of abduction."

"What nonsense," Verity said. "I asked you to take me on this voyage. It is beyond the pale that this stranger is trying to interfere in nothing of his concern."

Unfortunately, Hawkeswell had the captain's attention now. The man went to the end of the boat and cupped his ear again. Whatever Hawkeswell was yelling sounded like bird squawks to Verity, and she refused to believe that her fisherman would hear anything.

"He keeps yelling a name, I think. Yerl Awksell? Merl Fawksell?" He cupped his ear and leaned into the breeze. Suddenly his hand fell and he turned wide-eyed to his son. "I think he is saying he is the Earl of Hawkeswell."

"Could be he wants to sail north too," his son said. "Would be good to take him if he does."

The father chewed that over. The son ceased working the sail. Verity was horrified.

"If he is indeed the earl, which I think very unlikely, he would have his own yacht," she said. "He would not need to hire this boat to go north."

"True. True," the father said, scratching his chin. He looked to the shore, where Hawkeswell stood in a pose of noble power, arms crossed and legs parted. "Looks like a fine gentleman, though. He could be an earl. Never saw one before myself."

"I have," Verity said. "They look much finer than that man does."

"He be yellin' again," the son said. "I'm gonna take us in a bit closer to hear."

"No!" Verity cried.

"Won't take but a minute or two. If he is an earl, it won't do to just sail away, now, will it? M'wife will burn my ears if I turned down the chance of a lord's hire of the boat."

The boat began a broad, circular turn while the son moved the sail. Verity sickened when she saw that it would end up too close for comfort to Hawkeswell.

His image turned crisp as they neared. Blue eyes pinned her in place.

"It was wise for you to come back," he called to the captain. "Had you not, you would have answered to the magistrate."

The captain's eyes bulged at the threat. "For what?"

"That is my wife you are abducting."

"The hell you say!" The captain turned on her in shock.

"You are not abducting me. Should any magistrate become involved, which I doubt—he is only throwing false threats—I would swear that I had hired this boat and—"

"If I say it is an abduction, it is," Hawkeswell called. "Return her at once, or answer to me."

"If you do return to that shore, you will answer to *me*," Verity said.

The captain scratched his chin again. He removed his hat and scratched his head. He looked at Hawkeswell, then turned sheepishly to her.

"Don't want to get in the middle of a row, if you understand, Madam. Best we go back." He gestured to his son, and the boat aimed at Hawkeswell.

Verity fumed the whole way. Three more minutes and . . . Better to not have tried than to have success snatched from her grasp like this. She had screwed up her courage to brave the sea too!

Hawkeswell no longer glared when they drifted into shallow water. He smiled ever so graciously, as if he welcomed a friend's return from France on a ship decked out for royalty. She was not fooled in the least.

The boat glided up against the short, low dock. Hawkeswell strolled over to the boat's edge. "Testing your bravery, my dear?" He smiled at the captain. "She fears the sea. Five more minutes out there and you would have had a screaming lunatic on your hands."

"A narrow escape, then, m'lord."

"Oh, most certainly. Yes, indeed." Still smiling below blazing eyes, he gestured for Verity. "No need for you gentlemen to tie up. Come here, darling."

She obeyed, because there really was no place else to go. He grasped her waist and, as if she weighed nothing, swung her high over the railing and planted her on the dock beside him. The boat began drifting away again.

Hawkeswell looked down at her, none too pleased. She looked back, not happy either.

"You will be relieved to know that Miss Johnson is safely on her way."

"Thank you. I knew that you would see to that far better than I."

"The next time I obtain your promise not to bolt and disappear, I will have to phrase it like a lawyer, and cover all contingencies and modes of transport."

He did not appear nearly as angry as she expected. Barely vexed, if truth be told. More thoughtful than annoyed.

"Do you have such little faith in your powers of persuasion, Verity?" he continued. "You did not even give me a chance to accept or reject last night's offer."

"A rare opportunity beckoned, and I took it." They began walking. "Since you do not appear too angry, can I hope that you have decided to accept my offer?"

"I have been contemplating it at length. Putting aside pride. It is why I came back, looking for you."

"Have you made a decision?"

"Not quite yet. Let us walk back, while I contemplate some more, and try to put my irritation about this little adventure of yours behind me."

She gladly accompanied him back to the main lane, then onto the terrace. She said nothing at all, so he could contemplate all he wanted. She prayed that her attempt to get away had not changed his mind for the worse. He would not be so cruel, so stupid, as to keep her in this marriage over that. Would he?

She indulged in memories of home, and barely contained her joy. He was going to do it, she was sure. He was going to accept her proposal.

T hey walked the length of the village again, along the terrace. They went down to the beach once they had passed the shops. It was a fine day and other yachts were out on the water, their sails puffing in the gentle breeze.

Hawkeswell spotted Summerhays still fighting fish on his boat, a good ways out. It would be another hour at least before the yacht returned.

If he had stayed on that yacht, Verity would be many

miles up the coast before anyone even knew she was gone. She was succeeding in her goal to prove she was much more trouble than any man needed in his life.

"Let us walk this way," he suggested, guiding Verity away from the village's western end. They strolled west along the shore. The breeze picked at the narrow shaft of her pale yellow dress, pushing and pulling it against her legs and hips so her body's form was more visible than she realized.

The village lay in a little cove, and the land rose a bit toward its western point. He helped Verity up the cliff and hill, and found a spot where rocks gave way to some grasses. The prospect was impressive, with views of the entire cove and the coast in both directions. Tall ships heading into the Thames estuary could be seen on the southern horizon.

"I want to talk to you about your offer," he said. He shed his frock coat and laid it down so she could sit. It was utterly private up here. The world would never know what was said and agreed upon, and whether, having sold his troth for some silver, he now sold a bit of his honor too.

A better man would let her go free and accept no money as consolation for losing her fortune. He could not afford to be that good.

She settled down on his coat, smiling optimistically about the talk to come. She saw it in him, no doubt. The decision had probably etched his face. Her eyes sparkled with delight at her quick success.

He looked down at her and a memory flashed vividly in his mind, of last night and her naked leg. It had been surprisingly difficult to let her foot go. It had been deucedly hard not to kiss her leg, her knee, her thigh, and more. He inhaled, looked out to sea, and managed to banish that leg from his thoughts.

He sat down too. She had her legs straight out, like a girl's, and her ankles showed beyond the pale yellow hem. He noted that she could use some new shoes.

"I need to know something," he said. It was pride and conceit that needed to know and nothing more. "If I agree to your plan, do you intend to marry someone else? Is all of this really about another man?"

"There is no man waiting, if that is what you mean. I may marry, however, if I find the right man."

"One of whom your father would approve. One who would be a good steward of his legacy."

"Yes."

"A man like Mr. Travis?"

She laughed, and clapped her hands together. "Mr. Travis? Oh, my. No, not Mr. Travis. Why, Mr. Travis is even older than you are."

He might mind her speaking of him as if he were ancient if her mouth did not captivate him while she laughed and smiled. When in repose it appeared small and fashionably bowed. When she laughed it looked larger, sensual, and luscious.

"I am only thirty-one, Verity. Although ten years your senior, I am hardly ready for canes and false teeth."

"I only meant that Mr. Travis is much too old for me. It is not my intention to marry him. Also, if I marry anyone, you will still have the income I promised. As I said, we will arrange that before any husband can interfere, and in a way that a husband cannot break later. My father always said that in England anything can be accomplished with the right contract."

"Well, I had to know."

"I expect that you did." She said it kindly, as if she understood something of a man's mind, and why he would have to know. "Are we agreed, Lord Hawkeswell? Will you join me in trying to undo this wrong?"

"I am still thinking about it," he heard himself say.

He had intended to make quick work of this, and say something else entirely, but most of his attention had suddenly been distracted by a lock of her hair that had escaped her bonnet and teased at her brow. That one lock, and the way it feathered against her pale skin, looked unbearably erotic for some reason. It maddened him. All of her did.

"Perhaps you should try to persuade me."

"Persuade you?"

"With a kiss. If I agree, you will probably say that the kisses are over along with my claims to you. I would like one very nice kiss from you. While we are still married, and before our union is officially challenged."

He was teasing her, and she knew it. Her exasperated expression was not so much scolding as amused. "You want me to kiss you before you tell me your decision."

"Yes, only not like last night. A sweet kiss, not a bird's peck."

"It would still be a very fast one, sweet though it may be. I think that you are silly to care about kisses now. It would be wiser to kiss no more."

"What harm can there be in it? No one will see us here."

She eyed him suspiciously. "Only one. No more."

"Of course." He plucked at the ribbon of her deep-brimmed bonnet. "This was built to prohibit any kisses. It is like the wimples worn by the nuns in France. You will never be able to kiss me with it on." He untied the ribbons and removed the bonnet and set it aside on the grass.

She looked beautiful with the afternoon sun highlighting her hair and her cheek as she turned to him. She considered her situation, and rose to her knees. She appeared very serious, like a student puzzling out a difficult cipher.

She lowered her head. Her lips touched his delicately. She kissed softly. Sweetly. Her lips lingered a moment. Their velvet softness rested only one extra instant, but it was longer than needed, and that told him everything he wanted to know.

He cupped her nape with his hand so she could not end the kiss too quickly now. He encouraged her to linger a few moments more. Then a few more yet.

The reason for coming to this isolated rise escaped his mind. Only the delicate breath of her kiss mattered, and the heat flashing through him, destroying resolve and good intentions.

She trembled. Her lips pulsed gently against his own. The smallest pressure pressed against his hand, as if she thought to move her head away.

He could not allow that now. He embraced her with his other arm and turned her quickly, so she rested in his arms. She looked up in surprise, stunned by this change in position. He kissed her before she could speak.

Not sweetly either. He was beyond that. Beyond delicate lures and subtle games. He took her mouth hard, releasing a hunger that had been building for three days.

Her hand touched his shoulder and arm. Not in resistance. If she had thought to press and deny, that never emerged. Her hand just rested there, on the arm that circled and supported her body.

Hard now, furiously so, he seduced her mouth open so he could taste, explore, and possess. Her gasps and breaths spoke her shock and acceptance. Pleasure defeated her objections.

Yes. He ravished her mouth carefully, coaxing cries from her throat and sinuous flexes in her body. *Yes.* He laid her down and looked into blue eyes wide with astonishment. *Yes.* He kissed her neck, her pulse, and caressed down the side of that yellow dress while lovely sounds of feminine wonder sang in a halting melody of surprise.

Her form felt small under his hand. Almost frail. She did not fight his hold as he grew bolder, feeling her hip and thigh, smoothing along her leg, learning her body and seeing it in his head, naked beneath him, knees bent and raised and willingly open for him, for his hand and mouth and body—

The images compelled him. The desire owned him. He kissed down her chest to the top edge of her dress, then lower still to her breast. Her hand went to his head, to stop or encourage, he did not know. He kissed the hard tip pressing against the thin fabric and she cried in surprise into the breeze. He rose up and smoothed his palm over her breast and watched abandon claim her until her eyes glistened, unseeing.

He slid his hand beneath her, and felt for the tapes on her dress. Her eyes opened wider when it loosened. Her gaze sought the world. Sanity tried to emerge. He kissed her gently, then hard, while he lowered the garments from her shoulders and uncovered her breasts. Round and pretty, their hard, dark tips beckoned. He lowered his head and used his tongue to madden her.

Shock crashed into pleasure and pleasure into shock and neither could win in the confusion. She watched, horrified and fascinated, and aching with a frightening urge as his dark head lowered and his breaths titillated her breasts.

His bared teeth closed gently and a sharp arrow of pleasure shot down deeply. His tongue flicked and she thought she would die. She closed her eyes. This was wicked. Scandalous. Someone might even see them out here. She should stop this, end it, push him away. His mouth and hand made feelings cascade in her, however, that were too delicious to end.

He rose on one arm, and watched his caresses. He deliberately teased her, not unkindly, and saw the reactions that she did not know how to hide. "You like this," he said. It was not a question. "And this." His head lowered again and his tongue flicked at her other breast even as his hand kept devastating her. The sensations piled on one another, making her crazed and impatient.

He kissed her shoulder, her neck, and her ear. "And this." His caress slid down her leg, then up again beneath her skirt.

Alarm jolted her. She was not ignorant. She knew the danger now. His breath and mouth warmed her cheek and ear. "I will not know you completely, but this I will know and so will you. You are mine and this is mine and you will not stop me because you do not want to."

His warm touch already undermined her fear and objection. The breeze on her legs, the caresses on the bare skin of her thighs, evoked desperation within the pleasure. He sucked on her breast and a deep ache of pleasure flowed down, pooling near the warm strokes on her thighs.

One touch. A stunning shock that made her want to beg for more of them. Instead his hand covered her mound in an intimate gesture of protection and possession, briefly. Then he touched no more.

The aching pleasure dimmed. The tightness in her stomach eased. She opened her eyes. He was looking at her.

The emotions reflected in his eyes seemed dark, dangerous, and unresolved.

Her nakedness suddenly astonished her. She covered
herself with her arms, and sat up to set her dress and chemise to rights. She groped behind her back while her face
burned. He lay down, his head behind her, and she felt him
fix the tapes.

Embarrassment and anger streaked like a rocket through
her. She rose to her knees, turned around, and smacked
his shoulder as hard as she could. "You promised!"

He caught her hand. "I kept my promise. You are still a
virgin."

"Barely."

"You are too ignorant to know what *barely* means.
Trust me, it is more than barely still."

She scrambled to her feet and looked out at the sea.
She could not find Summerhays's yacht. Then she noticed
it, tied to the dock.

"We must hurry. They returned." She quickly looked
about, horrified that perhaps in seeking them, Audrianna
and Sebastian may have come this way.

Hawkeswell stood, brushed off his coat, and put it on.
He picked up her bonnet. She snatched it away from him.

"You lured me here because you said you wanted to
speak about my proposal," she said. "Were you lying? Was
this just more of the long game and the old plot?"

His severity had not softened. He still appeared much
as he had when he caressed her. His blue eyes watched
her too closely. Suddenly he was right in front of her, and
that male mastery that he exuded assaulted her.

He pulled her into an embrace, and kissed her again,
hard. The sensuality and familiarity of all those touches
were in the kiss.

"There is no game. No plot. It was the same as with you and that damned boat. A rare opportunity beckoned, and I took it," he said. He lifted her chin so he could look at her, and she had to look at him. "As for your proposal . . ."

She waited, holding her breath, praying she had not been wrong in seeing the decision she wanted earlier, before he got like this.

"No." He said it thoughtfully.

"No?"

"No."

She could not believe this. She had been so sure, from the way he had spoken, that he had accepted the sense of it. "Why not?"

"Because I say so."

"Because *you say so*? That is all the reason I am to get?" She wanted to scream. This had all been a trick. A way to get her up here alone so he could . . . could . . .

She smacked him again, then pushed out of his hold and strode away. She stumbled down the rise, refusing his help, not caring if she fell or looked like a clumsy fool.

Chapter Nine

Hawkeswell tried to take consolation in having been more or less honorable. Doing so had been difficult and painful, and he tried not to mind too much that Verity had not appreciated his sacrifice.

His body did not appreciate it either. It gave him hell for hours. His arousal never totally ended, because every time he looked at her he saw pretty, snowy breasts with provocative dark tips, and a woman mesmerized by her first taste of carnal pleasure.

She did not speak to him the rest of the day. She pretended he did not exist. The unfinished sensuality hung between them like a thick mist that kept blowing in his direction at the least convenient times, leading to inappropriate thoughts and a revival of his erection, and to erotic plots that would probably make her climb down that tree tonight and disappear forever if she knew of them.

Why not?

Because I say so.

It had been a poor and inadequate reason. Stupid. There had been nothing else to say, however.

He could hardly explain that he had decided he wanted her, and that desire had vanquished his earlier decision. She would never consider satisfying a hunger, no matter how compelling, a good reason for denying her the life she wanted. Yet, it was all he had.

Audrianna and Sebastian noticed her pique. Their valiant attempts at light conversation could not alter her icy expression one whit.

She excused herself and retired early. Hawkeswell excused himself in turn, and went out to the terrace to smoke. He was deep in contemplation when another cigar's glowing tip appeared beside him, and a hand set a glass of brandy on the terrace wall in front of him.

He and Summerhays puffed in silence together, gazing out at the flower beds where blooms swayed in the night air. The white and yellow ones caught what little light there was and dotted the expanse like pale sprigs on a woman's dark dress.

"You can thank me," Summerhays said. "Audrianna spied two people on the cove's point and feared you were up to no good. She insisted on coming in at once, but damnation if the sails just couldn't catch the breeze correctly to make fast work of it."

"Thank you."

"Your bride did not appear happy, however."

"Neither am I. Such are the wages of doing the right thing and allowing the inappropriate time and place to inhibit me. If I had been less considerate, we would both be more contented." He claimed more thoughtfulness than he possessed. It had not been consideration that checked him, but that damned promise he had made in the greenhouse in Cumberworth.

Summerhays chuckled quietly. "Time enough for contentment, I suppose. A whole lifetime."

"Here I thought your clumsiness with the yacht meant you were an ally after all. First you advise seduction, but now you insinuate the wisdom of forbearance. The latter is your wife's influence. Don't look so indignant. Do you deny that she sent you out here? Is she above, comforting poor Verity?"

"She has no idea what happened. When she saw Verity, she assumed the two of you had only had a good row."

"We did have a row. A short one. A few words, no more. But, yes, I think you would have to call it a row."

"The storm will have probably blown over by morning."

"Perhaps." *Probably not.* "Row or not, I think that we will go to London in three days."

They puffed away, their smoke snaking out into the night. Summerhays was good enough to talk about other things. He distracted Hawkeswell from thoughts of rows and discontentment, and vivid memories of the lovely passion awakening in Verity.

Verity spent the next day very close to Audrianna. While she tried to reconcile her shocking behavior with Hawkeswell, she also worried that she had lost the entire war through a demonstration of weakness in one battle.

She was almost positive that when he led her up to that grass, he had intended to say something quite different.

Perhaps, after a good night's sleep, he had rediscovered his more sensible inclinations.

She waited hopefully for some sign that he had changed his mind. But he did not address the question again at all. Nor did he apologize for what had happened on that little hill.

If anything he spoke to her, and looked at her, with a new familiarity, as if in having shared such a scandalous embrace, they now shared a private secret and sympathy. His presence pressed on her in invisible ways even when she tried to ignore him. Memories, both physical and visual, kept snaking into her head while she tried to pay attention to Audrianna's chatter.

That night, when she excused herself to retire, he did as well. Her heart rose to her throat while she walked up the stairs with him two steps behind her. She hated what his presence did to her. Hated the confused reactions of anticipation and worry.

At the first landing she turned on him. "Do not try to kiss me tonight. Do not dare. You had enough kisses yesterday and I owe you none for today."

"And you, Verity? Did you have enough kisses yesterday?"

"More than enough. Too many." The way he looked at her made her legs weak. "I did not like them either. It was all very unpleasant. We do not suit when it comes to kisses either. You should change your mind on that *no*. You really should."

He took the last two steps so he stood in front of her squarely. He displayed vague amusement at her protestations. "We suit just fine when it comes to kisses and pleasure, Verity. That will not frighten you so much after a while."

"I am not frightened. And you are wrong. I hated it. I—"

His finger came to rest on her lips, silencing her. "Do I have to prove that I am right tonight? You are challenging me to do so."

Her lips pulsed beneath that touch. Her whole body did, from his proximity and gaze. She gritted her teeth so she would stop reacting like a fool.

"I remind you of your promise," she said, after turning her face enough to break that contact.

"I need no reminders. However, I may have to stay the night in your chamber, to ensure you do not take advantage of another rare opportunity to bolt."

The suggestion alarmed her. Nor did she think he intended to sit in a chair in her sitting room. The scoundrel expected to again do those things that left her barely a virgin.

Sensations that she now recognized scurried with delight at the idea. Luring though they were, her susceptibility also dismayed her.

She could not allow herself to react this way if she wanted to have any pride left when they separated for good. She would never be able to convince him to change his mind if he kept kissing her and touching her like that. And eventually, when she married the right kind of man, she did not want to have to explain that this one had become most familiar before agreeing to let her go.

"No," she said. "You will not. You know that in sharing a chamber you tempt the devil, and your honor will be the worse for it."

He laughed. "How considerate of you, Verity, to worry about my honor on my behalf."

"It is of such concern to me that I promise you will not need to stand guard. I swear that I will be here in the morning. Phrased thus, my promise covers all possible rare opportunities that might arise."

Those blue eyes considered. They lured. Their color deepened. He smiled vaguely, in resignation. He stood aside, and held his arm out to the stairs.

"So be it. But run now, quickly, before I conclude that your pretty flush means you really hope I will be at your chamber door soon."

Verity did not sleep well that night. Hawkeswell had not said that he would *not* be at her chamber door, in so many words, so she kept listening for him there. That she continued to flush for most of the night hardly endeared him to her, and she tossed restlessly, wondering how she would get away now, worrying that she never might.

The situation vexed her, and left her jumpy and cautious. She decided that she needed to claim some privacy even from Audrianna. Therefore, the next morning she rose at dawn and dressed in her plain blue muslin. She tied on her apron and donned a shawl against the morning damp. Then she made her way down to the courtyard.

The gardeners were already bending to their labors with hoes and rakes, shears and carts. She peered over their shoulders and observed how they pruned. She admired the rich loam that the head gardener carted in from a field that had lain fallow the last planting year.

She almost forgot about Hawkeswell and those kisses, and her embarrassment that he had seen her half naked, and his insinuations last night that she really wanted to feel that way again. Therefore, when all the gardeners looked toward the terrace, and the head gardener made a little bow, it annoyed her to turn around and find Hawkeswell standing there.

He appeared dark and serious and too interested in her. The sensations from the hillside echoed in her body as if he commanded them to.

He gestured for her to come to him. Taking her leave of the gardener, she walked back the length of the courtyard and up the steps to the terrace.

"Come with me to the breakfast room," he said. "Audrianna and Sebastian are there, and I have news that they should hear."

She followed him inside and around the corner to the breakfast room that looked out over the courtyard from the lower floor of one of the wings. Audrianna ate there, and Lord Sebastian was serving himself from the dishes on the big sideboard.

"I hope that your aunt has not taken ill," Lord Sebastian said to Hawkeswell once they were all seated.

"Do you have cause to think that she has?" Verity asked, surprised.

"An express rider came with a letter for Lord Hawkeswell this morning," Audrianna explained.

"My aunt is in good health as far as I know. This news is of a different sort entirely." He removed the letter from his coat and set it on the table. He looked at it, then over at Verity. "It is from a solicitor in London. Mr. Thornapple."

"Mr. Thornapple? My trustee?"

"He had written to me at Surrey, then learned I was here instead." He unfolded the letter and scanned its contents. "He writes to inform me that he was successful in obtaining a new inquest into the probable death of Lady

Hawkeswell, born Verity Thompson. It will be held by the coroner in Surrey tomorrow, at the coroner's house. It will be a first step, and an incomplete solution, but will position us well for any appeal to the high courts. He was preparing to go down to Surrey even as he sent this letter off."

He set the letter aside. "We must go to there at once, of course."

"You must take the coach and four. I will give you the names of the staging inns where our spare teams are kept," Lord Sebastian said. "If the weather holds, you should be there by midday tomorrow."

Verity looked on, dismayed, as they made plans. Panic fluttered in her. She felt as if she drove a team of horses herself, and had suddenly lost hold of the ribbons.

"What if we do not rush to Surrey?" Verity blurted. Her question interrupted some advice Lord Sebastian was offering Hawkeswell. Everyone looked at her.

"What if that express rider had not found this house? What if we were staying another day's journey away from Surrey?"

"Do you mean, what if you were actually declared dead?" Hawkeswell asked. "We would then have to explain the mistake when we did arrive back in the county. It will be less complicated if a wrongful determination were not made in the first place."

"Well, I think if someone is declared dead, she should be allowed to be so for a few weeks if she chooses," she muttered.

Encountering only blank faces around the table, she conceded, "But, of course, that is not possible. We must ensure an error is not made. I will go to my chamber and prepare."

She took her leave to make ready for the journey. She

also needed to prepare for the implications of leaving this house.

The agreement forged in Daphne's greenhouse would end when the coach left this property. So would the promises. In the future she would have to rely on her own resources to hold off Hawkeswell.

S usan had most of the garments packed in ten minutes. Verity thanked her for her service, gave her some of the coins left from Hawkeswell's fifteen pounds, and dismissed her. Then she tucked her personal items, her hairbrushes and violet water and two haircombs, in the valise.

The door opened and Hawkeswell entered.

She gestured to the valise. "I am all prepared."

He looked at the valise, then at her. "You are unhappy."

"I thought we would remain here longer. I thought—" She picked up her bonnet and turned to the looking glass.

"You thought to have more time to convince me of your plan," he said.

"I think that you should give me the days in Surrey that I would have had here."

"One day or thirty, it will not matter, Verity. I no longer want to let you go."

No longer. Her heart sank. Those kisses on the hill had indeed changed his mind. He was going to force her back into this marriage because of a brief pleasure and a passing desire.

She glanced back at him, then returned to tying her bonnet's ribbons. She was on the verge of weeping.

Her situation was going to be much harder now. She had hoped to be home when the world found out she was alive and well. She had planned to use the months while she petitioned for that annulment seeing to her father's legacy, and discovering what had become of Michael, and ensuring Katy's welfare. Just her presence near the ironworks would help, and stay Bertram's hand as he dealt with those good people.

"Forgive my emotion." She wiped her eyes. "I see myself living among strangers now, people who have no reason to be kind to me."

"You fear your future too much. It will not be like that."

"Are you so democratic, Lord Hawkeswell, that you will permit me to go home, to visit the people I know?"

"I do not see why not."

"How often?"

"You can go as often as it is convenient for me to take you there."

"Why do I think that you will rarely find it convenient?"

He revealed no vexation with her. If anything, his expression looked sympathetic. "Because you are obligated to think the worst of me. If you do not, you will never be able to lie to yourself."

That took her aback. She turned from the mirror and faced him. "I do not lie to myself."

"You have spent the last two days lying to yourself, I think. You have been telling yourself that you can still convince me to want to be rid of you. You have been telling yourself that accepting this union means victory for your cousin and defeat for you, when it does not have to be that way."

"I may still be angry with my cousin, but my obligations to him, and his authority over me, are over no matter what happens, so that anger does not signify anymore."

"Then I must assume that the anger still in you is directed toward *me*, for being a party to Bertram's scheme. You do not want to give me victory either."

"I do not want to give the scheme itself victory. *Nor should I have to.* You pretended to understand that, but it was only one more ruse to get what you wanted and put me off my guard."

He half smiled. "Ah, you *have* been lying to yourself. Not only are you still claiming that you did not like that pleasure, which is a blatant falsehood; now you have been telling yourself that I importuned you on that hill, as part of the grand plot."

She glared at him.

"Did you pick through the memories carefully before concluding that, Verity? As you weighed my nefarious behavior, did you relive the pleasure of my mouth on your breast and my hand on your—"

"Most certainly not!" She flushed. "You are a scoundrel. I know your game, however." She snatched up her valise and strode to the door.

"You may think that I am a scoundrel, Verity, but I am also your husband. And if there is a game at work here, I have already won."

Chapter Ten

"Should this not be determined by a judge of one of the high courts, Mr. Thornapple? I agreed to hold this new inquiry because the disappearance occurred in this county, but since there is no body, my duties are unclear."

"In such cases, sir, there are no regularities, due to the situation being so rare. I begin with you today, and will then bring your determination to the King's Bench for an official declaration of death. As you say, the circumstances began here, and a local inquiry is as good a place to start as any."

Verity heard the exchange as the door to the library opened. The inquest was under way.

Hawkeswell paused at the threshold. She watched him scan the group who attended the proceedings.

"There is, as you know, a presumption of the continuance of life when a person goes missing," the coroner said. "Hence the tradition of waiting seven years."

She had expected an aging country squire to serve as

county coroner, not a fashionably dressed man no more than thirty years of age. This was a good property, and his library, which served the meeting, had tasteful furnishings and handsome bindings.

Mr. Thornapple cut a courtly figure himself, with his white hair and impeccable grooming. A solicitor of humble origins, he had been one of the few men her father trusted completely.

Mr. Thornapple cleared his throat. "The point of law that applies is the balance of probabilities, and that negates the presumption of which you speak. If a ship goes down, there is no longer a presumption of the continuance of life for the crew that goes missing afterward. There is no wait for seven years to pass before their estates can be settled. The balance of probability says the crew drowned. Hawkeswell's bride went missing, and evidence of her demise in the Thames has accumulated. Furthermore, if she still lived, surely she would have made her existence known by now. What other choice would she have, unless she wanted to starve? Furthermore—"

"I must interrupt, sir," the coroner said. "I see that Lord Hawkeswell has arrived. Join us, Lord Hawkeswell, since this inquiry is at your request as well as Mr. Thornapple's."

Heads turned toward the door where they stood. Verity did not see Bertram or Nancy, and the sick tightness in her stomach eased.

A dark-haired woman dressed all in lilac smiled brightly at Hawkeswell. Verity recognized her as Colleen, who had first introduced Bertram to her cousin, in the interests of helping Hawkeswell solve his financial problems.

Hawkeswell took Verity's arm and escorted her toward the desk where the coroner sat. "It was at my request, but I must withdraw it now. There is no need to continue."

"My lord, it is time to resolve this," Thornapple said in a tone both exasperated and confused. "You yourself encouraged me to—"

"The inquiry is unnecessary because my wife has finally been found alive and well, as you will see." He positioned Verity squarely in front of the coroner. "Please remove your bonnet, Verity."

She untied the ribbons and removed it. Mr. Thornapple gaped, then gave Hawkeswell a very severe stare.

"This is the young woman, Mr. Thornapple?" the coroner asked. "Do you know her on sight?"

"I do. It is she, Verity Thompson, heiress to Joshua Thompson's estate."

A wave of mumbles and exclamations flowed behind her.

Mr. Thornapple's expression changed from astonished to angry in a blink. "I should like to know where she has been these two years. Did you hide her away, Lord Hawkeswell? I cannot think of how that would benefit you, unless you thought this dramatic revelation would be amusing one day."

"It would not benefit me in the least, as you know better than anyone. I discovered her whereabouts by accident less than a week ago. I would have informed you at once, but I did not anticipate that you would find success in requesting a new inquiry so quickly."

"Fortunately, not too quickly," the coroner mused. "A day sooner and I might have found the balance of probabilities indicated she was dead." He scrutinized Verity, but not too critically. He seemed fascinated by the development, and not sorry to be hosting an event that would be the talk of the county by nightfall. "Where were you all this time, Lady Hawkeswell?"

"In Middlesex."

Mr. Thornapple all but spit. "Then you could not have missed the fact that your death was presumed."

"What were you doing in Middlesex? How did you come to be there?" the coroner asked.

"That is between my wife and me," Hawkeswell said. "For your purposes today, her living, breathing body is enough, don't you agree?"

"More than enough." The coroner could not hide his amusement. "I would say we are most thoroughly adjourned." He stood, and bowed to Verity. "It is my pleasure to meet you, Madam. Thornapple, let me offer you some brandy before you have apoplexy. Lady Hawkeswell, allow me to introduce you to some of your neighbors. Many were at your wedding, I expect, but you have probably forgotten their faces by now."

The sounds of moving bodies churned behind her. Mr. Thornapple positioned himself right in front of her and Hawkeswell. "I expect some answers."

"In due course," Hawkeswell said curtly. "We should be in London soon."

Mr. Thornapple's anger melted into something more troubled. He peered at Verity hard. "Is there anything that you want to say to me *now*, Lady Hawkeswell?"

I ran away because I did not consent freely. Should she tell him that, here, now? Would it make a difference if she did?

She looked around. The neighbors were dawdling, loath to leave a performance that had proven far more entertaining than they expected when they wandered here to pass the day. Most eyes were on her and Hawkeswell, but the coroner's brandy was being sampled by several men who had decided the shocking surprise called for fortification of their senses.

"I thank you for being a true steward of my property these last years," she said to Mr. Thornapple. "I indeed had reasons for not making myself known to you sooner. However, as Lord Hawkeswell said, they will be revealed in due course. I do not want to make this more of a theatrical event than it already is. I look forward to calling on you in London very soon."

Mr. Thornapple's nod turned into a bow. He took his leave.

Verity braced herself, and turned to Hawkeswell. He had heard what she said. His expression appeared much like it had been when they left Airymont. *If there is a game, I have already won.* The cost had been high, however. His neighbors examined her with curiosity, but the looks they gave him contained too much amusement for a man's pride.

"There is no way to remove you without greeting them," he said, indicating the people between them and the doorway. "We will make quick work of it. God knows I have no desire to be the dancing dog any longer." He led her into their midst.

Smiling mouths. Curious eyes. Surreptitious glances of mockery at Hawkeswell. Precise etiquette in every case, and elaborate expressions of relief. They all knew there was a very good story here, and hoped for a tidbit at least, and refused to drift away like they should.

Colleen waited on the outskirts of the group. She embraced Verity when, finally, Hawkeswell made it to her.

"Dear girl," Colleen cried. "What a relief to see you, and to learn at last that the worst did not happen. Do the Thompsons know?"

"We have not yet informed them," Hawkeswell said. "Perhaps you will do that for us. Please discourage them from coming down here, however. Verity does not need to be entertaining family so soon."

"I will write to them at once, and be firm on that. It would hardly do to host family now, no matter how excited they may be." She embraced Verity again. "I hope, however, that you will allow me to call. I could be of help, perhaps, as you take on your duties at Greenlay Park."

She appeared sincere, and Verity did not relish navigating Hawkeswell's estate without advice. She had not known Colleen well, except as the cousin of Hawkeswell and the person to introduce him to Bertram. She suspected that Colleen's kindness in befriending Bertram and Nancy had been exploited by them more than this pretty lady realized.

"Please do call. I will be grateful for your advice."

"But not that of your mother," Hawkeswell said, taking his hat and gloves from the butler. "We will go to her when it is time. I do not want her interfering now."

Colleen swallowed an impish smile that said she understood why anyone would want to avoid her mother.

Hawkeswell handed Verity into the coach. For the first time on this journey, he entered behind her. Verity saw why. The other people at the inquest had decided to depart right now too, so they could watch the resurrected countess and her earl a bit longer.

"Will they send out riders to cry the news?" she asked.

"In their own way, yes." He checked his pocket watch. "Their letters will reach London late tomorrow. We will wait it out here for a few days, before braving it out in town. Most of society will be long gone from London, of course, so you will never hear most of the talk."

"There will still be questions. What do you intend to say in response?"

"Damned if I know."

Not the truth, then. She could tell that this little drama embarrassed him. The coroner's humor and Mr. Thorn-apple's suspicions were the least of it. Those curious eyes, impatient for the details, had heralded what was to come.

He would hardly want to admit that his bride had never freely consented to marry him, so had run away and hid for two years until she came of age to have standing in a court of law. On the other hand, he could not lie and say she had lost her memory, even if she agreed to the ruse. Perhaps he would simply say nothing.

She watched the Surrey countryside that they passed. She had not noticed its beauty on the way to the coroner's house. She had seen nothing at all the last two days alone in this carriage. The entire journey had been passed in an effort to maintain her composure and to prepare for the shock her arrival would create at the inquiry.

Now she realized that this county possessed a lush rich-ness. A palette of greens decorated her view, with some dark browns in fields revealing good land for farming. Flowers flourished too, in beds at even modest homes, and as sprays of wildflowers running over low hills and road-sides.

They passed a small farmhouse blessed with many such blooms, but the summer display could not hide the house's bad condition.

"That family needs a new roof," she observed.

"They do not only need a new roof, but also a new floor. Improvements in irrigation would increase the yield of the land they work too. Regrettably, the man from whom they lease that land has not been able to help, much as he might like to."

She could tell from his tight tone that he was the man

in question. They were on his land now. "Can they at least sustain themselves?"

"Barely, and only because I took no rent two years ago, when the crops all failed for lack of warmth." A man walking down the road toward the farmhouse waved at the coach, and Hawkeswell waved back. "I have known that farmer my entire life. His people have been here almost as long as mine, for generations. I was educated to see him as a responsibility, and not only as a tenant. His fortunes depend on mine as much as they do the sun."

"It was the same between my father and his workers, even if the bond did not go back generations. To his mind their welfare was his responsibility. He knew that others who owned mills did not believe that, but he did."

He smiled at her reference to her home, and her past. "It appears we have something in common after all, then."

She rather wished they did not. She had assumed two years ago that he wanted her money to live in high style, not to put in new irrigation and build new roofs. More had compelled him than the chance to buy expensive indulgences, however.

That did not alter what had happened. It did not make her situation any more right or fair. It merely made it hard to blame him.

"Verity, I hope that you do not mind that I told Colleen she could write to your cousin," he said. "That would be better than receiving a letter from a ghost, I thought."

"I do not mind. It was not my intention to write to him at all."

"If you do not want to write, then I will do it. In a few days, so the surprise is well digested first."

"As you wish."

"He will probably want to see you."

"More likely he will want to see *you*. He will want to ensure that whatever the two of you agreed still stands. Promises were made, I am sure, that are important to him."

She did not have to look at him to know that he did not like that reference. His displeasure came to her through the air. It was odd how that happened. His moods could sometimes be felt now, even if he did nothing to express them.

"You should see him, Verity, if he comes down to London, whatever his true reasons for doing so. You said he did not mourn, but you really do not know that. He is your family, and some amends are in order for what you did. Apologies at least."

His scold angered her so severely that she barely kept her composure. She gave her attention to this man who refused to understand just who had to apologize to whom.

"I will not apologize to him or to anyone else. If you are determined that I must see him, I want your promise I will never be alone with him or his wife, ever."

He found her demand interesting. Or else her anger surprised him enough that he forgot his own. She was not hiding her emotions about Bertram well, and she heard her voice speak in hard, brittle tones.

"Verity, surely you do not—"

"*Ever*. Promise it, or Bertram will be in hell before I greet him again."

Again that curious, speculative gaze. "If it is what you want, I promise."

She had little memory of Greenlay Park's appearance, other than it was an intimidating house of ancient grandeur and old-fashioned furnishings. She had been too sad and worried when she was here for her wedding to notice much else. As they approached this time she took its measure, however.

It dominated its low hillside, and no forest obscured the view for miles around. The massive main block of the house faced the lane that led to it. The stones alone were big, and of a deep creamy hue, and the long windows marching up its facade spoke of many levels and high ceilings and a complexity of chambers that had made her feel tiny and perpetually lost two years ago.

Other blocks attached to the first, like a series of additions cobbled into wings spreading right and left. Classical, but in the old French style, Nancy had said on seeing this house. She meant the style of the old monarchy. The style of the aristocrats who lost their heads less than thirty years ago, to her father's approval.

She noticed that the landscaping surrounding the house for a quarter mile was in bad condition. At some point Mr. Repton's influence had been employed, and she could tell where ground had been moved to create artificial rises and falls, and a canal dug to wind picturesquely through banks of wildflowers and shrubbery. Lack of maintenance meant the banks had now returned to wilderness and the trees so artfully placed had lost good form.

She wondered, as the coach came to a stop and Hawkeswell opened the door, what her father would say if he knew his daughter was expected to live in such a place.

An old man and a woman of middle years emerged through the massive entry doors. The man hurried to the coach, buttoning his coat on the way.

"My lord. We did not expect— The messenger did not say that—"

"It is a long story, Krippin, and for another day, perhaps. This is Lord Sebastian Summerhays's coach, and it must begin its return to Essex tomorrow. Have the coachman and horses dealt with for the night."

"Of course, my lord. Mrs. Bradley, please see to my lord's guest."

Mrs. Bradley came forward just as Verity stepped from the coach.

"You remember Mr. Krippin and Mrs. Bradley, don't you, darling?" Hawkeswell drew her toward them. "The countess has returned home, Krippin. Please inform the servants."

Mrs. Bradley hid her shock, but Krippin's mouth gaped for an instant. Then the training of a lifetime summoned his formal demeanor again. "I will of course give them the good news, sir. Welcome home, Madam."

They all walked to the door as if she had been gone a mere fortnight in London. Inside, two footmen were summoned and sent to carry baggage.

"I would like to go to my chambers, Mrs. Bradley," Verity said before anyone could suggest something else. "I would like to rest from my journey."

"Certainly, Madam."

Mrs. Bradley mounted the stairs by her side. Both of them pretended ignorance of the fact that Verity had no idea how to get to her chambers, or to anywhere else in this house except the gardens.

Chapter Eleven

The Earl of Hawkeswell needed money.

Verity had not seen the evidence of that so clearly two years ago. Absorbed in her own worries, submissive in her decision, she had not paid attention.

Now a hundred little indications added to the ones she had already noticed in the farms and the landscaping.

There were few servants in this big house. Not nearly as many as at Airymont. Mrs. Bradley promised to send up a girl but it was doubtful the girl would be a proper lady's maid.

The furnishings showed wear too. The drapes should be replaced on the tall southern windows where the sun had done its worst to their fabric. There had been little effort to improve conveniences here either. At Airymont, there were water closets and even a new bathing chamber. It was apparent that this household still made do with pots and portable tubs.

Each observation discouraged her more. They served

as so many nails in the coffin holding her plan. The money denied him thus far from her settlement would continue to be out of reach during any petition, she suspected.

A huge sum was to come to him upon their wedding. It had not, he said. Perhaps she should promise to wait on any petitions until he received it. She would have to ask Mr. Thornapple if that would make a difference.

Mrs. Bradley brought her to the same apartment that she had been given when she came for the wedding. She realized now that someone had invested in these chambers at least. Recently. These drapes were new, as were the bed hangings in Prussian blue. The chairs featured unblemished upholstery and the fireplace sported scrubbed stones.

She pictured the earl ordering this done two years ago, so that his bride would not have to suffer the consequences of his finances. She wondered how he had paid for it all. Perhaps he had taken on debt.

He could have left it all as it had been and she would not have noticed that either. It would have made no difference to her. When one was in a sacrificial state of mind, one did not care if the stake on which she would be martyred was new and of good quality.

"All of your things are here, of course," Mrs. Bradley said. She led the way into the dressing room, and opened three wardrobes and two trunks.

Verity fingered the fine fabrics. She had all but forgotten this wardrobe, purchased in London during the months before the wedding. Nancy had dragged her to modiste after modiste, demanding the best lace and silks. They had ordered enough dresses to wear four a day and still not repeat one for two weeks. Nancy had enjoyed the spree far more than Verity herself.

She pulled out several dresses and held them to her

body and looked down. She had dressed very plainly at The Rarest Blooms, but not because she preferred humble garments. One did not garden in the best muslin or silk. Nor could she allow Daphne to lay out much money for her fabrics.

She found herself smiling at a lemon yellow sarcenet promenade dress as it flowed over her legs. It would be nice to wear pretty clothes. That was a feminine interest that she had never much indulged, but here was an entire wardrobe waiting to be explored.

"I will have water brought up," Mrs. Bradley said, after unpacking the valise of its few items. "Then we will leave you to rest, Madam. Normally we keep country hours here, but the cook will be surprised that my lord is in residence today, and will be a bit later than normal with dinner as a result. I will send the girl up in two hours, to help you dress."

Verity decided a rest before dinner would be wise. Resurrection had proven to be exhausting, and she needed to be in top form if she were going to spar with Hawkeswell at dinner.

He tapped at the door. When no one responded, he eased the latch down.

Verity's little sitting room was empty. No sounds came from the dressing room either. He entered her bedchamber. An artificial twilight shrouded it because the drapes were closed.

She lay asleep there, in her chemise and stockings. The vaguest frown marred her peace. Perhaps she dreamed of something distressing. Her legs, drawn up as she rested on her side, caused the chemise to rise high enough that her left thigh and hip were uncovered.

The lovely line of that hip and thigh, the gentle curve made by her body in this position, captivated him. Another day, soon, he would give in to the urge to join her and caress that soft, graceful form. Today he kept his arousal from having its way, much the way he had learned to control his temper.

He set a small box on the bed beside her, near her face, and opened it. The pearls within glowed in the dim light on their bed of blue velvet.

He had come close to selling them several times during the last two years, even though they were family heirlooms. A countess of Hawkeswell had received them as a gift two centuries ago from a royal lover, the legend went. Perfect and priceless, they would have gone far to delaying the decline of this house.

He was very sure it had not been sentiment that stayed his hand. Rather, he had not been sure the pearls were his to sell anymore. He had given them to Verity as a wedding gift.

He looked at the note he had written, decided against it, and slipped out the door.

Her nose hit something as she turned. The sensation nudged her awake. She rose out of a delicious weightlessness, and grew aware of herself and her surroundings.

She opened her eyes. Something odd blocked her view. She rose up on one arm and examined it.

A pretty wooden box, perfectly crafted and lined in velvet, rested on the bed. It was open, and strands of little creamy orbs lay within, contrasting in texture and color with their home.

The pearls.

A servant had delivered them while she dressed for the wedding two years ago. Nancy had been enraptured by their beauty and value, and insisted that Verity wear them for the ceremony. And she had worn them, just as she had done everything else demanded of her that day. But their beauty and rarity had done nothing to alter her mood, or make her any happier.

They had also been the first thing she removed after the wedding breakfast, because she feared breaking a strand. A clear memory came to her, one of the clearest of that day, of Nancy approaching her while she dropped those pearls onto the dressing table in the next chamber.

There are some things I must tell you now. That was how Nancy began that conversation that had provoked her rage and flight.

She lifted the pearls. No servant would leave them like this, on her pillow. Hawkeswell had been here.

He had returned her wedding gift to her, so she would have them as if she never left this house and this property that day. He expected her to wear them tonight, she was very sure. He would be insulted if she did not.

The strands fell over her hand and down her arm. Pearls felt like nothing else in the world, in their weight and surface and discreet luxury. These were probably worth a fortune.

She would indulge herself in their beauty for one dinner. They were not hers to keep, however.

Verity came down to dinner, as a vision transformed. Hawkeswell could not take his eyes off her when she entered the drawing room.

He had never seen her in anything except those simple dresses these last days. Even the memory of her wedding dress had been obliterated by unembellished, serviceable muslin.

Now the most interesting rosy brown silk encased her in a long, narrow, liquid shaft of elegance. The lace decorating its sleeves and hem and low neckline contrasted nicely with the unusual color and made the ensemble appear crisply fresh.

A sumptuous shawl in a paler version of the same color draped her arms and dipped low in the back. Multiple strands of pearls circled her neck and emphasized the elegance of her appearance, and of that particular way she had of tilting her head in silent query.

It tilted now, when she joined him. She noticed his glance at the pearls, and her hand rose and touched them for an instant. Her gaze carried an acknowledgment of what they were and how they had reappeared.

"The evening is fair. We are going to dine informally, on the terrace," he said.

"That would please me."

And him as well. There would be time enough for the crushing formalities of her new station. They did not have to spend this meal in a chamber that could seat forty.

They went out to the terrace where a table had been set. Candles flickered in the faint breeze, reflecting off silver and china still visible in the gathering dusk. The meal began arriving, more elaborate in courses and flavors than normally served here. Mrs. Bradley and the cook must have decided that the return of their countess required a bit of celebration and that frugality could be set aside tonight.

She peered through the dusk at the garden. "I remember it being bigger. Deeper."

"Wilderness has reclaimed the back half. It was the gardener's solution when most of his staff were let go. The grasses and saplings took over with astonishing speed. It is somewhat unsightly."

"The maintenance of such an estate must be costly."

"I have learned how little is essential. When necessary, one can sacrifice pretty vistas."

"That back garden could still be reclaimed. Or you could allow the wilderness free rein. In a few years it would be complete, and no longer unsightly."

She had drunk all her wine, and a servant poured her more. Hawkeswell watched the crystal rise to her lips. Last light had passed, and her mouth appeared very dark in the candlelight. Dark and erotic.

"There are not any trees of size in this garden," he said. "The light is good year-round. Perhaps, instead of rebuilding flower beds or leaving nature to do its work, a greenhouse would be in order back there."

"Their maintenance requires a great deal of work. If you have let the staff go—"

"The lack of servants on this property will be a problem soon solved."

"Then a greenhouse would be an enhancement. It would provide fresh flowers to the house year-round. If you reside here much of the year, a hothouse would be good too. Then the more exotic fruits could be grown for your table."

"How big do you think they should be?"

They debated the size, and she described the types available. She knew a good deal about greenhouses, and warmed to the conversation. She even laughed, which he thought unlikely tonight. She did not notice the servants drift away when the meal was done, so that the master and mistress might talk alone into the night.

"I do not think our old gardener is an expert at growing in greenhouses," he said. "You would have to instruct him if we do this. It would be your domain, if you choose."

The light made her blue eyes almost black, and caught the most subtle expression dramatically. Now he saw hesitation, and surprise at how they suddenly did not discuss his home alone, but both of theirs.

"There is room for one at the London house as well," he said. "You can continue your experiments, no matter where you reside."

She met his gaze for a long spell. Then she looked anywhere but at him. Her gaze roamed to the candle flames, the garden, the wall, as if in ignoring him, she could ignore the inevitable.

Finally she looked at the table's top. "I would prefer to continue them at The Rarest Blooms, until all is settled between you and me."

"No."

"Then allow me to stay with Audrianna. Lord Sebastian's coach will return to Essex tomorrow, you said. I implore you to allow me to go with it."

"No."

She did not ask why. It was in her eyes that she knew. She was not immune to the intimacy of this night, and the tightening, stimulating mood surrounding them now, full of compelling anticipation.

She finally looked at him. "And if I go anyway, without your agreement?"

"Since I am your husband, it is not my agreement that you need, but my permission."

"You know that I do not accept that."

He reached across the table for her hand. "You keep daring me to be harsher with you than I want to be, or need to be." He raised her hand to his mouth and kissed it. "This marriage has taken place, and it is time for it to begin in truth."

She gently freed her hand, and stood. He did as well, not only due to etiquette, but also out of respect. She was not a big woman, and one would not think her to be strong. Yet she had proven more determined and tenacious in her odd quest than he ever knew a woman could be.

She faced him in the night. Her head tilted in that memorable way. "When do you intend for this marriage to begin in truth?"

"Soon."

"I assume that you will at least give me fair warning first?"

He reached out and touched the pearls. "I have already done so." He skimmed the surface of the pearls, then let his fingertips slowly do the same to the skin right below the strand.

She closed her eyes to that stroking touch. She was too ignorant to know how much she revealed in that reaction, or in the way her body flexed with a tremble.

"And if . . ." She licked her lips. She had no idea how suggestive that looked. "And if I refuse?"

He had not decided how soon, but he'd be damned if he would give her time to open *that* front in her little war.

In a matter of seconds, soon became very soon, and very soon became now.

Chapter Twelve

He did not answer her question. He just stood there, too close, too tall, too dark. One might think that all his concentration rested on the slow, soft way he caressed her skin below the necklace.

She braced against the sensations. It was insidious how such a small touch could create rivulets of pleasure that diverted her attention from anything else.

Except him. His mere presence created a shocking intimacy. Her own essence responded as if she had no choice. A thrilling shiver of heat flowed through her.

Her body betrayed her horribly. The sensations from the hilltop returned even though he barely touched her. Indulging them became a compelling desire that obscured all the solid reasons why she should not allow this at all.

Outright denial proved impossible, but she managed to move back, away from him and that touch. There was enough fear within the thrill to allow that.

He followed, pace for pace. He did not menace her. He

merely stayed close, and prevented her from escaping his silent power.

Her rump hit the terrace wall, and she could back up no farther.

She placed her hand against his chest. Her palm pressed the silk of his waistcoat and her fingers the fine linen of his cravat. She did not do it to touch him, but to hold him at bay. Surely her gesture intended nothing besides that.

She thought she saw him smile in the dark. His hand came to rest atop hers and he pressed it down even more, so it turned into something of a caress. His heart beat under her palm and she felt his very life thrumming into her through her hand, and felt his body's warmth and the muscles of his chest.

He lifted her hand and kissed it. First the back, then the palm. Seductive, soft kisses stunned her arm. Sweet kisses, full of ardor and danger, so confident in their ability to mesmerize. On her pulse now, kisses of dark warmth that forced her blood to sing.

Closer now. Too close. His body not connecting to hers, but creating thrills as if it did. His palms now, warm and dry and too appealing in their masculine firmness, cupping her head and holding her, and tilting it so he could look at her.

She knew then, as she looked at him and the moonlight revealed his severe passion. She knew this would not be like the kisses of the past, and that all hope of freedom would end tonight.

She tried to conjure up memories of Michael, so she might use guilt as a shield. His face came as a mere phantom, and the kisses as childish, giggling things. She scrambled to find other sanctuaries, to stop him with words or

actions. But he kissed her while her mind ran, and he ensured no plan emerged.

A kiss designed to dazzle, to ensnare, to overwhelm.
A kiss that she could not escape. She had no choice except to submit to the ravishment of her mouth, first sweet,
then profound, then deep and so possessive she could not
breathe.

"The servants," she said on a gasp when he ended it,
finally, leaving her limp. Her first words and rebellion and
she barely managed either.

"They are long gone. Far away, above or below. They
know better than to linger in view or in hearing." He
kissed her again, softly, so softly that she wondered if she
had misunderstood his intentions. Then he embraced her,
and she knew she had not.

So hard to think, when your mind was forgetting everything except pleasure. Her consciousness savored the titillations to her body, to the exclusion of more rational ideas.

"I do not want . . ." The protest barely made it out, and
died as a caress skimmed her breast and her body cried
with delight.

"You do not want this?" he asked, while his mouth
pressed warmth and lures to her neck and ears and shoulder. His hand cupped her breast, and caressed again. "Are
you sure? Or are you lying to yourself again? There has
been too much of that today, don't you think?"

His hand did wicked things. Delicious things. She could
barely stand because of the way her strength dissolved.
Pleasure astonished again and again, robbing her of will
and thought and protest. She did not want this, but her
body did, and he ensured it spoke louder in this debate.

She could not deny it. She did not know how to. Desire

shouted down her small protest. He made sure it did. But he had heard it anyway, she knew. He had heard and understood but was making sure she would not protest again.

She tried once more to form the words, to escape the act that would bind her forever. Only instead her mind capitulated and acknowledged that there was no winning, no matter what the words, not now and not later. Her plan had been hopeless and she would never break this bond. She should allow the pleasure to have its way and revel in being so alive it seemed unearthly.

He claimed her mouth in a determined, dominating kiss and bound her closer in an encompassing embrace. She lost her weak grip on the lifeline to her intentions. She floated away on the sea of sensations, into a seductive mist.

No longer lying. No longer pretending. Hungry now, wanting more, not less. The touch on her breast no longer satisfied, but maddened her. The closeness no longer felt close enough. She melted into him, sharing breaths and scents and merging senses. He was in the mist too now; then he was the mist itself, surrounding her, entering her.

He sat her on the terrace's low wall and showered fevered kisses while his hands plucked at her back. She thrilled as the dress loosened. Low and deep, a cry pulsed and teased when he lowered the bodice and chemise and exposed her. She gazed down at herself, at her breasts rising full in the moonlight below the lustrous pearls, their dark tips so hard and sensitive.

Begging now, waiting, wanting. Watching his fingertips approach, breathless with anticipation. Then torture, sweet torture, and a building, excruciating need filling her, allowing no other thought except a crazed physical insistence for more and more and more.

His dark head dipped and his tongue laved and she

held his head to her so he would never stop, so the sensations would consume her. His caress moved to her legs, smoothing over hose and garter and higher to flesh. She parted her legs so he could, so the moist warmth there would be relieved, so the discomfort might abate. That caress, so firm and sure, so claiming and determined, rose higher yet, until it touched the discomfort itself and sent shocks of pleasure through her until she was spinning, spinning beyond hope in the madness.

Floating now, strong arms bearing her away. The terrace gone and the walls gone but the night and stars remained. Scents of fuchsias and pansies all around and moist, velvety petals on the skin of her back and arms and breasts.

He stripped off her gown, then her chemise. She looked down at her nakedness amid the flowers, her skin and hose and pearls alight in the dark. He knelt beside her, casting off coats, pulling off cravat, looking at her, those sapphire eyes absorbing her, commanding her, mesmerizing her. She waited, waited, her body throbbing and hungry for that crying pleasure again.

He gave it to her. He knew how. Oh, yes, too well he knew how. He joined her there in the flowers and made her cry for real, his kisses and tongue and hands promising ecstasy. She cried out, unable to contain the shocks of pleasure. She clung to him and cried and cried when he played at that hot center between her legs and tantalized her with touches designed to devastate.

He controlled the pleasure and desire and she had no say, no choices now. Her body could deny itself nothing and rejoiced when he came above her, even though she startled at being so helpless beneath his strength. He spread her legs and kept her crying again and again with those caresses and kisses until he pressed into her, filling her slowly but inexorably, forcing their bodies to join. The mist of intimacy turned heavy and dark and finally rained, drenching her soul.

Her body still hungered and wanted and desired, even as tearing pain and shock woke her from the daze. She opened her eyes to his dark form over her. Taut and hard and tense with control, he moved in her and she felt his own madness straining, his own desire aching for more and more and forever and fulfillment.

It all came hard. Hard enough to hurt badly. Hard enough to evoke renewed sensations of pleasure in her too. She submitted to a crescendo of power and tension that strained and strained, then snapped. After that there was suddenly silence and peace and the stars above and blooms below, and his deep breaths marking the pulse of time inside her and between them.

"We must go."
His voice, quiet and calm. Too close. Too real.
"You go. I do not want to yet." She had been watching the stars and smelling the blooms and finding herself again. The latter was taking some doing. He had just made sure, after all, that she could never totally find her old self again.

It is time for this marriage to begin in truth. He had made sure of that too. She had allowed it. She had not fought or protested much. Not nearly enough. She may have been unwilling when she wed, but she could not claim she was unwilling tonight. He had known she did not want this, but he had seduced her into wanting it anyway.

She had betrayed more than herself tonight. Also her

father and her home and the people who mattered in her life. The implications of this impulsive act waited right outside the daze still making her dreamy and listless.

She would have to face the fullness of her defeat soon. Tomorrow, or even sooner. She would never have most of the life she had wanted now. She wondered if she would be able to have any of it at all.

He stood, and lifted his coats. His shirt glowed and his form loomed above her. "It is damp, and unhealthy to lie thus. Come now." He extended his hand to her.

She grasped her garments to her body and stood. Her nakedness seemed foolish and scandalous. She struggled to get her arms in the chemise and dress without exposing herself to his gaze again.

He turned her and fixed the dress. Then he took her hand and led her through the garden and back to the terrace. She glanced at the windows and listened to the silence quake. Had the servants truly gone away, above and below? No doubt all guessed what had happened even if they had. She had been gone for two years, after all. Their master would be expecting his due.

She was glad that he did not speak while they walked up to their apartments. There was certainly nothing she had to say. However, by the time they arrived at her doors, a little anger had seeped into her because some of the shock had finally passed.

He bent to kiss her cheek and she let him.

"I think that you have been less than honorable tonight," she said, so he would not think that she did not understand what had happened, and why.

"Blame it on the pearls. They appeared so lovely above your naked breasts, Verity. You looked dangerously provocative, and I quite lost my good sense."

He kissed her again, then walked toward his own doors. She opened hers and slipped inside.

Blame it on the pearls. What nonsense.

Hawkeswell slept late and woke blissfully contented. He called for a bath, idled in the water until it cooled, dressed for the country, and ate breakfast while he quizzed the attending footman about county doings. All the while he contemplated what to say to Verity when he saw her.

He did not think apologies were necessary. She was his wife after all. However, he had not been as careful with her as he had intended. Odd, that.

Normally in taking pleasure he managed the requisite control to ensure he gave it as well. Damned if he knew if he had last night, though. The details were lost within memories of a rage of desire and an unearthly release.

Unfortunately, he suspected that the intensity of his experience indicated he had not been very careful at all. He had ravished her, and while he had little experience with innocents, he did know that ravishing was not the way to handle them.

When noon had long passed, he wandered up to Verity's apartment. He decided this might be a good day to knock. He waited for her response with less contentment than he had known on waking. More of the details were emerging in his memory now. Enough to cause him to suspect that a very icy wind might blow out once the door opened.

She did not come at all. Instead a servant did, a young blond girl who carried last night's dress and a needle.

"My lady is not here, sir. She was gone before I ever came to her."

Verity had not been down below this morning either, however. A shocking certainty jolted him. *She had run away again.* He had tried to force defeat on her. Worse, the seduction had been clumsy at the end, and he had hurt her. Now she had announced by bolting that she would never give up.

Fighting the rise of his temper along with a sickening worry, he strode down and called for Krippin and Mrs. Bradley. He paced while he waited, and planned the letter that he would send to Summerhays and the much firmer one he would write to Daphne Joyes. Only when Krippin and Bradley hurried into the library did he realize that he had been yelling for them.

"I want to know everything regarding my wife's movements this morning. Quiz the servants; talk to the grooms. Do whatever you can to discern where she has gone."

Krippin glanced at Mrs. Bradley. Mrs. Bradley cowered.

"My lord," Krippin ventured. "Lady Hawkeswell woke early, came down, asked for some tea, and drank it in the morning room. She then let herself out. She is in the garden now. I just saw her. I believe that she has been there the entire time."

The garden. Of course.

Feeling a fool, and more relieved than he liked, Hawkeswell strode out to the terrace.

He spied her at the back, where the wilderness tried to reclaim yet more ground. She wore the blue muslin and bonnet that he had first seen in Cumberworth. She bent and rose, bent and rose, while he watched.

He went down and walked toward her. The old gardener was trimming some boxwood near the terrace, right beside a bed whose center section of flowers had been flattened. Anyone looking at those crushed plants would guess what had happened there. Hawkeswell was sure that he saw the distinct impressions of a woman's head, shoulders, and hips.

"This bed should be cut back, Saunders."

Saunders stopped his clipping and bowed. "I set about that this morning, milord, but milady came out and saw me and forbade it. You cut a flower and it does no harm, but to cut a whole plant down at this time of year can kill it, she said."

"Is that true?"

Saunders nodded. "She said the poor plants should not suffer because of some fool's carelessness."

"Did she say anything else?"

Saunders flushed. "I can't remember. My memory is not what it used to be, milord."

Hawkeswell strolled down the path until he reached Verity. She bent and rose once more, and threw a plant into a bucket by her side.

They faced each other across the derelict plot of garden. Some flowers grew here amid the wilder greens, lilac ones with rough leaves and many petals, like small purple daisies.

"Have you decided to restore this section?" he asked.

"I think so." She returned to her work.

"Saunders said that you would not permit him to cut back those flowers we ruined last night."

"Please do not presume to think it was on account of sentimentality."

"I did not think that."

"There is no reason to kill the plants. The servants all know what happened anyway. Mrs. Bradley was far too solicitous about my health when I came down. She kept asking how I fared this morning, and if I needed anything." She pulled out another weed. "They were all far away, above or below, indeed. You have your witnesses, as you wanted, I think."

"I am sure that they did not see or hear us, Verity. They just assume. It was two years, after all."

"No doubt they felt bad that I forced you to live like a monk for so long. Down here in Surrey, they did not know that you hardly abstained all that time. They do not read the London scandal sheets and do not know about all your lovers."

He almost said that a lover was not a wife. That, he was learning, they were very different in many ways. Common sense prevailed and he did not venture there.

He smiled. "What else did you say to the gardener? He claimed he could not remember, but he was only being discreet."

She pulled off one glove to have a clean hand. She used it to dab a handkerchief at the beads of sweat forming at the base of her neck like tiny pearls. "I said the evidence of the night was so plain that perhaps we should set out a sign and be done with it. A memorial plaque. *Here did Lady Hawkeswell lieyeth while her lord taketh her the first time.*"

He could not tell if she was angry, or teasing.

"And what did you say when Mrs. Bradley proved too kind, and asked how you fared, Verity?"

"I told her that I had difficulty walking this morning at first, but that it was passing."

"You did not really say these things." The notion left him aghast. "Did you?"

She swung another clump of plant and root into her bucket while she eyed him with a twinkle in her eye, too satisfied with his reaction. "My people are bawdier than yours, Lord Hawkeswell. But no, I did not really say them."

At least she was not too angry to make little jokes.

She continued her weeding. Silence reigned. Perhaps some apologies were in order after all.

"It was not my intention to hurt you, Verity. If I did—"

"I know *exactly* what your intentions were, my lord. The good and the bad."

And the less said about that, the better, he could see. He was not so stupid as to respond.

"As for any hurt, I was warned to expect it. I am indeed walking fine today. I thank you for your concern."

She bent and twined another tall stem around her arm and yanked. She shook off the dirt and tossed the weed toward her bucket.

"What do you plan to grow in this bit of garden?" he asked.

"Bulbs. I will plant them in the autumn for next spring."

"The gardener can do this preparation."

"He is too old. It is hard work."

"We will be hiring younger ones before autumn."

"I want to do it myself. It is good to have a purpose."

He removed his coats and draped them onto the ground. She froze at the movement. Half-bent, glove wrapped with a vine, she watched him warily.

He had done the same thing last night, of course, right before he ravished her on the ground. "Lady Hawkeswell need not be so cautious. Her lord is not planning to taketh her again while she lieyeth in the garden today." He surveyed the overgrown bed while he rolled up his sleeves. "Do you want all of this out of here? This little tree too?"

"Yes, all of it should go. We must start afresh."

He bent beside her, grabbed an errant sapling, and pulled.

Chapter Thirteen

For three days the curious neighbors stayed away. On the fourth day they began calling. Carriages came and went in the afternoons. Ladies examined her and gentlemen smiled indulgently. Eyes gleamed with more curiosity than mouths dared express.

Verity learned to garden in early morning, then wash and dress for their arrival. She sometimes pored over her stack of newspaper cuttings, and reorganized them by the dates of events instead of dates of publication. She also wrote letters while she waited, to Audrianna in Essex and to her dear friends at The Rarest Blooms.

She received mail as well. Daphne wrote to tell her that Katherine had arrived safely, and still visited with them. She went on to describe how four Mayfair households had asked to contract privately for flowers and potted plants. Audrianna also wrote, to report that she would return to London whenever Verity did.

No letters came from the north, however. Audrianna

forwarded nothing at all. Verity had hoped that the vicar would at least let her know that her own letter had been received and read to Katy. She wrote to Mr. Travis, but he never responded to her request that he describe the state of things at the ironworks either. She was left to worry that her own letters had not made it to their destinations.

Frustrated and worried, she finally wrote to Mr. Thornapple, asking after Mr. Travis and the ironworks, and requesting his help in learning about some of her old friends there. In the least she hoped Mr. Thornapple would find out for her if Michael Bowman still worked there, supporting Katy and improving his craft, or whether he had been arrested and tried.

Mr. Thornapple's response arrived on her sixth morning in Surrey. His letter both encouraged her and disheartened her. After reassuring her that Mr. Travis still performed his duties, he reminded her that the particulars regarding the business were her husband's concerns now. He politely but firmly suggested that she devote herself to her domestic responsibilities.

She needed to go home, of course. It was the only way to learn what she wanted to know. She would have to cajole Hawkeswell into allowing it. It vexed her that fulfilling even part of her plan would now rely on his permission. She had hoped that she could at least learn a few things by letter while she arranged that journey, but fate was not cooperating.

She was folding away Mr. Thornapple's letter when a very fine carriage rolled up the lane. She watched from a drawing room window as a lovely woman stepped out, a vision in white punctuated by one red plume in her straw hat. Colleen had arrived, and she had not come alone. An older woman in her late middle years, narrow as a reed in her ensemble of Prussian blue, emerged too.

Verity sent for Hawkeswell. He had sequestered himself in his study with his land steward. He had been almost invisible to her these last few days while he tended to this estate. He rode out early and sometimes returned late, his boots covered with mud.

He joined her just before the ladies entered the drawing room.

"Colleen," he said in greeting. "Aunt Julia, welcome. Darling, this is Mrs. Ackley, my mother's sister."

"You must address me as Aunt Julia too, my dear. I shall address you as Verity. Our family does not hold with formalities among ourselves."

Verity was not sure she wanted to call this woman Aunt anything. Her narrow face wore a wizened expression of scrutiny. She looked to be a thinner, older, less friendly version of her daughter Colleen.

"I know that you said you would call on us soon, Hawkeswell," Colleen said when they had all seated themselves. "However, Mrs. Pounton said she had called here, and that she was not alone in being received, and Mama would not be put off any longer."

"Those calls themselves delayed us, along with my duties," Hawkeswell said. "I intended to pack Verity off well before anyone intruded tomorrow and bring her to you, Aunt Julia."

Mrs. Ackley acknowledged the intention as her due. They gossiped about Mrs. Pounton and a few other local people. Then Mrs. Ackley turned her attention pointedly toward Verity.

"So, my dear, where were you all this time?"

The question, posed so baldly, startled everyone in the room except Mrs. Ackley herself.

"The others dared not ask, and of course you could not be expected to answer if they did, but I trust that you will both indulge me and count on my discretion."

"Mama, please," Colleen said, casting Hawkeswell a glance of apologies.

"Aunt Julia, all that matters is that she is here now," he said. "I will not have her quizzed by anyone, including you."

Aunt Julia retreated, but her pursed lips displayed displeasure at his scold. Colleen rushed to ask what improvements Verity planned for Greenlay Park.

"I was visiting with friends, Mrs. Ackley," Verity said. "Hawkeswell has met them, and he knows the truth of this. As we trust your discretion, so can you trust my explanation."

Mrs. Ackley tasted that morsel. "Friends, you say."

"Yes. Lady friends."

"Odd that you visited so long."

"I expect so," Verity said. "I was claimed by a childish impulse."

"I trust there will be no more such impulses, let alone one that lasts two years."

"I do not expect there will be. Now, perhaps you will advise me on that which your daughter asks. How should I improve this noble house?"

Aunt Julia had a very long list of improvements to recommend. It took her a quarter hour to list them. Then she moved on to Hawkeswell's London house and, finally, to her own properties.

"My London house has been closed a year now, Hawkeswell. You must promise we will open it again. I will send

Colleen up to town when you go, to begin the refurbishment."

"We will talk about that, and the long list of expenditures that you have advised, another day, Aunt Julia. I have responsibilities to others who are more in need than anyone present in this chamber now."

His aunt did not take the rebuke well. She turned a keen eye on the newcomer among them. "You are a very quiet young woman, Verity. One might forget you are even present."

"She can hardly contribute to talk of redecorating a house that she has never seen, Mama," Colleen said.

"As a countess, you will have to learn to converse even when you have nothing to contribute. Otherwise you will get the reputation for being too proud, Verity, and with your background that would not sit well with society at all." She bestowed a sympathetic expression. "Being a countess frightens you, doesn't it? That is why you left. Have no fear, my dear. Colleen and I are going to help you rise to your station to the extent that is possible, so that my nephew will not be embarrassed more than cannot be helped."

"You are too kind."

"Yes, too kind," Hawkeswell said. "Excessively so, which is why we must decline your generous offer. Take time from your considerable obligations to tutor Verity? No, I will not hear of it. I doubt that I will ever be embarrassed more than cannot be helped, so the schooling you have in mind is unnecessary. As for Verity's silence during your visit today, I too have been silent. As has Colleen. Your eloquence has always left others tongue-tied and in awe."

Mrs. Ackley's surprise at this soliloquy turned into vague

suspicion. She peered at Hawkeswell, trying to determine whether an insult were buried in all that verbiage.

Colleen stood. "We must take our leave now. Come, Mama. You wanted to call on Mrs. Wheathill today, and the afternoon is passing."

While Hawkeswell escorted his aunt to the reception hall, Colleen stole a private moment with Verity. "I wrote to your cousin, as requested. The response came yesterday. The Thompsons are shocked, of course, but also overjoyed. They will travel to London next week and are hoping that you will go up to town too, so they can call on you and express their relief and happiness."

"It is my intention to go to town soon, so perhaps I will indeed meet with the Thompsons."

"You must inform me when you plan to depart. I will join you, and make introductions to a few friends of mine who reside there all year. There will be little other good society in the summer, but perhaps that is best for such an odd homecoming. It will also leave us time to plan all the decorating we intend to do. It will be great fun."

Verity remained noncommittal, but gracious. She hoped that Colleen's plans did not fill every day. There were other things she needed to do this summer besides decorate and make morning calls.

That night they dined in the great chamber with the huge banquet table. The vast surface of the polished table struck Verity as humorous, dwarfing as it did the two places they had at one end. Rain pattered on windows in a gentle downpour that had begun an hour prior to the meal.

Hawkeswell addressed the matter of his aunt and cousin while they ate pheasant in a good brown sauce. "I have never understood why relatives believe a family relationship permits one to be rude. My apologies, Verity. My aunt can be trying on the best of days. Her pique that we dallied before calling to pay homage made her forget herself this afternoon."

"I do not think she forgot herself at all. I am glad she spoke as she did. Now it is said, and need not be said again. Speaking one's mind, even to the point of rudeness, avoids misunderstandings."

"You handled her splendidly, no matter what her mind."

"No, you did. If you had not put her in her place, she would have pecked and pecked. I thank you for defending me." It had touched her when he did that, and the gratitude she expressed was heartfelt. He could have allowed her to dangle instead, like a toy for his aunt's amusement.

"Colleen would like to be a good friend to you, I think."

"Because I handle her mother splendidly?"

"Perhaps. Maybe she suspects what was behind your absence, and feels some responsibility."

Might Colleen's ready offer of friendship be a way to make amends? She had still sounded like an ally of the Thompsons this afternoon. More likely Colleen did not begin to comprehend Bertram's character, and had been an innocent pawn herself.

"She had written to my cousin as promised and received a response," she said. "They would like to call on me in London."

"Would you prefer that?"

"I do not want to receive them at all, either here or in London. If I must do it someplace, however, let it be in town. I certainly do not want them as houseguests here."

"Then we will go to London in a few days. I need to go anyway. There are some matters to settle."

"I assume that you will be calling on my trustee, Mr. Thornapple."

"Yes. There will be papers to sign."

"Should I accompany you?"

"That is not necessary."

Of course not. She no longer had any say in the use of her inheritance. In the eyes of the law, she had ceased to exist. Mr. Thornapple's letter had all but said so outright.

Going forward, her husband would receive the income from the company, along with whatever had accumulated in the trust into which that money had been placed since her father's death. That trust disappeared upon her marriage and it all went to her spouse now, with no diversion at all.

She had intended to meet with Mr. Thornapple on her own, to seek counsel for a petition of annulment. There would be no reason to do that now. She could hardly claim lack of consent to a marriage when she had given consent to its consummation.

Which she had. Try as she might the last five days, she could not lie to herself about what had happened that night.

He had seduced her, to be sure, when he knew she wanted to avoid marital intimacy. He had taken advantage of her ignorance and her innocence, but he had not forced her to do anything.

That intimacy had changed the way they treated each other these last days. Hawkeswell wore the confidence of a man who had settled an important matter. She in turn suffered an increased disadvantage, with him and with herself, while she decided how to live this life she was never supposed to have.

"Are they dependent on you?" she asked, returning to

their visitors. "They spoke as if they expect you to lay out a good deal of money now."

"My mother asked me to see to her sister's care, so I do. Aunt Julia married an army officer, and he left her very little. Ladies can be quite expensive, so fulfilling my promise has caused strains."

"I am sure that you did all you could. They are very well turned out, so you were probably very generous."

"I have regretted not being able to enhance Colleen's fortune. Her trust is very small. It is fortunate, I suppose, that she has expressed no desire to marry. She still grieves for the fiancé of her girlhood, who had the misfortune to die from a fall from his horse."

"Perhaps now that a larger settlement can be arranged, young men will woo her out of her grief. I will see if I can encourage that."

"It would please me if you did. She and I have been very close since we were children, and I think of her like a sister."

"Then I will do my best to see her as your sister too, as long as I do not have to think of your Aunt Julia as a mother-in-law."

"Heaven forbid."

The rain caused dusk to come early, and shadows had gathered in the chamber by the time their meal was finished. Verity rose. "I think that I will retire to my apartment and listen to the rain while I enjoy a good book."

He took her hand, so she could not depart at once. He gazed up her length. At the pale dinner dress and the Venetian shawl. At her bodice, and the neck that had never again worn those pearls. Finally he looked in her eyes.

"Verity, in your dressing room there is a door. It opens to a narrow corridor. Have you noticed it?"

"Yes. It is an odd little passageway with no purpose, but it has a window with a lovely prospect."

"That passageway has an important purpose. It connects our apartments."

She puzzled out the lay of the chambers in her mind. It had seemed to her that his were much farther away.

"Verity, I would like you to be sure to unlock the door at your end of the passageway tonight."

"Yes, of course." She was not surprised. She had no idea how often these things happened, but she knew it was just a matter of time before it happened again.

He kissed her hand, and released her. She went above, to prepare for another ravishment.

He expected that the door would probably be unlocked, but with Verity, one never knew. So he was pleased when the latch turned without incident.

She had behaved oddly these last days. Her demeanor had turned formal, as if, now that being the countess was inevitable, she summoned all those drills and spent the days rehearsing them. She had acquitted herself admirably during those calls from the county neighbors, and even managed a bit of imperious hauteur with Aunt Julia. Unfortunately, she treated him with the same cool distance.

Desire's howling winds had swirled in him for six days now. She would sit there at meals, back rod straight, lifting her fork in a slow, studied ritual, but a part of his mind had been on explicitly erotic considerations. Now, as he faced the pitch black of her bedchamber and tried to remember just where the furniture was situated, a raging storm wanted to break inside him.

He waited for his eyes to adjust, but the chamber remained an inky void. It entered his mind that she might have planned this, and set out chairs and trunks designed to trip him. He laughed to himself at the idea she might plot such revenge, but went back to his own dressing room and fetched a small lamp anyway.

Its light revealed that no traps waited. Verity was in bed, her dark hair streaming over the white sheet that covered her.

He reminded himself that tonight's goal was to give her pleasure, that he had some amends to make. Wife or no, rights or no, wisdom dictated that he ensure she never thought of this as a painful chore. He approached the bed while he fought a rear guard action against the effects of an erection so hard it amazed him.

She was little more than a shadow under that sheet. Her eyes were closed but their thick lashes fluttered. He set the lamp on a far table, shed the robe, and walked to the bed.

To his surprise she opened her eyes. She watched him. *Examined him.* She was a mere six days away from being an innocent, and she observed his nakedness with the frank curiosity of a practiced courtesan.

He slid under the sheet and reached for her, and had another surprise.

"You are undressed already."

"As are you."

"Yes. However—"

"Was I supposed to wait in my dinner dress? Or an undressing gown? No one explains these things, at least not to me. You tore my favorite dress the last time. My girl plies a good needle, but it will never be right again. If I have made a mistake, I am sorry, but I thought to spare my wardrobe from your impatience."

"Your solution is both practical and welcomed." He gathered her soft warmth close to his body. "There will be no impatience this time, and it is only uncomfortable for women the first time. You will know pleasure to the end tonight, Verity. I promise."

Warmth. Strength. Flesh pressing flesh and frightening physical intimacy that assaulted all her senses. She hid her shock, but his naked body touching hers in so many ways kept stunning her, as if her own nakedness had not expected the boldness to go both ways.

It was different for her from the first kiss. No feeble protests. No attempts to collect herself. No struggle to deny the power. She had accepted how it would be when she dismissed her girl, removed her favorite nightdress, and climbed into this bed.

He took his time anyway. He lured and seduced with deep, claiming kisses. His hand caressed with a mastery that demanded her whole body join her decision to surrender to the inevitable.

The sheet fell down their bodies so nothing covered them. She was exposed to the light he had brought in, and to his gaze. She watched his kisses move over her, forming tiny brands on her, each one making a thrill enter her blood. Awkwardness faded under the onslaught of sensations that woke and captivated her body.

She watched his hand move over her. A very masculine hand, strong and hard and darker than her skin. He caressed around her breasts while he kissed her neck and shoulders in ways that created a pulse far below, where her body trembled from the memory of what was to come.

Desire. That was the meaning of that tremble. All the

pleasure encouraged its spread and growing intensity. She noted what was happening, how every caress and kiss lured her with titillations that soon preoccupied her consciousness.

She did not resist the descent into pure carnality. There was no reason to anymore. She released the last of the awkwardness. She submitted with both relief and resignation. As with the last time, pleasure banished the guilt for a while. Later, perhaps, most likely, she would contemplate how she had betrayed her hopes, her legacy, even her very life by succumbing to this man. Later she would think of Michael and his crooked smile with nostalgia and worry about his fate.

When Hawkeswell's fingertips started teasing at her hard, sensitive nipple, she closed her eyes so nothing distracted her from the delicious excitement he gave her. His head lowered and he intensified the effect with his mouth and tongue and teeth on her other breast. She held on to him, clutched at his shoulders and arm. Her back arched and her breasts rose and she begged for more with her body and thoughts.

All of her was alive. All of her was sensitive to the slightest touch. All of her was wanting. Desire beat like a soft drum, in her head and in his breaths and through her body. It merged with her very pulse, and throbbed in rhythm to physical cravings. More, yes, more. Joyful, excruciating pleasure. Kisses and caresses both gentle and rough, and madness, wonderful madness, destroying all restraints and reveling in the primitive glory.

That hand now, that powerful hand, sliding lower, too slowly, far too slowly so that moans sounded in her head and ears. Moving down her body toward that pulse. Nothing mattered now except that. It was all there, all the desire and pleasure. She grasped his head and held it to a kiss. Her kiss. Her fury, wanting more, urging more. She spread her legs as that hand neared and she whimpered within the kiss.

"You are too impatient," he chided quietly. His hand closed on her inner thigh. Her hips rose instinctively, a reflection of the cries in her head.

"Is this what you want?" His fingers brushed against flesh that wept and waited with furious desperation.

A devastating shock of pleasure streaked through her. Then another and another. Madness growing now. Awareness constricting to a small circle in which nothing but need existed.

Finally one profoundly different sensation, starting more intensely and rising sharply, then splitting through her whole body and essence, through her blood and flesh, in one long, deep tremor that stunned all her senses.

He had been waiting for her astonishment. He came over her then, his lower body meeting hers. He pressed into her and she did not know if it hurt or not. The remnants of the tremor still echoed and her awe left no room for awareness of pain. She felt the intimacy, though. The scent and closeness. His body's dominance of her shouted into her daze.

His masterful hand positioned her legs as he wanted them, then pressed against the headboard to leverage his moves while he filled her and took her and overwhelmed her body and soul.

"Will you always tell me when to leave that door unlocked?" Her voice inserted this practicality into the long silence, but after the power had begun to pass.

He did not mind, although his head was hardly up to discussing logistics. He was accustomed to negotiations of one kind or another with women in bed.

"You should probably do so every night. I do not believe that formal announcements are customary."

"Then I am never to know? Am I supposed to wait, awake, to be sure I am ready if you choose to do this? If you do not make a visit, I could wait all night when I should be sleeping."

"I do not think there will be any danger of that."

"Are you saying that you intend to come here *every night*?"

He had meant that she would fall asleep, and not really wait all night no matter what her notion of duty. However, her question was a fair one, and her astonishment a timely reminder of her ignorance.

"Probably so. For a good while, yes, I will most likely come to you every night."

He did not ask if that would be agreeable. He was not inclined to open those kinds of negotiations.

"I do not think that will be so distasteful," she said. "Perhaps you were correct, and in this one way we will suit well enough."

He rose on his arm and looked at her puckered brow. It matched her voice, which was full of deliberation. "We will suit more than well enough, if you remain bold and honest."

"Bold and honest? Is that how you perceived me?"

"They are as good as any other words to describe how you take pleasure." They also described much about the rest of her too, he decided.

"I was taught by my governess that husbands prefer modest and virtuous."

"I am glad that you proved such a poor student of the lesson."

"Then you did not find my lack of restraint shocking?"

"Not at all."

"I did. I expect you did not because you have experienced such things before with all those other women."

Rather suddenly she had led him onto swampy ground. He heard no accusation in her voice. She was only being her bold and honest self. He stepped carefully all the same.

"Other women? Oh, from my distant past, you mean. Here I had clear forgotten about them."

She giggled, then laughed hard. When she had caught her breath, she angled up and gave one of her bird pecks on his cheek, then fell back on the bed. "I thank you for trying, Hawkeswell. Being the bold and honest sort, I have no illusions, however."

The swamp fairly oozed now. He decided this little conversation had gone on long enough so she would not feel neglected.

He kissed her, and lingered when pleasant memories flowed on the intimacy, then left the bed.

Chapter Fourteen

Hawkeswell's house on Hanover Square appeared less tired than Greenlay Park. Not the best address, Celia had written in a letter. Fashionable society had long ago moved on. That the Earls of Hawkeswell still lived there reflected their fading fortunes over the last few generations.

Certain chambers encouraged Verity to think that living here would be very pleasant anyway. The library might need redecorating the way his aunt Julia said, but Verity liked its jewel-toned upholstery and dark woods, and the fine, large windows that looked down on the square.

In contrast, the drawing room seemed cold, with its fastidious, fine-boned furniture and severely classical decor. She suspected that the drawing room had not been used often in recent years. She doubted Hawkeswell entertained much at home. If gentlemen friends called, he probably received them in that nice library, or up in his apartment.

"Here is the garden," Hawkeswell said, opening one of

many French doors in the long back gallery that also served as a ballroom. "Promise that you will not scold."

She stepped onto a fine, deep terrace paved in what looked like rough marble. The garden stretched before her, broad and deep, all the way to a brick wall at the back that masked some buildings that she assumed were coach houses and necessities.

"Oh, dear."

"The gardener is not the best, you mean."

"He is incompetent. The yews are ruined, and all the shrubbery poorly pruned. He does not know the first thing about landscape, I fear."

"I trust that you will correct him."

She went down the steps and stood amid the disaster. "I am not sure that I can. This may be too much for me."

"Get whatever help you require. Release this gardener and hire another. Hire three. I leave it in your hands."

She surveyed the series of silly little flower beds that broke up the walkways. The entire property needed a new design.

They completed the tour, ending at her apartment. As with her rooms at Greenlay Park, these had been treated to new fabrics not so long ago. She wondered if Colleen and Aunt Julia had seen to it at both houses, and not Hawkeswell at all.

Yet it seemed to matter to him if she approved. He watched her finger the bed drapes and look out the window. He strolled behind her as she opened doors and drawers in the dressing room.

She spied a door on the far wall beyond the dressing table. "Another odd passageway?"

True to his word, he had used that passageway every

night since the first time. She had begun waiting for him. Sometimes, while she waited, she saw him as she had that first night, walking toward her, naked and aroused, his eyes dark and his expression taut. She would sense her body stirring and her breasts getting sensitive in anticipation of what was coming.

"No passageway this time. The dressing rooms adjoin directly." He opened the door to show his own, with its wardrobes and tables and some chairs. A manservant stopped hanging a coat and bowed. "This is Mr. Drummund. He has been my valet for . . . How long has it been now, Drummund?"

"It has been my honor for twelve years now, sir. Since you were at university." Drummund seemed touched by the attention.

"He had his hands full early on," Hawkeswell said. "Life has become much duller the last five years or so, has it not, Drummund?"

"Never dull, sir." He returned to the coat. "There is mail. I was about to send it down to Surrey."

Hawkeswell turned his attention to the letters. Verity returned to her own apartment and found mail waiting for her as well. It had been sent just that morning.

Audrianna wrote to say that she and Lord Sebastian had also returned to town. Verity sighed with relief at the reassurance that one of her dear friends would be close by.

Hawkeswell dipped the pen and signed the stacks of vellum that Thornapple had set before him. With each scrawl of his signature, he took control of Verity's fortune.

The solicitor had been the image of professional indifference about the entire matter. However, as the last
heavy page turned, he removed his spectacles and examined Hawkeswell while he folded each page just so.

"I hope that you will accept a little advice about this
inheritance that your wife received, Lord Hawkeswell."

"Of course."

"This is an industrial enterprise. It is more subject to
economic vagaries than wealth derived from land. The potential is much greater, but so is the danger. Lady Hawkeswell brings a handsome income to you, and with the
dissolution of the second trust that collected her profits
while she was a minor, a good deal of money reserved from
that period. There is no guarantee, however, that the income will continue."

"I expect that the need for iron will increase, not decrease. While there are no guarantees, there is also no
reason to assume a decline."

"You are wrong there. The decline is at hand as we speak.
The ironworks are solid, but currently are suffering from
a postwar depression. Furthermore, over half the amount
each year derives from the boring and machining. Currently they have an advantage, due to Joshua's ingenuity
in devising a new method. He never patented it, you may
know, because to do so would mean revealing the method
itself, and he did not trust others not to steal. Should it
become known, however, the advantage would be much
depreciated."

"And if it should become lost entirely?"

"Then they would have no advantage at all."

The dependence of this fortune on fortune itself had
not escaped Hawkeswell. He had been weighing it ever
since Verity spoke about that business in Essex.

"Lady Hawkeswell is well? Her adventures have not taken a toll?" the solicitor asked casually.

Of course, Thornapple was as curious as everyone else. Unlike everyone else, he had known Verity's father and, as her trustee, would be truly concerned for her.

"She is none the worse for those adventures, perhaps because they were not very adventurous. She was not far from London all that time, and living with a widow whom she counts as a close friend."

Thornapple relaxed back in his chair. "I will say that I am grateful that you told me that. Just as I was relieved to see her walk into that library. My reaction may have appeared harsh, but in truth . . ." He thought better of his intended words, and returned to all that folding.

"In truth?"

"In truth I assumed she was dead. Didn't we all?"

"Her cousin did not."

"It was not in Bertram Thompson's interest for her to be dead. He is not a blood cousin, and would not inherit her share. I can see from your surprise that you did not know that."

"No, I did not."

"He was the son of her uncle's wife by her first husband. Bertram thought he should have inherited more of the business, but an argument could have been made that he should have received nothing at all."

Interest in that testament had receded, due to those progressing events, but now the solicitor's reference piqued it again. "Her father still left her the much higher share, however."

"Seventy-five percent. Bertram Thompson received twenty-five percent. His stepfather, Jeremiah, helped build that company, but that half share went to Joshua when Jeremiah died. Bertram probably assumed he would receive that half back, at least, when Joshua in turn passed away. He was not pleased to learn the truth of it."

Thornapple stacked the documents neatly in two piles. "According to Joshua's testament, the property must remain in her name and be bequeathed to her bloodline. I think there may be distant relatives in Yorkshire. No, Bertram would not have liked those strangers coming in and putting him aside. I daresay that even after seven years, he would have argued that, lacking a body, she should be presumed alive."

Hawkeswell took his leave and carried his stack of documents to his horse. He pondered Thornapple's revelations while he rode from the City.

They explained why Bertram had been so content with the limbo of the last two years, at least. His hold on that business remained secure only while Verity lived. And, perhaps, he had also prayed that Verity was alive because he knew that she was one of only two people in the world who knew her father's secret inventions.

"I think it needs to go right here," Daphne said, planting her feet on a path in the back half of the garden. "If you want a proper greenhouse for propagating, it must be here, so there is sufficient light."

"I think that she is correct," Celia said. "You will need to direct its manufacture too. It should not be an ordinary structure if it is to grace the town garden of an earl."

Verity eyed the placement that Daphne recommended. No matter where it sat or how lovely its form, it would be a modest greenhouse by the standards of The Rarest Blooms. She would not be growing for commercial purposes, however.

"Are you sure that Hawkeswell approves of this?" Audrianna asked.

"You would not want to strain his temper," Daphne added dryly.

"I told you that it was his idea," Verity said. "He has handed both gardens over to me, to do as I like."

"It sounds as if you intend to be here long enough to see it through," Daphne said. "Have you reconciled yourself to this marriage?"

"You are prying, Daphne," Celia scolded with a little laugh. "But don't let me stop you, *please*."

Verity's own smile turned into a small grimace. "I expect to be here a good long while. I have reconciled myself to the truth that there will be no annulment unless Hawkeswell fully supports such a petition and I produce incontrovertible proof of coercion. Neither will happen, so here I am."

Celia was standing closest, and gave her an embrace. "It is not where you wanted to be, I know. However, it is not a bad place compared to most others."

Marriage to an earl and access to a huge fortune is not a bad second best, is what practical, worldly Celia meant.

"That is true, and I am not so stubborn as to be miserable with my circumstances, now that they have become inevitable. I am finding contentment."

They returned to the terrace and debated the rest of the garden plan from that prospect. Celia drew what they described as it would be seen from the house.

"I should like to make a winding path, that passes by a series of little garden rooms," Verity explained. "In this way, the greenhouse would simply be one more chamber."

Celia drew more. "I will leave you to use colors on it, Verity," she said. "I will make some copies, so that you can plan for different times of the year."

"Only make one copy," Daphne said. "Bring it back, and Katherine will make the rest. She is a gifted artist, Verity. I must buy some pigments for her before we leave town today."

"Will she be staying with you?"

"Oh, yes," Celia said. "I think she will be with us a good long while."

Verity's and Audrianna's eyes met. They traded curiosity. They had acknowledged during one of their recent private talks that it was much harder to obey the Rule now that they no longer lived under it.

"I trust that she is like us. Not dangerous," Audrianna ventured. "Sebastian has always had concerns about that."

Daphne leaned over to see Celia's sketch. "I expect she is no more dangerous than you were, Audrianna. She has shown no interest in my pistol, for example."

Audrianna blushed at this reference to a misadventure with that pistol that led to her alliance with Lord Sebastian.

"Will he be returning soon?" Daphne asked. She meant Hawkeswell. Daphne had only agreed to visit today because Verity had mentioned in her invitation that the earl would not be here.

"Sebastian is meeting him at their club," Audrianna said. "I expect it will be some hours before either one rides back."

"Then Verity has time to show me her new wardrobe," Celia said while she held up her two drawings to compare them.

"I would much rather show you something else. I have need of your good minds."

A half hour later, all of them were arrayed in Verity's bedchamber. Daphne, Celia, and Verity sat on the bed, poring over scraps of paper. Audrianna had pulled a chair close so she could see as well.

"I always found your taste for newspapers excessive," Celia said. "I can see you put it to good use, and had a bigger purpose than I guessed." She gestured to the stacks. "Some of these are two years old, from right when you came to The Rarest Blooms. Worker uprisings. Demonstrations." She picked up a little stack. "Arrests and executions."

"Here are some about Brandreth and his followers," Daphne said. "There is trouble enough down here in the South. We even had to enter town other than the normal way today, because of a gathering on the main road. However, we have been spared revolutionaries like Brandreth."

"I think he was entrapped, the way Mr. Shelley's poem implies. Many agree with that view," Audrianna said, perusing the articles that Verity had saved. "I will say, however, that your home county and those near it look to be fairly dangerous, Verity. Perhaps it is wise that you will be living here instead."

"I did not save these writings to keep a record of the danger. I have been looking for names of people. Look here. These are stories from the counties near my home, of people gone missing. Men, almost all of them. Then, these are reports of people found, after being lost or hurt. And these are names of those tried for crimes. If you match them up, there are six men who went missing and for whom there is no other information."

"Why have you saved these?" Daphne asked, fingering one of the stacks.

"I was keeping track of which court sessions I had read about, and which I had missed, at first. I was looking for one name in particular, which is absent totally. Only recently have I noticed this oddity."

"So you were seeking information on a particular missing person?"

"Yes. He is the young man I told you about, whom my cousin threatened to harm."

Celia slid a sidelong glance to Daphne.

"He was an old childhood friend," Verity explained, but she felt her face warming. "I must find out what happened to him, if Bertram indeed betrayed my trust."

"Of course you must," Daphne said. "The unexplained absences of these other men do not signify, however. They may have just run away from their families and lives. Some will do that."

"Normally I would agree. However, look at this." She set out several articles. "Both of these men were from Staffordshire, near Birmingham. Both of them had been questioned by the justice of the peace there about complaints from landowners. This JP did not arrest them, but then they went missing. And this one here, he disappeared after a confrontation on the road with Lord Cleobury. This other one was arrested in Shropshire after my cousin laid down information that he was causing trouble at the ironworks, but was freed. Then he disappeared too."

"They all probably ran away once attention turned to them," Audrianna said.

Probably, Verity thought. Yet the more that she had rearranged stacks of articles the last few weeks, the more she sensed that something was amiss with all these missing men.

I can cause trouble for that son of hers. None will stay my hand. I can have him transported or worse, and who will feed her then? That was what Bertram had said when he made those threats. He had been smug in his power. Confident and hard.

Daphne picked up the articles recently laid out. "It is odd that they all had run afoul of important people, but if they were instigating trouble, these are the people who would notice and try to stop them. You have told us plenty about your cousin, and Lord Cleobury is known for his hard views. This magistrate's name is familiar to me as well, only I do not know why."

"It is not familiar to me," Verity said. "I do not remember my father or even my cousin ever speaking of Mr. Jonathan Albrighton."

The name elicited a response from one of their party. Celia snatched the article from Daphne and peered at it.

"Do you know of him, Celia?" Daphne asked.

Celia frowned over the notice. "He was known in London a few years ago. I believe he went abroad. It appears he has returned, if it is the same man."

"Perhaps I will meet him when I go home," Verity said. "I should like to, in order to assess his character and whether he finds any of this peculiar." She swept her hand over the newspaper cuttings.

"Are you planning a journey north soon?" Audrianna asked.

"As soon as I can arrange it."

Her friends were too good to lecture her, but it was written on each of their faces, according to their characters. The possibility existed that she would not be arranging it soon at all, if her husband had a say in the matter.

"Damnation." Hawkeswell muttered the curse while he watched a tall man darken the threshold to the card room at Brooks's. "What in hell is he doing here?"

Summerhays looked over his shoulder at the man in question. "He is a member, of course. He rarely comes, but—"

"He is coming this way. He probably dragged himself

from some whore's bed just to seek me out to be clever at my expense. Prepare for a good row, Summerhays, because I'll be damned if I will sit peaceably while he slices with that wit of—"

"Castleford," Summerhays greeted, as the man now loomed over their table. "Odd to see you here prior to nightfall, and at least half-sober at that. It is not even a Tuesday."

Tuesdays were the Duke of Castleford's days of duty, when he devoted himself to the business of being a peer and a man of disgustingly huge fortune. The rest of the week he went to hell.

Hawkeswell and Summerhays had once joined in the debauches. Maturity and responsibility had tempered their behavior the last few years. Castleford, however, had managed to escape any curtailment of the fun, but still managed to exert more influence in government and society than was fair for someone with such a dissolute life.

The young duke looked down at them, amiable of face and bright of eye, his fashionably dressed brown hair falling with appropriate recklessness about his face. He was the picture of an old friend greeting the fellow sinners of his youth. Yet in those eyes the devil's spark gleamed.

Hawkeswell's temper began coiling and not a word had been spoken yet.

"What? It isn't Tuesday?" Castleford drawled with mock shock. "I clear lost track. It is good to know, however." He swung a chair over to their table, collapsed in a lazy sprawl on it, signaled for one of the servants, and ordered a very fine and expensive bottle of wine.

"Your favorite, as I remember," he said to Hawkeswell. "I hope I got it right, because I bought it to share with you."

"That is generous."

"It is incumbent upon friends to celebrate each other's good fortunes. I hear that your bride has been found. You must be very happy, and relieved."

"Of course he is," Summerhays said.

The wine came. Castleford insisted three glasses be poured. He raised his toward Hawkeswell in silent salute.

"So," he said after the toast. "Where in hell was she all this time?"

"Damnation, Tristan," Summerhays said. "If you joined us only to be rude—"

Hawkeswell gestured for Summerhays to stand down. "Did you wake early and refuse to imbibe all day just to be able to appear civilized when you asked me that question? Is your life so bereft of purpose that contemplating this meeting amused you for days now?"

Castleford smiled slowly. "Yes. To both questions. Two days ago, upon hearing the news, I snapped sober at once. Zeus, there is a good story here, I said to myself. Perhaps the making of a comic opera." He sipped some wine. "I have been trying to meet you accidentally ever since."

"If you wanted to find him, you could have called at his house," Summerhays said.

Castleford reacted as if that were a peculiar idea. He returned his attention to his quarry. "You should tell me the truth. The rumors that are raging do you no credit. I can hardly defend you if I do not know they are rumors in fact."

"What kind of rumors?"

"You have not told him?" Castleford asked Summerhays.

"Hawkeswell, you do not need to listen to this," Summerhays said. "He is more besotted than he appears."

"*What. Kind. Of. Rumors?*"

Castleford sat forward, to speak confidentially. "You will be happy to know that I have taken note of who said what, in case you want to call anyone out."

"How good of you."

"That is what friends are for, is it not?"

"*No,*" Summerhays said with exasperation. "Friends do not pour oil on fires just to amuse themselves. Damnation, if he does call someone out, you are going to regret this game."

"Summerhays still fears my temper, but the truth is I have been a citadel of calm for the last five years at least. I am not going to call anyone out. Now, what kind of rumors?"

Castleford had more wine poured. "First, there is the gossip that she ran away out of girlish fear of the wedding bed. That story isn't interesting at all. Much more colorful is the one that says she ran away *after* her experience in the wedding bed, because you bungled it to the point of horror." Castleford offered a man-to-man gaze. "You will be happy to know that I offered to line up twenty women who would publicly testify on your behalf on the matter."

"No one would believe such nonsense," Hawkeswell said. "The fool saying that will be known by his own stupidity."

"Exactly. Then there was the man who confided to me that he had it on good authority that she had been with her lover all that time. That is, I fear, a commonly held assumption, and the most popular *on dit*. That you were cuckolded even before the ink dried on the license."

The gossip had turned to impugning Verity. That Hawkeswell had suspected the same thing did not matter. He had a right to wonder, but others did not have a right to speak the lie as if it were fact.

His temper began casting off the bonds. Like a sleeping dragon prodded awake, it strained against chains until they snapped, slowly, one by one.

"Who confided this last bit to you?"

"*Do not* tell him," Summerhays warned.

"If you are going to duel with someone, that is not the man who needs it," Castleford said with a dismissive wave of his hand. "Besides, as I said, that is on everyone's lips, and you can't kill them all. No, the one you want to kill is the one who told me that your wife has been in Shrewsbury, where she established herself as an abbess of a brothel of some renown among the radical elements of society."

The dragon burst free and roared fire. "What was this damned liar's name?"

"Bloody hell," Summerhays said. "Castleford, do not give him that name."

"There is no need to, because he is not available for killing. I advised the rogue to make himself scarce because he was a dead man once Hawkeswell learned of it, and I would make certain he did. I heard this morning that he hopped the packet to France."

"Then why have you done this? *Look* at him." Summerhays swung out his arm in Hawkeswell's direction.

Hawkeswell was sure that Sebastian appeared far more agitated than he. He drank some wine and contemplated taking a packet to France himself, and drawing and quartering this man who had insulted Verity.

Castleford scowled at Summerhays. "Would you have remained silent if *you* heard his wife so dishonored? Would you have wanted me to remain silent if I had heard *your* wife spoken of thus? He needs to know it has been said, and he needs to call out the next person who repeats it."

"It was good of you to inform me," Hawkeswell said. "And at such inconvenience to yourself too. I trust that you will send me word if you hear it again, so I can do what I must."

"Of course. However, I have had some time to think. A solid two days of abstinence permits that. I have devised a plan to divert attention from Lady Hawkeswell's ill-timed marital interlude."

Hawkeswell caught Summerhays's eye. Castleford appeared very pleased with himself. He assumed his plan was brilliant, which was normal. What was peculiar was that he had concocted a plan to begin with.

"A plan?" Summerhays ventured.

"A very good plan. Trust me, Hawkeswell, in a little over a month's time no one will be whispering about your wife's disappearance because they will be whispering about something more interesting instead. I will call on her this Tuesday, to set everything in motion."

"Your plan requires you to call on her?"

"I need to see if she is worthy. That glimpse at your wedding hardly sufficed. If I am going to include her in my circle of friends, I should at least chat with her for a few minutes first."

Hawkeswell caught Summerhays's eye again. Neither of them liked the sound of this.

"When you say your circle of friends, you mean your Tuesday friends, I trust," Hawkeswell said.

"Initially, yes."

Hawkeswell had images of Verity lured into orgies and

debauches. That he had enjoyed such things in his time did not mean he was going to allow his wife to.

The dragon had begun dozing, but now it breathed fire again.

Castleford became distracted by some men nearby who loudly argued politics. Hawkeswell tried to call his attention back. "Castleford . . . Tristan . . . *Your Grace*."

"Mmm?"

"You can of course call on my wife tomorrow, while I am there. Or any other time, while I am there. But, I warn you now, never call on her when I am not there."

He thought that very funny. "Don't be an ass, Hawkeswell."

"Hear me out. If your plan is benign, I thank you. However, if you think to end speculation about her absence by providing society with a better scandal about her behavior in your circle, do not even try it. And God forbid your pickled mind has decided to encourage speculation regarding an affair with you—"

"You barely said the vows and she left you for two years, my friend, and that is the hard truth of it. I doubt she needs all this protection you now give her with such a heavy hand. However, I do not seduce the wives of friends, and while you and Summerhays have become boring, I still count you as one. My plan is simply a dinner party, with the very best of society. That is all."

"You do not give dinner parties for the best of society."

"No, I do not. They are tedious. However, in a fit of nostalgia for our old friendship that emerged from who knows where, I have decided to host one to which you and your wife will be invited." He stood, annoyed by the suspicions expressed, although he knew damned well he had no right to be. "A month from this Tuesday. Expect invitations, both of you."

Before he could leave, Summerhays raised a finger to announce one more point. "Castleford, the best people will not attend your dinner party. You have offended almost all of them."

"That is true, but I said the very best, not the best. And the very best will come."

Chapter Fifteen

E very morning Verity ate breakfast in the morning room
prior to going out to the garden. She always had tea,
as a little indulgence to remind herself that being a countess had its benefits.

The mail would arrive while she was there, and a few
letters were always for her. Colleen would write to invite
her to call on one of her friends who remained in town.
Daphne or Celia would write to describe the progress on
the new hothouse that they had decided to add at The Rarest Blooms. Audrianna would jot a note to arrange an out-
ing.

She recognized all the hands, so when a letter arrived
that bore a different penmanship, it all but jumped out of
the stack. She recognized this hand too. Nancy Thompson,
Bertram's wife, had sent a letter.

Verity considered not opening it, but knew she must.

Nancy addressed her by her title, then expressed excessive relief at her good health. She finally indicated that

she and Bertram had taken lodging at Mivert's Hotel, and asked for permission to call.

The temptation to be very much the countess almost overwhelmed her. Cutting responses strolled through her mind, each one designed to sever any ties with her cousin and his wife. She might have used one if she thought it either possible or wise to create a permanent estrangement with the man whose business decisions would directly affect her fortune. Instead she went to the library, sat at a writing table, and suggested in a brief response that they all meet in Hyde Park this afternoon.

She then jotted another note, to her husband, informing him of the appointment, and sent it above to await his wakening.

Hawkeswell thought Verity appeared splendid as they alighted from the carriage in Hyde Park. She wore a hat that framed her delicate face with fair blue crepe and white plumes, and a promenade dress that emphasized her willowy form. She popped open a white parasol to protect her from the low sun, and together they entered the flow of people enjoying the fashionable hour.

It was not crowded compared to the season, and so he spied Bertram Thompson from some distance away. Bertram's needle-straight brown hair and middling, wiry form did not herald his arrival so much as his very fair skin and sleepy eyes. Always at half-mast, those lids looked either haughty or bored no matter what Bertram's actual mood.

The woman at his side had taken as much care with her appearance as Verity had. The angled brim of Nancy Thompson's hat ensured that her golden hair could be admired, and she held her parasol so the world could appreciate her proud expression, severely handsome face, and large green eyes.

What had he thought when Colleen first introduced them? Graspers. Climbers hoping to grapple up faster than others by means of this marriage. He did not hold it against them. Having been born at the top of the heap, he understood why others would strain hard to clamber out of the lower parts.

Except Verity, of course.

The Thompsons came into clear view. Nancy paused when she saw Verity, then rushed forward with her arms open. Passersby noticed, as she had intended they would.

"Lady Hawkeswell," she exclaimed, forcing an embrace on a very stiff Verity. "My dear girl."

Bertram managed an awkward kiss on Verity's cheek. "We are relieved and gratified that you have returned to us, and that you are well."

Hawkeswell hoped Verity never looked at him the way she looked at Bertram then. Although her cool fury was for him too, if one got down to it. All of her resentment about this marriage was in her eyes. Even if the gaze of blame focused on Bertram, the other two people present had been his accomplices.

"I am glad to see both of you as well. That is a very lovely ensemble, Mrs. Thompson. That silvery gray suits you."

Neither relative missed the address, or its significance. The Countess of Hawkeswell had just signaled that henceforth formalities would be maintained.

"Shall we all continue our walk?" Hawkeswell suggested. "We are creating an unwelcomed island in the river."

They paced together. Bertram muttered pleasantries and

Hawkeswell muttered some back. The ladies carried the conversation, such as it was.

"Is all well in Oldbury?" Verity asked. "I obtained county papers whenever I could, but I know that I missed most of the news about the people there these last two years."

"There is so much news that I can hardly give it all now. I will write to you with what I remember, however," Nancy said.

"Is Mr. Travis still with the mill?"

"Of course." Nancy's voice fell into minor key. *We have no choice on that, do we?*

"And the vicar, Mr. Toynby— Is he still putting his sheep to sleep every Sunday?"

"Mr. Toynby left us over a year ago. There is a new vicar now."

Verity's profile firmed. "And Katy Bowman's son, Michael. What finally became of him, Mrs. Thompson?"

Both husband and wife reacted strongly to the question, but not in similar ways. Nancy flushed red and cast Verity a cautious glance. Bertram flushed with anger.

"Gone a good while now, he is," Bertram snapped. "Good riddance, I say. Nothing but trouble, the ungrateful scoundrel."

"Gone where?" Verity pressed.

"Who knows? To town, perhaps. To join his revolutionary friends. Wherever, it is fine with me, so long as he is far gone from my county and my works."

Nancy remained silent. Verity kept looking at her, as if she found that silence interesting in itself.

"Your works, Thompson?" Hawkeswell felt obliged to say. "Your devotion to the family concern is admirable, but you misspoke."

"Yes, you did misspeak. Thank you, Hawkeswell, for saying so. It spared me the necessity of reminding my cousin myself." Verity looked over at Bertram expectantly.

Thompson flushed more deeply. "I stand corrected. *Our* works, Lady Hawkeswell."

This meeting had not begun well, and it was turning worse fast. Hawkeswell decided to end everyone's misery. He took Verity's arm. "It was good to see both of you. It has been too long. Thompson, I will write to you with some questions that I have about that business. Come along, my dear. We have a full night ahead."

He guided Verity away after some awkward good-byes. Mrs. Thompson did not appear happy that no invitations were extended first.

Verity remained thoughtful while they retraced their steps to the carriage. He handed her in and settled across from her.

"Did you enjoy yourself?" he asked. "If your goal was to inform them that there will be no sentiment on your part, and that they are now reduced to mere acquaintances, you succeeded."

She barely appeared to be paying attention to what he was saying. "I thoroughly enjoyed myself, thank you." She spoke absently and dully, while something else occupied her mind.

The sound was unmistakable. It penetrated the wall and door while he undressed. It broke through his contemplation of that meeting in the park, and of Verity's curiosity about someone named Michael.

The sound came from the chambers next to his own, probably the bedchamber. Verity was weeping.

Drummund pretended he did not hear, until Hawkes-well paused and lifted a hand for silence so he could listen. Then the valet's eyes sought his.

Hawkeswell dismissed him. Still dressed in shirt and trousers, he passed through Verity's dressing room.

She was standing near the bed when he entered, and crying no longer. She had swallowed her sorrow on hearing his footsteps. He considered leaving again, so she could release her emotions without his interruption.

"I am not ready. I am sorry." She slipped off her shoe and propped her foot on a chair. She began to roll down her hose, as if his appearance in her chamber meant only one thing.

Which it always had. Still, he did not care for the way she now felt compelled to become "ready" when she really wanted to cry. He wondered if this transpired often, and he had missed it on nights past because he was not in his dressing room yet when she wept.

Maybe she cried every night, then dried her tears, removed her clothes, and climbed into bed to wait for the performance of her duties. The idea angered him.

She set her other foot on the chair and began on the other hose.

"Stop that, Verity."

He startled her. She set her foot on the ground and faced him.

"You were weeping just now, before I entered. Why?"

She just looked at him, her blue eyes blank and hiding her thoughts. That only angered him more.

He wanted to insist that she tell him. He almost said that as her husband he had a right to know everything he wanted to know. Except he did not, and she knew it. He could demand she give him her obedience, her future, and her body, but if she chose to keep her heart and soul to herself, he could not stop her.

To his amazement, her gaze became watery. She wiped her eyes, sniffed hard, and turned to her bed. She lifted a paper lying there.

"Nancy did not waste time in complying with my request. She sent the news from Oldbury by messenger tonight. Here it is. A list of the neighbors who died, young and old, while I was gone and unaware, and unable to mourn them. She also includes an explanation of those who left, and even a few notes on those who have arrived."

He took the page from her and sat on the bed near the lamp. It bore columns of names, each with a title. Dead. Removed. Arrived. Missing. Rather prominently, Verity's own name had been listed below that last heading, then crossed out. Nancy had found a way to express her pique in the end.

Katy and Michael Bowman were listed under Removed.

"She does not write that Katy is missing or dead," he said. "That is a good sign, is it not?"

"I suppose. I will not know until I see her, however. I wrote to the vicar, asking after her and requesting he read her a letter I included. Only he is on that list now, under "Removed." If the letter is following him, it could be lost or traveling the length and breadth of the land."

"Were you weeping at Nancy's cruelty in listing these names with no thought to how you would receive them?"

She shook her head. "I was moved because I know many of them. Or did." She stepped close and pointed to the list labeled "Dead." "That is a little girl. She would be no more than ten now. A pretty little thing with red curls. My father helped her father build their house when she was born, as he was wont to do sometimes."

She pointed out a few more names, of people from her girlhood, and described who they had been to her.

She smiled toward the end of her explanation, the memories warming her instead of bringing sorrow. He decided to wait another day to ask about the young man named Michael whom she had been careful to ask Nancy about.

She took the letter and folded it. He took her hand and kissed it.

"I will leave you to your memories, Verity."

Her eyes misted again. She did not release his hand. "For a man who has known countless women, Hawkeswell, you really do not know women very well at all. I do not want to be left to mourn, and to spend the night with ghosts."

"Then I will stay, if you want me here."

She appeared grateful, which touched him. She turned away and began undressing. There was nothing seductive in her movements. Her distraction meant she barely noticed what she was doing.

He had to watch, of course, while he removed his own garments. The domesticity of her matter-of-fact disrobing charmed him.

They met under the sheets and he guessed that she had not asked him to stay for pleasure. She truly did not want to be alone. She required company, nothing more.

He pulled her close and tucked her against him so he faced her back and she curled against him. She sighed deeply and stilled, and her breathing calmed into a steady rhythm.

Soon he thought she slept. He weighed slipping away so that he might sleep as well. That would be unlikely if he remained here, with her bottom nestled against his loins.

To his surprise, her hand took his, the one on the arm embracing her. She moved it, until it cupped her breast. He caressed, and she sighed again in a little melody of contentment.

He needed no more encouragement than that. He fondled until her breath shortened and her bottom snuggled more closely against him. She tried to turn.

"No. Stay like that," he said. He instead turned her slightly away from him and braced on his other arm so he could kiss her cheek and shoulder, her back and hair. He used his hand to arouse her, stroking down her body and circling her nipples until her little cries sounded impatient and her bottom rose higher, pressing his erection, seeking more.

He caressed her bottom. His fingers followed her crevice until they touched her softest, warmest flesh. He watched her face and the way pleasure transformed it, until she clutched at the bedclothes beneath her and cried out her need and her assents and finally her release into the night.

He took her just as she was then, half hugging the mattress, and watched her pleasure climb again while she arched erotically into his thrusts.

"I need to go home."

"This is your home."

"I want to go to Oldbury," she said, rephrasing. "You said that I could."

They had not moved. His body still curved along hers. His hand rested on her breast, much as she had invited, but in comfort and possession now, not to titillate. It had been a long, slow joining, and at the end, when her need had grown to the point of frenzy from his repeated thrusts, he had reached around her body and rubbed the nub below her mound.

The result had been her spectacular second release that had demanded his own. She had cried into the night with abandon, and pulled his head to her so she could kiss him aggressively, with a savagery that intensified the climax. Her violent ecstasy still echoed in his head.

All of which left him ill-prepared for her unexpected announcement.

"I said you could go when it was convenient for me to accompany you. It is not now. Parliamentary sessions begin soon, and we must be here a month hence in any case."

"I will return long before a month passes." She plumped her pillow, hugged it, and nestled in. "I am going to go."

"And if I forbid it?"

She said nothing.

"Well, at least I will know where you are this time if you run away, Verity."

She turned to her other side so she faced him. "I have things I must settle there, and people I must see. I warned you that I would not forsake my past life for you, but I think that you expect me to anyway. It will not happen, no matter what you forbid, or how much pleasure you give me."

"It is far too dangerous for you to go alone. We will talk about it tomorrow." He'd be damned if he were just going to capitulate. However, right now, with visions of her beautiful passion still haunting his mind, he did not want to argue, or think about how to end this rebellion.

She smiled contentedly. She assumed she had won. Well, she would learn the hard truth tomorrow.

"Why must I be here a month hence?" she asked.

"You will be invited to a dinner party hosted by the Duke of Castleford. It will be a month from this Tuesday. I think that royalty will attend."

"Whoever thought that the daughter of an iron worker would sit with royalty? Such are the benefits of marrying an earl, I suppose. I will hide behind you and muddle through it."

"You will not be riding my coattails into that milieu. Nor will you be able to hide. The party is in your honor, in a manner of speaking."

She rose on one arm. She frowned thoughtfully while she watched her fingers walk over his chest in a pleasant tapping march. "Why would this duke bother with me?"

"He and I were good friends until a few years ago, and he has been moved by nostalgia to ease your way, it seems. He will be calling on you tomorrow. I will be here."

He debated whether warnings were in order. Unfortunately, with Castleford they probably were, for all his talk of standards. Tristan would undoubtedly be fascinated with Verity, especially if she did not act in awe of him. He might consider that a challenge he could not allow to stand.

"He has a reputation for being dissolute and a libertine. It would be best if you only received him when I am present too."

"I know about his reputation, from the scandal sheets. Celia seems to know a bit more, but then, she often does, and she has added glosses to those notices. If you were his good friend, you must have been dissolute once as well." She cast him a critical glance. "Orgies and such."

"I no longer find such diversions amusing."

"Why not? I think they must be eternally amusing."

She might be asking why he now preferred blue to brown, and calmly observing that while she had never worn brown herself, she assumed the habit of wearing it would not grow tiresome.

"When a man is nineteen years of age, getting roaring drunk is fun, audacious, and rebellious. One needs to be good and foxed to join an orgy without inhibition. About five years ago I decided that I would never get that foxed again. At which point orgies became peculiar, not amusing."

"You mean that your tastes changed."

"Yes. My tastes became much more boring."

"Or simply more private. You did not become a monk. You just stopped swiving women in a room full of other men swiving other women."

Never let it be said that Lady Hawkeswell minced words or worried overmuch about the appropriateness of the words themselves.

"Why did you decide to never get very foxed again?"

That was the trouble with women. No matter how carefully a man sidestepped and circled, no matter how cleverly he diverted and obscured, women possessed an uncanny ability for spotting that which was being avoided and honing in on it with relentless precision.

"You may have noticed that I have a bit of a temper."

She giggled. "No? You do?"

"Being drunk makes controlling it difficult. In my efforts to learn restraint, I accepted my limitations."

She appeared to find that a sensible explanation. She expected nothing more. She may not have wanted anything more even if she knew there was more.

She adjusted her position, yawned deeply, and closed her eyes.

"I almost killed a man. That is why I chose not to get foxed again."

Her lids rose and her blue eyes sought his face. "But you did not kill him."

He shook his head. "Summerhays was there, as drunk as I was but of better character to start. He saw how it would end and dragged me off the poor fellow. He thrashed me senseless, to be sure I stopped. When I came to, and sobered up, I knew how it would have to be henceforth." The memories of that night remained vague, lost in a haze of false euphoria giving way to red rage. The only thing he remembered clearly was swinging his fist again and again while fury drowned his mind. "The man had insulted me somehow. I do not even remember what he said. If Summerhays had not been there . . ."

He had often wondered how it would have been, to live with knowing his lack of control had cost a man his life. That, more than anything, had taught him the restraint itself.

"Most men would not admit they had been wrong, or accept how it would have to be, especially if the resolution meant an estrangement from a good friend, as it seems to have caused with Castleford. It is understandable if sometimes you miss him, and envy his freedom from the necessity of good sense."

"I do not miss him. I certainly do not envy him." Except sometimes he did. How like Verity to realize the nostalgia went both ways with Castleford.

She did not argue. He liked that quality in her. She expressed her opinion but displayed no compulsion to convert anyone else. Nor did she sigh at his density or smirk at his denial. She merely closed her eyes, to go to sleep.

Drowsiness claimed him as well, and his body relaxed into the mattress and against her softness. The first was very comfortable and the latter oddly comforting, and a pleasant peace lured him. He struggled back to consciousness and began to cast back the sheet, to return to his own chambers.

"You do not have to leave, if you do not want to." She sounded half-asleep. "Unless it is a rule that I was never told, that is."

It wasn't a rule, but it might be wise to go. Maintaining a few formalities was not a bad thing with a woman. However, she had said she did not want to be alone with the ghosts, and perhaps they still lurked on the edges of her dreams.

He decided that he would stay this once. For her sake.

Chapter Sixteen

Once more Hawkeswell found himself following a carriage on horseback in the rain. The journey to Shropshire had turned into more of a drama than he expected.

Colleen was to blame. Upon hearing from Verity that the journey was planned—a journey that Hawkeswell had not yet agreed to when Verity revealed the news to his cousin—Colleen asked to join them. She had not seen their mothers' cousin Mrs. Geraldson, who lived near Birmingham, for two years, and accompanying Verity would also hit three more targets with one ball. Colleen could leave London's late-summer heat and stench, enjoy good company while touring the countryside, and avoid returning to her mother for at least a fortnight. The last point won Hawkeswell's reluctant agreement.

If Colleen came, so did Colleen's lady's maid. Both servants now rode with their mistresses in the baggage-laden carriage.

He spent most of the time enjoying the country, which still left a good deal to contemplate the lessons he was learning about marriage. Foremost was that, while Verity might not be the sort to cajole jewels out of her husband when pleasure had turned him weak with her, any request not immediately refused would be assumed to be granted. *We will talk about this tomorrow* only announced defeat.

The rain proved light and fleeting, and the clouds broke in the sky ahead. They would reach their destination soon. Mrs. Geraldson had insisted they all stay with her, and since her property was an hour's carriage ride to Oldbury, he had agreed.

He may be allowing Verity this visit, but he did not like the idea of her taking lodgings too near the ironworks. An hour away seemed a good way to maintain a variety of necessary distances.

Mrs. Geraldson lived right across the Staffordshire county border. Hawkeswell already knew her to be a plain-speaking lady of middle years who relished her quiet life in the country. Her property was of good size, with airy apartments and several outbuildings, and Verity and Hawkeswell were given the best chambers. Their quarters were not luxurious, but more than adequate.

Once settled, they joined their hostess for light refreshment. Along with Colleen, they sat in a pleasant and feminine drawing room drinking punch and eating tiny cakes.

"I am honored to have you as guests, Lord Hawkeswell, Lady Hawkeswell." Mrs. Geraldson smiled indulgently at Verity. "Perhaps I can be forgiven for a lack of modesty if I claim some small part in your happiness. One never knows the power of a simple letter, and how it can initiate a serendipitous series of events."

"Hermione is referring to the letter of introduction that she gave the Thompsons when they came to London for their first extended visit," Colleen explained when she saw Verity's confusion. "Although I had known Mr. Thompson from when I visited here as a girl, her letter reintroduced us."

"You know my cousin?" Verity asked Mrs. Geraldson.

"I should hope that I know any person of consequence near Birmingham."

She had known Verity's father too, it turned out. She even had news about the ironworks.

"Trouble is brewing there, it is said. Well, it is brewing everywhere these days, isn't it? All these radicals and demonstrations. Lord Cleobury says there are secret revolutionary committees everywhere. One does not feel safe to go out in one's carriage, for fear of assault by those who the natural order decreed should have only wagons and carts."

"Has there been actual violence?" Hawkeswell asked. "Have there been recent assaults such as you describe? We have heard nothing of this in London."

"It is only a matter of time, after what happened in Derbyshire last summer and Manchester in the spring. Mr. Albrighton is doing his best to keep an eye on things, but he is only one man."

"Albrighton?" Hawkeswell asked. "That would not be Jonathan Albrighton? If so, I did not realize he had property here, or that he was even back in England."

"That is indeed his name, Lord Hawkeswell. Do you know him? He received a legacy from a relative, and has taken residence in Losford Hall."

The revelation fascinated Hawkeswell. "I will go visit him tomorrow. It has been at least five years since we spoke."

"How has Mr. Albrighton been keeping an eye on matters?" Verity asked. "Does he warn men off? Send them out of the county?"

"With so many counties bordering each other here, that would do little good. They could hop right back, couldn't they? Lord Cleobury fears that the close county borders breed trouble all by themselves, and that rebellion will begin right here. He has brought cannon to his property. They are lined up on the terrace, in preparation for an attack."

"I doubt there will be open rebellion," Hawkeswell said. "People are angry and restless; that is true. The end of the war has brought hardships. Most of the demonstrations express that discontent, not treasonous beliefs."

"I fear that you think too kindly and that Lord Cleobury is correct. They will never be satisfied until they have destroyed all that is good," Colleen said. "A firm response is required. The army must be used, as it was with Brandreth and his rabble."

"If you had experienced that treason almost in your garden, Lord Hawkeswell, you would understand the concerns of decent people up here," Mrs. Geraldson said.

"People only want to be able to feed their families," Verity said. "It is in everyone's interest to help them do so."

Mrs. Geraldson was not accustomed to disagreement. "Your own family feels differently. Mr. Thompson has informed all his workers that if they participate in such seditious activity, they will be put out of his mill and out of their cottages. He did not hesitate to call up the yeomanry last winter when some men were talking trouble there."

"I cannot speak for my cousin. However, my father would have never forbidden men to speak their minds, to him or anyone else. We are a free people, are we not?"

"Indeed we are," Hawkeswell said. He saw a row coming. A change of subject was in order. "Tell me, Mrs. Geraldson, what news is there of my other relatives in these parts? I confess that I have never met some of my mother's people. Are there many in the county?"

"There are more in Derbyshire."

Talk moved on to a long report on cousins many times removed. While Hawkeswell distracted their hostess from talk about rebellions, he suspected that Verity worried about Mrs. Geraldson's revelations about Bertram and the ironworks.

The next morning, Verity dressed early in a carriage ensemble. She was breaking her fast when Hawkeswell entered the breakfast room. He eyed her garments, parasol, and reticule while he ate and chatted with Mrs. Geraldson.

"Are you going somewhere?" he asked, when their hostess excused herself.

She assumed a casual, airy tone and hoped that would help. "I intend to call for the carriage and visit Oldbury."

"Not on your own, you are not."

"You spoke of visiting Mr. Albrighton today, so I must go on my own. I will return by afternoon, and will take great care with my safety."

He got that look on his face. The one that said he was trying hard to be reasonable. Only his idea of being reasonable usually meant he expected her to agree with his reason, and relinquish her own, after he stated his opinion a few times.

"Verity—"

"It is why I am here. I will be unable to sit still, let alone play the part of a polite guest." She lifted her parasol and reticule to emphasize her resolve.

"Put those down. You are not going anywhere if I do not allow it. The coachman will never disobey me, even if you will."

"My home is mere miles away. Why allow me to come this far if you will deny me now?"

"I am not denying you anything, except dangerous independence. This may not be Manchester, but you heard Mrs. Geraldson describe the mood abroad here. It is not safe."

She wanted to tell him that Joshua Thompson's daughter would always be safe at the ironworks. Only she was not sure that was still true. She might not be seen as Joshua's daughter, but as Bertram's cousin and a peer's wife.

She set down her reticule. "I knew we would not suit."

His expression firmed and his gaze pierced her. "Do we not? No decent man would act differently. Would you prefer I proved indifferent to your safety?"

No, she realized. She would find that disheartening. But she had lived independently for two years and did not like being forced by another to set aside her plans, either on a whim or for reasons fair. She did not like being expected to obey even if she disagreed with the command.

"Perhaps it is not you and I that do not suit, but marriage and I," she said. "I would be vexed by any husband's interference."

"You will have to learn to live with that. Since we are married and I am your husband. Now, come here."

He was angry. An old, ugly fear spiraled through her, wanting to take hold. She scolded herself that to react thus was stupid. This man had never been cruel, or lost hold of his anger in her presence. Still, that visceral sensation from the past stirred, and she hesitated before she walked around the table to him.

He pushed back his chair and patted his lap. "Sit."

She lowered herself until she perched on his lap.

"Now kiss me the way you did the night I stayed with you, the way you did right after you screamed from pleasure into the night."

Her face burned. She glanced over her shoulder, to see if anyone might see.

She was not even sure that she knew what he meant. She touched her lips to his, and as she did she remembered that kiss, so much the result of intense sensations crashing through her. She was not sure that she could kiss like that while sitting in a breakfast room.

She tried, however. She met his mouth more boldly, and did what he did to her with her tongue and her teeth. Her body responded when he accepted and took and finally gave in return in a flurry of mutual, hungry kisses.

She forced herself to stop, because the door might open at any moment. She wondered if she appeared as flushed and aroused as she felt.

"Now, ask me to accompany you to Oldbury today, so you will have protection and help if you find trouble."

She swallowed the prideful impulse to refuse. "I should very much like to go to Oldbury today. Will you take me there?"

He bared his teeth slightly, and closed them gently on her finger. A brief, intense, feral heat entered his eyes. She could not look away. In his gaze she found the vivid mem-

ory of that night, of him moving so deeply into her body
and of her going wild from the sensation of being filled so
fully.

He set her on her feet and stood. "I will call for the carriage, and see Albrighton another day if necessary."

"Thank you," she said, too aroused for comfort.

He lifted her chin and kissed her. "See? We suit very
well, Verity."

I t always surprised Hawkeswell that most industrial
sites appeared very rustic. Almost agricultural. The ironworks a mile outside Oldbury, in an isolated, disconnected
bit of Shropshire wholly circled by other counties, were
no different.

The buildings were made of brick and local stone. They
sat on the property much as outbuildings did on farms, with
trees and bushes, greenery, and even a few wildflowers
scattered between them. In the distance, perhaps three hundred yards away, a stone house could be seen on a low
hill, its side facing the works and its size indicating the
owner or manager lived here.

A community had grown up north of the works, with a
good number of cottages. A broad stream ran along its
edge, pouring toward the ironworks where a dam controlled its flow before it turned the big wheel of the tilting
hammer.

Home, Verity called this. He had not realized just what
she meant. She had grown up in that house up there, with
the furnace and forges all but in her garden. He pictured
her running down the hill, to join the workers' children in
play.

"Do you want to go to the house?" he asked. "The

Thompsons had not yet left London when we departed, so I do not think they are here now. The housekeeper would let you in."

She gave the house a good look. "I do not need to go to the house. Nothing of him remains there for me. He is still here, however, in the forges and furnaces." She pointed to the stream. "He drowned in that. It is hard to believe it became a rushing river that spring. He was helping the workers save their homes when he was swept away."

She strolled down the hard-packed dirt that served as the street. Every eye she passed followed her and the gentleman by her side. At the end, beyond most of the buildings, they came upon tracks set in the ground.

"The iron is brought to the canal by special wagons that run on this track," she explained. "It is not far. There are not many ironworks like this one. Everything is done here, from beginning to end. Raw ore comes in, and split rods and castings and wrought iron leave."

A more modest house, but still of good size, stood down here at the other end of the works. "That is Mr. Travis's house. He will not be there now. He should be in the boring house."

He followed her while she retraced her steps to a low building with few windows. No one entered or left as they approached, and no smoke came from its chimney.

Six men worked lathes inside, fitting thick iron rods on clamps and feeding them to the tool that ate their interiors. Work stopped when Verity entered. Suspicion and silence slowly gave way to shocked stares.

"Mr. Travis," an old man called. "The master's daughter is here. She should be a ghost, but I don't think she is."

A door opened, revealing yet another chamber, this one full of smaller lathes and a long table covered with bits of iron and steel. Mr. Travis peered through spectacles, then removed them and peered some more.

He was a big man, with sandy hair going white, and a ruddy face as hard as the iron he worked. The smile that broke did much to soften it, however, and for a moment Hawkeswell thought the man would weep.

"That can't be Miss Thompson, Isaiah. That there is a lady born if ever I saw one. A fine lady who has lost her way, I think."

"It is truly I, Mr. Travis," Verity said, playing along.

Travis advanced on them, peering hard and frowning like a comic actor. He came very close and crouched down so he could look up under the rim of her hat. "I'll be damned. So it is. The years have made the girl a woman, and the woman a lady at that."

Verity embraced him, then introduced Hawkeswell. "I would like to visit with you for a short while, if it will not interfere too much, Mr. Travis."

"No one here to say you can't, so I take that to mean you can," he said. "Best if you visit as long as you want and need, because when your cousin returns, he'll not take kindly to another visit."

He led them to that other room and closed the door. Hawkeswell examined the bits and pieces of metal on the worktable, and the tools and lathes. This must be where the secret lived. Those other lathes used bits formed here by Mr. Travis, and the nature of the bit itself was probably the secret.

"I wrote to you, Mr. Travis, to tell you that I was alive and well," Verity said. "Did you not receive my letter?"

"It came, and it gave me such joy and relief. It is an odd thing to grieve for someone, and later learn she is still alive. A most peculiar experience."

"So peculiar that you could not write back?"

"Your cousin also learned that you still lived. He came down here, to forbid me to write back. Said he would let me go if I did, and the mill be damned. Said I would be responsible for all these people having no work. He will not be happy to learn we talked today." He lifted two chairs off pegs high on the wall and set them down.

Verity sat. Hawkeswell declined.

"We have much to discuss while we have the opportunity, Mr. Travis. Before we talk of the business, I need to ask you where Katy is. I wrote to her as well, as soon as—" She glanced to Hawkeswell. "As soon as I felt able, but sent it through the vicar, who I now learn has left."

"Left he did. Lost the situation. The man with the living put a relative of Mrs. Thompson in his place. Mr. Thompson believed the last vicar had used the pulpit to foment discord. That means he often spoke of your father with more praise than he used in speaking of the current occupant of the big house."

"And Katy?"

"She is nearby, just not right here. She lives on the parish's charity now, in a cottage not far from the canal."

They moved on to talk of the mill itself. Hawkeswell listened, but he also studied all those bits of iron and machines that Travis used in here.

Travis described the trouble last winter, which he thought Bertram handled in the worst way, and the general discontent of the workers on account of a decrease in wages now that the war was over and cannon and muskets were not needed.

Verity took her leave of Mr. Travis with promises to return very soon. Once outside she expressed her concern. "I always suspected that Bertram had not filled my

father's place well. He forbade me to come down here
once he became my guardian, and it has been years since I
spoke to Mr. Travis alone. He has much more to tell me, I
am sure."

"You mean, tell you when I am not with you."

"It is no insult to you. He does not know you, or where
your mind is on all of this."

"He is not sure that I am not in collusion with Bertram,
is what you mean." He could hardly blame Mr. Travis,
when Verity also was not convinced of that.

"You are an *earl*. He will not speak freely in front of
you, whatever he thinks of your involvement with Bertram. The House of Lords has hardly been sympathetic to
such as these people." She strode down the lane with purpose. "Now, I must find Katy."

Chapter Seventeen

The cottage near the canal lock proved to be a hovel of stone and old thatch. A kitchen garden grew in the rocky soil surrounding it, and only shutters would hold out the elements or cold.

Verity's heart broke when she saw it. She wanted desperately to see Katy again, but she almost hoped they had been directed to the wrong place.

Hawkeswell stepped out of the carriage. She handed him the basket of food that she had bought in Oldbury.

He handed her down in turn. "I will wait here," he said.

She had been debating how to ask that of him. It touched her that he understood how she would want time alone with Katy. Not only were there things to discuss that she did not want Hawkeswell to hear, but there were emotions that required privacy too.

"It may be some time. Do you want to take the carriage and come back?"

"I will walk down to the lock and watch the show for a while. If I decide to take the carriage, I will let you know."

She carried the basket to the door of the cottage. Her knock caused movements within; then footsteps approached on a wooden floor. The door opened to reveal Katy, thinner now, and her hair whiter than it had been, but still sturdy and unbowed.

She frowned at the fine bonnet and dress in front of her, and angled her head to see the carriage beyond her little garden.

"It is I, Katy. It is Verity."

Katy gripped the threshold, stepped outside, and peered hard at Verity's face. Recognition entered her eyes, along with tears. She pulled Verity into an embrace so encompassing, so warm, so *familiar*, that Verity wept too.

"My child," Katy cried softly. "My dear child."

"Was that your husband out there?" Katy asked. She had insisted Verity take the one chair and she sat on a stool not far away. "He is a handsome man."

"He is at that." Too handsome, perhaps. It had been her undoing, and continued to be. Combined with his station it made him very sure of himself, which made her a little less sure of herself in turn. "He can be very kind," she added, because she did not want Katy worrying about her. He *could* be very kind. "He brought me here so I could find you and let you know that I was alive and well."

"I had long given up hope of seeing you again. This is like a miracle to me. If he can be kind, why did you run away, child?"

How like Katy to know at once she had run away. But then, in the past, when she ran away, she ran to Katy.

The embrace outside had reminded her of why, and filled her heart with nostalgia. Those arms had comforted a child after a mother's death, and a girl again after a father's. When that governess scolded too much, or Nancy chastised, she would slip away sometimes, knowing all the while that she would pay for it, and go down the hill to Katy's cottage to be embraced and comforted again.

The scent and softness of this woman had stayed with her the last two years. Now, sitting in this little sad cottage with its rough plank floor, she felt more thoroughly herself than she had for many years.

Yet she could not honestly answer Katy's question. She did not want to worry her by describing what Bertram had threatened.

"I ran away because I did not truly agree to marry." She explained her plan, and how she had hoped to get free once she came of age, and come home and put Bertram out. She told Katy all of it.

"It was the plan of a child," Katy said. "Your father's child, for there was much of his mind in it, but still a child who knew little of the world. You are here now, though, and if that lord can be kind sometimes, being back in that marriage will not harm you. You will be safe, at least."

"I have learned more of the world now, and I am content at last, now that I have seen you." She leaned toward the stool and gave Katy another embrace. "And Michael? How does he fare?"

Katy's eyes closed, and Verity knew she had touched a sorrow. Her heart sank.

"He has been gone a long time now. Longer than you. I thought nothing of it at first; it was not the first time he left as you know, but . . ."

"Where did he go?"

Katy slowly shook her head. "I do not know. Sometimes I would dream of him and you, together the way you were as children, and worry that the dream meant he also was dead." She dabbed her eyes and forced a smile. "But since you were not, as I can see with my own eyes now, perhaps the dream meant nothing at all."

"Was he possibly arrested? He could be rash in his talk, Katy. Perhaps he was involved in something and put in gaol."

"If so, not in Shropshire or Staffordshire. If he had stood at the sessions, I would have been told. Mr. Travis would have heard of it."

Verity took Katy's hands in hers. "So all this time you have been waiting, not knowing whether to mourn him or not."

"Or you, child. Or you."

"I will discover what became of him, Katy, even if it is not happy news, so you do not have to wait much longer." She looked around the tiny cottage, dark with its two small windows. "This must be uncomfortable when it rains, and in winter."

"I count myself lucky to have it. After Michael left, I was put out of the works' cottage where we lived."

It was not supposed to happen that way. Part of the agreement with Bertram had been that Katy would never be put out. This further evidence of Bertram's betrayal infuriated Verity. She had difficulty hiding her anger.

"I will see that you have more comfort in the future." She wanted to be more specific. She almost was before she remembered that she had no power to promise anything. She would have to request permission from Hawkeswell to help Katy. She would have to petition him in order to have a crumb of her own inheritance used to benefit this dear woman.

She stood, and went to the small table on which her basket rested. "I have brought you things for later, but a few for right now too." She unwrapped a meat pasty and a hunk of cheese. "Let us share, while you tell me all about my neighbors. Give me only the joyful news, Katy. I already know the rest."

Hawkeswell watched the barge waiting for the canal lock to do its work. Held in place by two hefty gates, it floated higher as water rushed in. The piles of coal on its bed could not defeat the forces of nature, and its deck rose until it lay higher than the gates themselves. Then the gate ahead opened slowly, and the barge floated away.

The Birmingham canal curved ahead, one of many twists as it followed the lay of the land between Wolverhampton and Birmingham. Even so it could not avoid some hills, and steam engines had been set up to pump enough water to ensure the canal could function on them.

Bills regarding canals kept being proposed in Parliament, as men eager to make money either moving goods, or making the goods to be moved, petitioned for permission to cut these waterways. As a result he knew more about canals than most. He knew that this was not the best canal, but rather narrow, and complicated by the big curves of its serpentine path. Even so, it was far better than trying to haul that barge's coal overland.

He walked back toward the carriage, checking his pocket watch as he strode. Verity would probably want to stay with Katy a good while longer.

He had thought, when she spoke of the woman, that Katy had the place of a nurse or governess in her affections. Seeing their reunion, watching their joyful embrace and the tears flow, had disproven that. Instead Verity had meant exactly what she said. Katy was like a mother to her.

The area appeared safe enough. He decided to take the carriage after all, and sent the coachman to inform Verity that he would return in two hours.

L osford Hall rested on a hill, at the end of a lane that wound through trees. As Hawkeswell approached he thought it a handsome property, but its setting lent it an air of mystery. That would be appropriate for the man who lived there now.

Jonathan Albrighton received him in a library stuffed with books and papers. Not all had come with the house. Unbound volumes and stacks of pamphlets mixed with the neat bindings normally found in a country house of this size.

"I am pleased that you called. I was hoping that you would," Albrighton said.

He appeared thinner than Hawkeswell remembered, but still carried himself with a manner that implied both deference and arrogance at the same time. His dark hair was pulled into an old-fashioned tail, and his dark eyes, his whole countenance, invited one to confidences and trust, as always. Hawkeswell knew, however, that no matter how long one looked and how often one confided, the mind behind those eyes would forever remain unknown.

"So you knew I was in the area." He did not bother to make it a question. "Word does spread quickly in the country, doesn't it? As a JP, you no doubt hear it before many others."

"It only confirmed what I expected. You would have to come eventually, to see about your wife's inheritance."

They sat in comfortable chairs, the kind a man could read in for hours. No doubt this man did. Albrighton had been a most studious student at university, and everyone assumed he would become a don himself. Instead he had chosen a nomadic existence, traveling far and wide, his stays in London always of uncertain duration.

That, combined with an income of ambiguous origins, had led Hawkeswell, Summerhays, and Castleford to conclude that Albrighton was involved in activities of ambiguous legality, perhaps even for the government.

"So you have become a country gentleman," Hawkeswell said, admiring the library. "Although it suits your intellectual interests, somehow I can't see you contented here long. Of course, serving as a magistrate gives your curiosity more active purposes."

"It was an unexpected appointment. I try to execute my duties well, however."

"I am sure you execute them admirably. Will you be doing so for a good while? Are you planning to stay in England now?"

"That remains to be seen." Albrighton smiled pleasantly. The eternal depths of his dark eyes drew one in but, as always, revealed nothing once one became submerged.

"I have had my ears filled with stories about seditious doings in the region. My hostess is sure revolution is at hand. She reported some nonsense about Cleobury buying cannon. I have seen nothing today to warrant such fears."

"People will talk. Fear is abroad, more than is warranted, as you say. I have become more circumspect in talking to men who may be fomenting discontent, lest my attention only feed the worry. As for Cleobury—well, he was never very smart, was he?"

"It is believed by many in Parliament that the Home Office is instigating trouble rather than calming it. That there are agent provocateurs at work up here, in Home Secretary Lord Sidmouth's employ. Would you know anything about that?"

Albrighton just looked at him, a vague amusement playing at his mouth and in his eyes. "And here I thought this was a social call. Did the peers send you to investigate these rumors? If so, I cannot help you. I have not met any agent provocateurs, if they really exist."

"I was sent by no one. I am just curious for my own purposes." Mostly he was curious why Albrighton was here. Of course, the work for spies would have decreased with the war's end, much like the demand for iron. With his skills no longer needed, the man would have to go someplace.

Hawkeswell stood and went to look out the window. It overlooked a small garden that gave way to a wilderness area. "Have you been back in England long? It is odd that no one in town knows of it."

"A year, perhaps. I passed through London quickly, and had no time to call on old friends."

Hawkeswell did not think he was a friend who would have been called on in any case by Albrighton. He wondered if any man was. "This is a fine property. Part of a legacy, was it?"

"Thank you. I think it is a fine property too."

Hawkeswell laughed. "You will have your mysteries, won't you?"

"I think of it as privacy, not mystery."

"I doubt Cleobury permits much privacy, if you have become friends with him."

"I would not presume to describe Lord Cleobury as my friend."

Hawkeswell turned around. "What the hell are you doing here? Not retiring to the sweet country air, I think."

"Would you have me lie to you, Hawkeswell? Make up a tale that fits your assumptions about me? I will do so if you insist. I would prefer not to. We have known each other too long, and shared some fine times in the past. You and a few others deserve better."

Yes, they had shared some fine times. Albrighton had sometimes stood with Summerhays, Castleford, and him through good and bad. Not shoulder to shoulder, however. Albrighton was always a little apart, and a lot unknown. Privacy, he called it.

Hawkeswell returned to his chair. "No, do not lie. Tell me how things are in Paris, instead. I am sure that you have been there more recently than I."

"Are you finished with your calls for the day?" Hawkeswell asked when Verity emerged from Katy's cottage that afternoon.

"Quite finished." She settled into the carriage and he climbed in with her. "Where did you go?"

"To see the countryside."

Verity watched him with a speculative expression. To his surprise, she moved from the seat facing him, and snuggled in by his side. He put his arm around her, so she could get as close as she wanted.

"My cousin will be back in a day or so. Nancy wrote to their housekeeper that they are returning, and of course word has spread," she said.

"I did not expect him to dally in London once you departed, so I am not surprised."

"I intend to speak with him about Katy, but he will not hear me. He will deny his lies and promises to me."

She snuggled closer, then turned clumsily and managed to slide upon his lap. She kissed him aggressively, much as she had in the morning at his command. Since he had not commanded it this time, her forwardness delighted him.

"Are you certain that you want to start this here and now?" he asked, when she finally ended the kiss. Already he could not keep his hands off her.

"Very certain." Her breathless, warm voice made him harder. Heat burned away vague considerations of restraint.

She kissed him again to prove her certainty. He hardly needed more encouragement, although her bottom moved and flexed just enough on his lap to render concerns of time and place mute.

Fevered now, he set her feet on the floor. She bowed over him, holding the back of his seat to steady herself. He held her head to a savage kiss with one hand while he raised her skirt with the other.

He hitched it high, draping it from her back, and the chemise too. "Hold it up."

She gathered the fabric in one arm, clutching it to her breast. Below its soft billows she was naked to her garters. She remained bent toward him. Her bottom rose as her back arched, and her spread legs sought balance in the moving carriage.

He thought her unbearably erotic looking, but picturing

her from the other side almost undid him. He wanted to turn her and taste her and take her hard while her pretty bottom arched up and her legs spread more and—

Not now. Not here. No time anyway. He raised his head to a kiss and caressed the damp curls of her mound, then stroked deep and long until her first cries spoke her own impatience. He teased ruthlessly, gently stimulating the sensitive flesh until she cried out with each touch.

He lifted her, and settled her on his lap again, facing him on bended legs. He shifted forward and pushed her knees back and entered harder than he intended, so hard that she gasped.

He stopped and waited for her body to accept him, as he often had to do. Finding restraint had never been more difficult than this time. He gritted his teeth while her velvet warmth softened and found comfort around his flesh. Then he cupped her bottom in his hands and guided her movements and let the fire burn out of control.

She rested against him, her head on his chest, not even attempting to move. The dress had draped down some, but her bottom still showed beneath its edge, pretty and white and so feminine in its lovely shape.

He thought she slept. He let her, and kept her in place with an embrace. Eventually, however, they neared Mrs. Geraldson's house. They could not arrive there like this.

With his slight movement she sat upright and became aware of her extreme dishabille. She backed off his lap and let her chemise and dress fall. They quickly made themselves presentable.

"I suppose that was scandalous," she said.

"Not nearly as scandalous as what I considered doing."

She appeared to puzzle that out, trying to imagine just what else he could have possibly done.

"Do not tie your head into knots, Verity. I will show you sometime."

She nodded, and allowed a minute to pass before speaking again. "I am very distressed by how Katy is living. Such a place can ruin a person's health. She has to walk all the way to the canal for water too. The parish barely gives her enough to buy food."

"Her circumstances are unfortunate."

"I would like to send her to Surrey, to Greenlay Park. Surely there is a cottage there that she could live in, or she could help the cook or housekeeper. I would say we should bring her to London, but she does not know town life and I do not think she would be happy."

"Surrey is better, I am sure."

"Thank you. This is very important to me."

She assumed that his response meant he had agreed already. She appeared very pleased with herself.

"Verity, did you seduce me in order to obtain my permission on this?"

"You implied this morning that kisses and such would help win your agreement on matters of my preference."

He would have allowed it even without her boldness. After seeing the love expressed in that reunion and hearing that woman call Verity her child, how could he refuse? There had been no need to use feminine wiles on him.

He decided it was not in his interest to tell her that.

Chapter Eighteen

"I hear that the Thompsons have returned," Mrs. Geraldson announced two days later. "No doubt you will want to call on them, Colleen. Perhaps you intend to as well, Lady Hawkeswell."

"We can take the cabriolet and drive over ourselves," Colleen said. "I have a good hand at the ribbons, and Hermione's mare is very mild, Verity."

"My wife was complaining of a headache this morning," Hawkeswell said. "Nor should you go that far without protection. I will go with you, Colleen. I have some things that I need to do at the works anyway."

Verity appeared grateful that he had saved her a lie by lying himself. He knew she would not want to see her cousin at all, let alone pay a call with Colleen in tow.

An hour later he took the reins of the cabriolet and, with Colleen by his side, headed to Oldbury.

"You must convince Verity to be more careful with her health," Colleen said. "She was up very early this morning, walking outside while it was still damp from a heavy dew. She was not even wearing a shawl."

He had not been aware Verity rose that early. "I do not believe she is frail. I suspect her health would have taken a bigger toll by now if she were. However, visiting here has troubled her mind."

"It probably only reminds her of how difficult it will always be in society. She will never feel at home there, especially while she still has such ties to Oldbury. It is not for me to advise, but perhaps this should be her last visit. She can always see the Thompsons when they visit London, and they are her only relatives."

"No, it is not for you to advise."

Colleen stiffened enough at the scold that he regretted speaking so directly. He took her hand to let her know he was not angry.

She twined her gloved fingers though his. "Forgive me. You are correct. I do forget my place sometimes."

"Not at all. It is only that the best advice is not always advice that it would be wise to follow."

He released his hand to have both for the reins, but made sure to smile at Colleen until her careful passivity passed.

Her advice had been well-meaning, and perceptive. This visit was reminding Verity of the differences between their stations. That had been the very first reason she gave for not wanting the marriage, and now here she was, back home, and the degree to which her people wanted nothing to do with him was clear. She anticipated, correctly, that his circles would prove even less open to her than hers were with him.

He left Colleen at the Thompsons, but excused himself

from lingering long. Mrs. Thompson expressed disappointment, and hoped he would return soon.

He took the carriage down the hill, and sought out Mr.
Travis. Caution was evident as the man greeted him, and
perhaps more so when Mr. Travis insisted they go to his
home for their conversation.

There was a Mrs. Travis, a small woman with a happy,
full face. She brought some ale to the little drawing room,
then disappeared.

"I have some questions about the ironworks," Hawkeswell said. "My wife has great confidence in you, so I decided to ask them of you instead of Mr. Thompson."

Travis did not permit the slightest reaction to move his
rough-hewn face.

"Verity tells me that she and you are the only ones who
know Joshua's secret. Having seen that part of the works,
I do not see how that can be."

"Boring is boring, sir. Lathes are lathes. There is nothing new in that. It is the tool used to bore that matters. Its
craft is not visible to the eye, and it is made of steel, not
iron, and I work it just so. Those men that you saw use
those tips, but they do not make them, and describing
their form will do no one any good. I set them on those
lathes, and I collect the tips afterward so none go missing."

"Could Mr. Thompson not just take one?"

"He could, I suppose, if he could get them off my dead
body. Then if he does, what is he going to do with it? Take
it to another man to copy? That secret gets out and it is the
ruin of him, so there is little point in it."

"It would mean he could get rid of you."

Travis chuckled. "That it would. There are days he would

like to, but those special jobs are the only things keeping the works alive, now that the demand for casting has all but disappeared. He would be wanting to keep things going for a few years at least. There's big changes coming in the world, Lord Hawkeswell, and there will be a need for iron to make them happen."

"In the meantime, however, I gather the works are not busy."

"Let us just say you should not be spending this year like the income will be the same as it was ten years ago. No doubt in my mind that the elder Mr. Thompson would have weathered it well, but this one does not take the care that is needed. Goes down to London a lot, doesn't he? The industry is up here, not down there. Better he should go to Manchester and Leeds, and dine with other men of trade and industry, not earls."

Hawkeswell gazed down the lane, at the hamlet of buildings that housed the works. They were smelting today, and billows of smoke floated out the huge chimney on the blast furnace.

"Tell me about the elder Mr. Thompson."

Travis quaffed some ale. Hawkeswell drank too, to encourage him to loosen his tongue.

"Not an easy man, if you know what I mean. Crusty outside but maybe too soft inside. Like a fine loaf of bread. He had his own mind; that was certain. But no man could work iron like he could. Whether it be at the forge or it be casts, he understood it like it was made of the same substance as he."

"It sounds as if perhaps it was."

Travis laughed at that and nodded. "We all respected that. He was one of us, wasn't he? To the end, some days he'd come down and take off those costly coats and strike the iron. It's hard to stand against a man who has sweated with you. And he was honest, but he knew that was a rare thing. That is why there is no patent. To get one you give out the secret, make drawings and such, and others who don't give a fig about patents will steal."

"Yet he trusted you with it."

Travis shrugged. "He could not do it all himself. Run the works, find the trade, make the bits. He had to trust someone, and I was as good with machining iron as any."

"But Bertram Thompson was not."

Travis said nothing.

"Why did he teach his daughter the secret? She does not work iron."

"I expect he taught her with pictures and such, so she could draw it if she had to. It could be done, just like if he went for a patent. As to why, it was so it was not left to me to decide the future of it. He passed it to the next generation. And through her to another who would take his place, I expect."

He meant her husband. If Joshua Thompson had not died in that flood, he would have arranged his own marriage for Verity. To a man much like himself. A man who worked iron, and who was crusty on the outside and maybe too soft inside, when it came to his workers and his family.

Hawkeswell suspected that Verity was correct, that Bertram had especially liked marrying her to a lord because there would be no danger then of another man competing with his hold on the business. No lord would dirty his hands with it, and Bertram would be safe.

"If you had to hand the secret to another man, Mr. Travis, to whom would you give it? If Verity must make that decision someday, to whom should she turn?"

Travis grew sober, as any man might when allusions were made to his death. "Well, now, sir, that is a problem. It would have to be a man with both the skill and the integrity, wouldn't it? Neither is easy to find in the quantity required. If I had to pick, though, it would be a young man whose skill held much promise and whose character I trust even if others might not."

"Is there such a man?"

"Hard to say. There was, but he isn't in these parts anymore. It would be Michael Bowman, Katy Bowman's son."

That would be the Michael that Verity had asked Bertram about. Hawkeswell had avoided dwelling on that query or putting too much significance on it, because he had suspected that he would not like what it all implied.

Now it turned out that this Michael Bowman might have had the qualities that Bertram lacked, and have been a candidate for taking Joshua's place.

He did not expect me to marry someone like you. No, her father had not. He had expected her to marry someone like Katy's son, the man Verity had married the Earl of Hawkeswell to protect.

Hawkeswell found himself counting out his paces as he walked to the cabriolet.

Verity spent the morning restlessly, trying to avoid Mrs. Geraldson's unctuous concern about her headache. Whenever she could, she spied out the windows at the lane.

Finally she saw a rider cantering toward the house. She tried to reach the door before the manservant who had this duty, but she was too late. She had to watch him carry the letter to his mistress, so Mrs. Geraldson could examine it and direct it to its intended recipient.

The inconvenient seal vexed Mrs. Geraldson. She frowned at the letter. She held it up to the window to attempt to read the contents. Verity made herself known with a little cough.

Mrs. Geraldson swung around. She had the decency to blush. "There is a letter for you, Lady Hawkeswell. Not posted. A rider brought it, but not an express rider."

"How peculiar. If you will excuse me, I will go outside and read it."

Once out of the house she tore it open. Someone had written in Katy's name, as they had arranged prior to their parting two days ago. The letter reported that Katy had managed to complete the little duty that Verity had given her.

Verity returned to the house, and informed Mrs. Geraldson that she was feeling much better, and would be taking Hawkeswell's carriage out to enjoy the day.

The three young men barely fit inside Katy's cottage. One of them, like Hawkeswell, was tall enough that he had to bend if he stood, so he sat on the floor.

They filled her ears with the kind of local news that Mrs. Geraldson would never know. Two of them worked at the ironworks, and they described the discontent there. The war's end had affected all ironworkers and the ones at Oldbury were no exceptions.

"The special work is what keeps it going," one said. "The machining and boring. But Mr. Thompson—well, milady, he is not your father when it comes to getting that work, so some of the older men have been let go, as has

Timothy here. Forced on the parish like Katy, their families are, but that charity only goes so far."

"He took the wages down last winter too," another
complained. "And he is cheap with fuel where we labor in
winter. Needs more for hisself, I guess, so he can buy his
lady her jewels."

Katy sat quietly, her body subtly rocking in agreement.
Verity sought her gaze sometimes, to be sure this was not
just lads talking the way they did at times, complaining the
way young men are wont to do in their restlessness.

It had not been hard for Katy to summon these particular young men, who had all been friends of Michael. After
they voiced their views about the mill, Verity asked them
to come outside to fix a little fence that Katy had around
her kitchen garden.

She positioned herself as far as possible from the house
so she would be out of Katy's hearing. She gestured for
Timothy to join her.

"I did not want to speak of it in her presence, Tim, but
I want to learn what you know of Michael."

His mouth firmed. "I know little, and what I know isn't
good."

"Tell me."

"He was more talkative than most, in complaining. He
did not wait for the master's daughter to invite it, like we
just did. Braver, he was, I guess. And he was involved with
others, in the big towns. Would go up to Liverpool at times,
and to some secret meetings near Shrewsbury. Mr. Travis
told him not to, but he would anyway." He shrugged. "Then
one day, he went, and never came back."

"Was he arrested?"

"We never heard if he was. Odd, that. Hard to try a
man without no one hearing of it."

Hard, to be sure. But impossible?

"Some think he just left, for better things," he said. "Can't blame him. He was good with the iron, as you know. Better than any of us. Skilled, like your father. The master took a liking to him when he was a boy partly due to that. The new master, though—he didn't like him at all, did he?"

No, not at all. Her father had liked Michael, and not only because of Katy's place in their house. He had gone to the works a few times, and shown Michael how to do things with wrought iron that only Michael seemed to learn quickly.

Now he had disappeared, right around the time Bertram was threatening to have him transported. No one here had heard of his arrest and trial, though.

Bertram might have arranged to have Michael arrested in another county, of course. Even so, a trial of radicals or revolutionaries would attract attention, and most likely even be reported in the London papers.

For two years she had worried that she had no idea of his fate. She had allowed herself to hope Nancy had lied, and Michael was at the works still, growing in his skill and caring for Katy, ready for the day she came home and offered him a special partnership. It was obvious now that Nancy had not lied, though. Bertram had indeed done something to make Michael go missing.

"Is he the only one who has left so abruptly?" she asked. "There have been others, haven't there?"

Timothy pondered that. "There was Harry Pratt, from the works, earlier this year. His wife wouldn't believe he ran away, but there had been a bit of trouble for him with Mr. Thompson, so most think he did. There's rumors of a few others over in Staffordshire, but with the way laws are now, I'd leave too if someone took too much notice of me."

"I would like to speak with some of the others," she said. "Perhaps one of the older men knows things you do not."

Timothy shook his head. "I'd not be going to the works alone, milady. It ain't the way it was with your father. There's angry men there, and they are not hoping for much good from this lord you married. There is fondness for you still, but . . ."

But she was no longer mostly one of them. It had been years since she ran down the hill to play with the village children. As a married woman, she was worthless to them too. As a countess she could not even be trusted.

Timothy's gaze shifted, as something down the road arrested his attention. Without his saying a word, his companions reacted to his unspoken warning. They left Katy's little fence, and came over so they all stood together.

Verity turned to see what created the united stand. A horse galloped down the lane, bearing a tall rider. Hawkeswell.

She strode forward, so he would stop long before he drew up to Michael's friends. His eyes were all for them when he stopped his horse anyway. He could intimidate a person with only his size and strength, but his anger ensured that he did now. He contained it well enough, but it was in his eyes and taut body. She had not seen him this furious since that first day in Cumberworth.

Finally, unfortunately, he looked down at her. "A peculiar assignation, Verity."

"I asked Katy to collect them here, so I could learn the truth of how the mill fares."

"To what end? You have no legal voice in the matter,

and your cousin will not be sympathetic to your interfering. Your likelihood to do so is probably why he married you off."

It was part of the cruel truth, and he did not hesitate to lash her with it. He was even angrier than she thought.

His expression held no softness as he gazed down on her. "You deceived me today. I can only assume that you have before too." He did not wait for her to respond. He trotted his horse a few paces, to where the coachman had moved the carriage upon seeing his lord arrive. "Take her back to the house now."

She had no choice except to enter the carriage when the coachman opened the door. Hawkeswell did not follow when the coach began rolling. She looked out the window, and saw him pacing that big horse toward Timothy and the others.

Chapter Nineteen

When Verity arrived back at the house, she learned that Colleen and Mrs. Geraldson had taken the cabriolet for a late-afternoon call on the closest neighbor.

Had Hawkeswell asked them to vacate the house so he could deal with his errant wife in privacy? Or had Colleen recognized his mood, surmised the reason, and sensibly removed her hostess and herself from the premises?

Verity went up to her chamber, removed her hat, and sat in the chair. It would not take him long to follow on horseback. No matter what he was saying to those young men, and she doubted it was friendly, he would be here soon.

She struggled to control herself from succumbing to stomach-churning dread. It had been a long time, so wonderfully long, since she had needed to do so and she was out of practice. The whimpering fear kept sneaking out of where she blocked it. Hideous docility whispered that she must beg forgiveness and hope that made it end quicker.

Within minutes she was a girl again, an isolated, lonely girl who could only pray the anger passed quickly and that the punishment would be over. Sensations and sounds and images from the past crowded into her mind, undermining her composure. She tried receding, away from the world and into herself. She found some solid ground for her emotions there.

The horse outside destroyed that reprieve. The sounds of a rider made her nauseated. Steps down below had her blood pounding in her head.

He had it in him. All men did. Everyone did. He admitted how much of that anger he possessed. He controlled it now, he said, but the world gave him the right to release it on her if he chose.

She wanted to believe he would not, but she did not really know. Anger could bring out an unknown cruelty in people, and lead to the step she knew was sadly easy to take.

She heard his steps outside her door and she braced herself. Her thoughts scattered, wildly. The fear made her tremble. Anger shouted in rebellion.

She would apologize if she must, but she would not beg. She had asked for *none of this*, had agreed to *none of it*, and she would be damned before she became that half-broken girl again.

Hawkeswell was ready for a good row when he opened Verity's door. He had many things to say, some commands and some questions, and they would be said, by Zeus, now, for certain.

He did not know what he expected inside that chamber, but he knew it was not what he found.

Verity sat in a chair, much as she had sat in Cumberworth that first day. Her expression was similar too. Resolved. Calm. Strong, he had to admit, although it was an inner strength exuded invisibly. Her manner pricked his temper more, just as it had that day too.

Her gaze rose from where it had been fixed on the floor. What he saw in her eyes stunned him.

Strength, to be sure. Rebellion. But also resignation. And fear. Real fear, hidden beneath the other things, but so real it soured the air.

She feared *him*, he realized. His anger. She feared that he would physically punish her.

It shocked him. Insulted him. He had never given her cause to—

A thought came to him. An old suspicion. It only made his anger spike, now toward a different target and for a different reason.

Later. Not now. He stayed far away from her, to reassure her, but he still spoke.

"I hope you will never deceive me like that again, Verity."

"They would have never agreed to meet me if you were with me."

"*I don't give a damn.* As I said back there, you are worthless to them, so their information is worthless to you."

Her head bowed. He wasn't fooled. He waited for it, and she did not disappoint him.

"It was not supposed to be this way."

"No, it was not. You were supposed to marry one of them. It is why you were taught the secret."

"Not one of them. Not necessarily. But, yes, as I have

said, my father expected my husband to be in control of the works."

"Did he decree it should be this Michael, about whom you have been so concerned?" For all his annoyance, he faltered on the question, and waited for the answer with a peculiar sort of dread.

"Michael and I were children when my father died. My concern has been for Katy, and I ask about her son because I think my cousin did Michael harm."

"I think it was more than that. I want the truth now. I want you to swear it. Did you—?"

"If you need me to swear, do you trust my word enough to believe my sworn oath?"

"I don't know, damn it. It is the best I can get, though, and will have to do." He approached his question differently, so she would see how it did not come out of pique alone. "When Katy first saw you at her door, there was shock, then grief."

"Not grief. Tears, yes, but not grief."

"I have seen her in my head many times since, and it was grief, I am sure. I saw her face during that embrace. You did not. Her words to you, about her child—I thought she spoke to you, but now I think not."

"Then who—"

"Her son. Her poor child. She thought he was *with you* these two years, Verity. She thought he had left, to join you when you ran away. She never thought you were dead, but instead somewhere with her son. Your arrival here proved that was not so. Her worry and grieving did not end when she opened that door. It began."

She scoffed at his view of it, but he could tell she was seeing that afternoon again in her own head.

"Did you also expect him to run away to join you, Verity?"

Again that insidious dread, heavy and visceral. Too much like grief. Too much like fear. He hated it, and the weakness it implied, and drew on the rumbling anger to obscure it.

"I have wondered since I found you alive whether that was the real reason you left. Now, as you worry so for him, and try to learn his fate, I think that his failure to join you is the reason you are so sure ill has befallen him."

"It was not like that between Michael and me."

"Wasn't it? When you slipped away to see Katy, you also saw him. The friend of your childhood became the friend of the girl." He glared, as another memory came to him. "That first kiss. It was him, damn it. *Wasn't it?*"

She looked away, but her rising color said he was right. A new emotion grew within his fury. An unexpected one, which fulfilled the dread and gave it meaning. Disappointment. Disappointment so intense that even the anger could not hide it.

She had loved this young man, and still did. She had expected to marry him. She had agreed to another marriage to save him, and had run away to be with him. Her current marriage and station and husband were parts of a life she never wanted and would never want. *It is not supposed to be this way.*

He turned away as the fullness of it settled on him. He laughed at himself inwardly. Hell, she had told him, hadn't she? Point by point, she had explained most of it, and offered him a way to be free of her. So why this . . . dismay, and sense of loss? None of this really mattered, after all.

"I did not leave because of a pact to join him, or he me.

I swear this. On my father's name. I left for the reasons I told you. I have been concerned for Michael because it was he whom Bertram promised to harm, and whom Nancy said had been harmed anyway, and I need to know what became of him."

"So you married me to protect *him*?"

"He is Katy's son. Her family. Her breadwinner. I have known him my whole life. *Of course* I did what I had to in order to protect him. For all the good it did."

He stepped toward her, to speak his mind clearly without fifteen feet separating them. As soon as he moved, she stiffened and backed up, to keep that gulf as broad as possible.

Fear again. In her eyes and pose. Of him. Of the anger she had seen on the road near Katy's house. Of whatever she saw in him now.

She was not lying, but not being truthful either. She was putting a better face on it because she feared him, and feared what he would do if she admitted that she loved this young man.

His mind turned to that other suspicion that had become more certain when he entered this chamber.

"Verity, when you said you were coerced, before the threat to this man and Katy, what did you mean?"

The change in topic confused her. She did not answer at once. Her big eyes watched him, but that closed blankness entered them.

"Did your cousin beat you, Verity?"

She shrugged. "It is common with children. Were you spared?"

"Tutors and schoolmasters used canes, that is true, but I did not live in eternal fear of it. Did you, those years with Bertram?"

She stood abruptly. "I do not want to talk about this. It is long in the past."

"Is it? You looked like a woman who assumed I was going to hit her when I walked in this door. I have given you no cause to think that."

"That man. You said that you almost—"

"I was drunk, he insulted me, and he was a man. And it was wrong. I ask you again, Verity. Did your cousin ever raise a hand to you?"

"Why do you ask this now? It was years ago. It has nothing to do with you."

"I think it has much to do with me. Tell me."

His insistence distressed her. She would not look at him. Her gaze darted around. Her expression twitched and her eyes carried flashes of anger and fear and . . . loathing.

"He did not do it often. He let Nancy do it for him." She rubbed her eyes with the back of her hand. "She hated that he had not received more in the legacy. He hated that I existed. I could not please them. I could not—"

A sob choked the words. She covered her eyes and turned away. "God forgive me, I wanted to kill them toward the end. I still do when I see them. They took pleasure in my suffering." She managed the furious words between gasps for composure. "I barely dared to breathe in that house. I could not permit myself any joy. I was within view of all that I knew, in a house that was mine, yet separated from who I had been."

His anger had hardly disappeared, but there was little left for her now. He expected some would return soon enough, when he contemplated what he had learned today about Michael, but her distress made it insignificant at the moment.

He went to her and turned her into his embrace. She broke, and sobbed with strangled, frantic sounds, as if the tears alone could not relieve what was inside her.

He held her while it poured out, trying hard not to picture a younger Verity hiding her nature and burying her presence and hoping there would be no whipping or beating this day.

She calmed. Her breathing returned to normal. He patted her head and spoke before he released her. "Did he know? Was Bertram aware of his wife's treatment of you?"

She nodded. "When she was trying to force me to agree to the marriage, he would hand her the cane."

He kissed her head. "I must go now. I will end this conversation as I began it, Verity. Please do not leave this property without me."

The grooms had not finished unsaddling his horse, so it was quick work to make him ready again. Hawkeswell swung up and headed toward Oldbury at a gallop.

Dusk was falling when he presented himself at the house on the hill overlooking the ironworks. The servant took his card away, then hurried back to escort him to the master.

The Thompsons had posed themselves in their drawing room. Verity's drawing room, if one wanted to be accurate. Hawkeswell gave them both a good look while they expressed delight with his call, peculiar though the hour might be.

"I learned something very shocking today, Thompson. I am hoping you can shed some light on it," Hawkeswell said, setting aside his hat and whip.

"I would be honored to light any path for you, sir."

"I learned from Verity today that in the course of trying to convince her to accept my proposal, your wife beat her with a cane many times, and that you not only permitted it, but encouraged it."

Nancy's face fell in shock. Bertram gaped at the accusation.

"She is vile to say such a thing," Nancy said.

"Are you saying it is a lie?"

"She was willful and stubborn, Lord Hawkeswell, simply for the sake of it. She had no true objection to the marriage. What young lady could?"

"You still have not said whether it is a lie, Mrs. Thompson. Did you, or did you not, use a cane on Verity when she lived under your husband's protection?"

"Only when she was disobedient."

"For example, when she would not obey the command to marry me?"

Silence rang in response.

Bertram sputtered. His heavy eyelids actually rose to reveal his anger. "See here, Lord Hawkeswell, I do not like the way—"

"Mrs. Thompson, it would be a good idea for you to leave your husband and me alone now."

Head high and expression haughty, she swept a dramatic turn and left the drawing room.

Bertram stuck his hand in his waistcoat and puffed up his chest. "I do not take well your coming here and speaking thus to my wife, sir."

"I only asked her some questions about a matter much on my mind."

"A little late, don't you think, to be worrying about my cousin's state of mind in accepting you? You did not care much about it then, so why should it prey on your mind now?"

"I had no idea that you had beaten her into it then."

"You hardly cared to find out one way or another. Let us be plain, sir. Her fortune was all that mattered to you, and it was not in your interest to know the particulars regarding how that money found its way into your purse. You left that to me, and I saw to it."

Hawkeswell's temper had not been in the best form for hours now. Mrs. Thompson's demeanor, and now Bertram's accusations, opened the lock that held back what had become a rather deep flow with many currents. That Bertram touched on more truth than Hawkeswell liked did not encourage restraint.

"It is in my interest to know now, Thompson. Your cousin is my wife and responsibility, however badly that came about."

"Don't be blaming us that she has given you trouble from the first day. We had no difficulty handling her."

"With the threat of the lash or your hand or fist? That is not handling. That is breaking. You were her guardian. You were supposed to protect her. Not misuse her."

Bertram's face twisted in a sneer. "I broke no law. She was fed and clothed and lived in this house. I had to be reminded of Joshua's betrayal every day by her presence in our family. I have nothing to apologize for regarding her, and I'll not be upbraided by *you* because of a belatedly awakened sentimentality. I delivered her fortune to you as promised, so you have no complaints."

Hawkeswell reached out, grabbed Bertram by his coat, and pulled him close. "You are a scoundrel," he snarled into Bertram's astonished face. "You hit a defenseless girl. What kind of man are you?"

"I did not often! Ask her!"

"Once was too often, you coward, and you allowed your bitch of a wife to beat her regularly."

"I was within my rights. She was rebellious and disobedient. I was her guardian. There is naught you can do about it."

"You are wrong there. I can do *this*." He swung his fist and slammed it into Bertram's face. Bertram's head snapped back. His legs buckled.

"You are mad! Insane!" Bertram held his face and staggered, trying to stay on his feet. "I heard about you, about you being quick to engage in fisticuffs and being of a violent temper. Well, I won't stand for it. I will—"

"You heard about me?" He thought he might really go mad now. "You believed me to be a violent brute, and you still gave her to me? *Damn you to hell*."

Bertram cowered and held up his arms to protect his face. Then his gaze slid sideways. He lunged, and grabbed Hawkeswell's horsewhip. An instant later the sting of the whip landed on Hawkeswell's shoulders and arms. Sneering with hateful victory, Bertram swung the whip again.

Hawkeswell grabbed the whip's lash as it fell and jerked it out of Bertram's grasp. Furious now, terrified beyond sense, Bertram flailed with his fists and landed a blow.

Hawkeswell's head roared in a way it had not in years. He defended himself, but every time he hit Bertram, it was really Verity for whom he evened the score.

Chapter Twenty

Knocks and calls woke Verity. Someone was pounding on a door, yelling Hawkeswell's name, demanding his attention. A woman.

Verity rose and peeked out her own door. Colleen stood in the narrow corridor, her white undressing gown all that was visible.

She pounded again and called his name in a furious voice.

Verity slipped out of her room and watched. Hawkeswell's door opened. Enough light flooded out to indicate a lamp still burned. He had not been sleeping.

The door stood open and Colleen strode in.

Verity walked the twenty paces to his door and looked in. Hawkeswell was still clothed in trousers and shirt. Colleen faced him, hands on hips, face distorted with emotion.

"Have you gone mad?" Anger stressed her voice so it

sounded almost like a hiss. "Is it your goal to be known in these parts as a man without good judgment, who must be avoided by decent people?"

He turned away, and fingered a paper on the writing table. He lifted a pen and bent to jot something. "You are referring to Thompson, I assume."

"Yes, I am referring to him. Word just came."

"So that was the horse I heard outside. Has he raised the hue and cry?"

"Nancy sent a messenger to me."

"One wonders what she expects you to do. I trust that you sent back word that you are sure there is more to the tale than she shared with you." He set down the pen.

Very curious now, Verity stepped into the chamber. "If there is a tale about Bertram, I want to hear it."

Colleen glared at Hawkeswell. "Please tell her to leave. I need to speak to *you*."

"Say what you want. She will learn of it anyway."

"Hawkeswell—"

"If she wants to stay, she stays. She has far more right to be here than you do."

Colleen's face fell at the rebuke. She found composure, and addressed him as if Verity had not chosen to stay at all.

"Is it true? Did you thrash Mr. Thompson?"

"I did."

"Hawkeswell!" She paced, astonished and agitated. "Dear heavens, I thought that you no longer— Had you been drinking?"

"I was stone sober."

"Then why?"

"That is between him and me. I do not blame you for introducing me to the man, Colleen, but he is a scoundrel.

I'll not have anything to do with him in the future, aside from the necessary contact regarding Verity's estate."

"Blame me? How could you even consider blaming me?"

"I said that I do not. However, much has transpired from that introduction that has not been good. I do not believe you knew his true character."

"Whatever you think of him, your behavior was inexcusable."

"I had one of the best excuses in the world. If Mr. and Mrs. Thompson want the world to know, we will air it publicly. I promise you, however, that no decent man would favor Bertram in the argument."

"Are you at least going to tell *me* the cause of the argument?"

He glanced at Verity. "No, I am not."

Colleen noticed the glance. Her mouth pursed. "I *see*. Forgive me. My worry that you had reverted to your old ways made me react too strongly. Good night."

She rushed past Verity, her face flushed and eyes burning. Verity closed the door behind her.

"You thrashed Bertram?"

He shrugged. "Odd that Mrs. Thompson sent a rider to Colleen. Perhaps she expected my cousin to call me out on it." He smiled at his own little joke.

"She did not send that rider to ask Colleen to upbraid you. She sent a message begging Colleen to try and mend the rift."

"I humiliated her husband. I doubt she wants any mending."

"Nancy is ambitious. She would sacrifice Bertram to hold on to the connections this marriage gave her." She walked over to him. "Since everything about my cousin and you also involves me, are you going to tell me why your anger got the better of you?"

"Let us just say that I lost my temper with good cause." He set about folding the letter he had been writing.

She took the letter from his hands, and set it down again. She guessed he was not proud of allowing fury to rule him again, but he did not appear apologetic about it either.

"Did you do it because of what I told you this afternoon?"

He gazed down at her, and brushed strands of hair away from her face with his fingertips. "He did not deny it. Nor his wife. I could not thrash her, of course."

"Of course."

Still that tender, light touch. His voice was quiet now, and thoughtful. "I imagined you in that house, fearful and unhappy, and that woman— I only hope that you will not be even more afraid of me because of it."

She pressed his hand against her cheek, then turned her face to kiss his palm. "I am not afraid now. I will not be in the future either." She was astonished that it mattered to him how she felt. She kissed his palm again. "It may be wrong of me, but I am moved that you were so angry on my behalf, and bothered to confront him at all."

There had been no such protection since her father died, and it touched her deeply.

He circled her waist with his hands. His gaze deepened until it entrapped her. So seriously he looked at her. So thoughtfully. As if he sought much more in her than would ever be found.

"You were indeed forced into this marriage, as you said. You were well broken before he made the threats against Katy and her son."

She should feel vindicated, she supposed. Or relieved that he believed her completely now. Instead his deep thoughtfulness troubled her.

"Bertram said I had not cared then," he said. "He believed that meant that I should not care now. That was his defense of his misuse of you."

How foolish of Bertram, to provoke Hawkeswell that way. Had he and Nancy not seen the fire burning?

"He was correct," Hawkeswell went on. "As were you, in your accusations in Cumberworth and Essex. My thoughts were on your fortune, not your happiness. I assumed, in my conceit, that of course you were willing." He kissed her on her forehead. "I have done you great harm."

"You cannot be blamed for what you did not know."

"I did not know then, but I knew when I seduced you in Surrey—or I strongly suspected. But I did not bind you to me in that garden that night because of your fortune, Verity. If that was all that was at stake, I might have acted differently."

"Then why?"

"You. I wanted you. I desired you. Two years ago you were a meek, quiet girl. But the woman who faced me down in Cumberworth—she raised the devil in me, and I knew how it was going to be. It is the oldest male reason in the world, and no excuse . . ."

She considered its weight and cost while she fingered the edge of his shirt's gap near his neck. Being desired by Hawkeswell had never been as lacking in significance as he thought. Both excitement and pleasure had played big roles in where they now stood. He had seduced her, but she had not refused to be seduced. Even now, in his arms, having this conversation that was long overdue, his hold affected her in so many ways.

Desire, intimacy, comfort, protection—they were all
expressed in the calm way his strong hands grasped and
supported her, and in the thrills and ecstasy that he gave
her too.

"What is done is done," she said, too aware that she
accepted him with those words in a manner that she had
avoided before. She experienced no regret in doing so.
Instead, the acceptance released a surge of joy. "There are
worse rocks on which to build a marriage than fortune and
pleasure." She playfully tugged at his shirt. "Since I have
provided the fortune, I trust that you will take responsibility for the pleasure."

He laughed, and it made her happy to see his humor
lighten. "If you continue to cooperate."

"Already you seek to shirk that responsibility and leave
the duty to me. It is for you to ensure that I *want* to cooperate, Hawkeswell."

She turned to go on that saucy note. After she took two
steps his arms imprisoned her and he warmed her back.
His kiss scalded her neck.

"You cannot throw down a gauntlet like that and expect
me to let you walk away from the duel, Verity." His caresses skimmed her body. "I think that the less I permit
your cooperation, the more you will want it, considering
your rebellious nature."

"I do not see how you can forbid it."

"Don't you?" His voice warmed her ear. His hands
cupped under her breasts. His thumbs rubbed her nipples
through the cloth of her undressing gown.

She began to understand then how he could prevent her
cooperation. She could not embrace him while he stood
behind her. She could only take the pleasure while stand-

ing on weakening legs. The sensations sank low in her body fast in this position.

She reached behind her, to hold him too, to touch him.

"Ah, ah," he scolded. "No flanking maneuvers. I will have to find a way to stop that. This may work." He plucked at the ribbons that bound the neck and front of her gown. His hand pulled at the bows' ends one by one and the gown gaped more with each one's demise.

He eased the gown off her shoulders and down her arms until the fabric hung from her hips. The sleeves' cuffs meant it did not fall off completely, however. She tried to reach one with her other hand but the fabric confounded her.

"It appears that you cannot move much," he said. "You will just have to take it."

Take it meant accepting his caresses passively while they stood there. His kisses pressed the flesh of her shoulders and neck. She watched while his handsome hands teased her breasts to unbearable sensitivity. Arrow after arrow of maddening excitement shot down but she could not even relieve the thrumming need with movement.

He scooped her in his arms and carried her to the bed. He laid her down and rolled her over, so her face pressed a pillow and the cuffs imprisoned her even more.

He stretched beside her, resting on one elbow, facing her. With slow care he raised the hem and skirt of the gown, and folded it at her waist until she was naked above and below a thick belt of fabric.

His gaze drifted down her body. Slowly, almost languidly, he bent to kiss her back. Each kiss was a little pleasurable shock. She closed her eyes and wondered how something so small could affect her so profoundly.

The kisses reached the small of her back and stopped.

She opened her eyes to see him regarding her again. He slowly skimmed her back with his fingertips, but did not stop at the gown this time. Instead that light caress slid over her bottom and to her thigh and played there like a feather, torturing her.

"You appear unbearably erotic like this," he said, watching his hand move again. His palm smoothed over the curves of her bottom. Trembles of anticipation shivered deliciously. She was almost painfully aroused, and they really had not done anything much.

His caress dipped down, between her thighs. Her breath caught and she closed her eyes and waited. He let her wait until she was half-mad, then touched surely, perfectly, and her breath caught again.

"You are ready. So quickly." He slowly stroked again and her whole body trembled. "Should I take you now? While you lie there so ready? Or have I ensured that you want to cooperate, as you instructed?"

She did not understand. She looked at him, confused.

"Cooperating does not only mean accepting or submitting to pleasure, Verity." He played with the buttons on the cuff on her wrist near his hip. "Cooperating means giving and sharing too. Have I ensured you want to?"

Had he? This *was* erotic. The passivity that he had forced excited her. He invited her to something else now, however. Something more, perhaps.

"You are the one who bound me like this, so I could only submit or accept."

"The sleeve is loose now. You can free yourself. Or not." He fell on his back and unfastened his own cuffs. "In a few minutes the choice will not be yours. Seeing you there, waiting and ready, I am thinking that cooperation can wait for another night."

She decided it would be submission that would wait. She pulled her arm out of the sleeve and sat up. She made quick work of the other cuff too, and fought her way out of the volumes of fabric.

Hawkeswell had shed his clothes by the time she cast the undressing gown away. He reached for her, pulled her on top of him, and held her to the first real kiss of the night.

Sharing, he had said. Cooperation. She knew that he liked when she kissed him. She made sure this kiss went both ways.

She looked down at him afterward. "I am not very experienced. My cooperation may disappoint."

"It has not so far. Nor do I think it ever could."

She moved her knees forward while she knelt. She sat back on his thighs. Blue eyes alight with humor and sensual challenge dared her to be bold.

She set her hands on his shoulders, then watched their paths as she slowly stroked down his chest. She splayed her fingers and caressed back up, fascinated by the firm muscles under the soft velvet.

This would not be so difficult, she realized. She had only to do what he did, adapting for the obvious differences. Bracing on hands and knees, she kissed him, then moved her mouth lower, to his neck and finally to his chest.

Feeling very bold now, she kissed and tasted. A sweet emotion stirred in her while she did. Caring. She wanted to give him joy, not just pleasure. She wanted him to feel how she was grateful for his caring too.

The intimacy moved her in ways she had not expected. She did not know how to contain it. Kissing him, touching him, she could not run from it or put it away. Emotion

filled her heart and drenched her and she could only press
her lips to his skin again and again to release it.

She sat back again and looked at him while she caressed. At his mussed dark hair and wonderful blue eyes.
At the fire in him as he gazed back. She had accepted this
marriage, and pleasure and fortune would be its foundations, but much more was inside her.

Still, the pleasure and fortune mattered to him. And to
her. She moved her gaze to his phallus, rising between them.
She then glanced back at his face. His eyes and vague smile
carried a challenge.

She touched the tip, and knew at once what to do. She
ran her fingers down its length.

His head leaned back and he closed his eyes. Jaw tight
and face hard with control, he accepted the pleasure while
she caressed and rubbed and learned what pleased him.
Her discoveries fascinated her.

Suddenly he reached for her. Eyes hot and teeth bared,
he lifted her forward and lowered her.

She held him so they joined, then let him fill her.

She adjusted her seat. "It feels different." Deeper, was
what she meant. "I may like cooperation."

He smiled. "It is for me to make sure you do. Remember?" He stretched his arms toward her body and circled
her nipples with his fingers. Down where she sat, a silent
physical hum began in the flesh that surrounded him. The
more he caressed, the worse it got. The lighter his touch,
the more intense the sensation.

She leaned forward and braced on her arms. Sliding
up, she stopped right when their joining would be broken.
Then she moved her hips down and absorbed him again.
Wonderful pleasure shivered around their union. She did
it again, shifting a little so he was in even deeper.

His hands rested on her hips but he did not guide her. She moved harder, faster, trying this and that. The hum became something more, a deep awareness and heat that hinted at a new mystery.

His hold on her hips tightened. Guiding now, he held her to his thrusts. She surrendered to the power of it, and met him breath for breath and thrust for thrust. The hum gave way to the most wonderful shivers. Unearthly sensations, unlike anything before, centered deeply where he moved in her. Then they rippled out with a compelling tremble. Almost immediately the ripple became one crashing, violent wave.

She cried as it inundated her with its dark brilliance. She cried again and again when it broke once more during Hawkeswell's final ravishment. It was unlike any release she had experienced before and it awed her.

She collapsed on him, spent and disoriented, sore from the way they had shared without restraint. His arms wrapped her and he held her close, pressed against his chest, long into the night.

He slept, but she did not. She looked into her heart, at the emotions of the last days. She turned and kissed his chest again, without him knowing, and lingered there, pressing her lips to his skin and feeling close to him in so many unexpected ways.

She had accepted fate in admitting that this marriage would stand, whether she had chosen it or not. Had it been only that, though? If she could still get free, would she want to? The question shocked her even as she asked it.

She did not know the answer, but she did know some things. She would grieve if they parted now. She would miss the intimacy and the passion. She would have never been this bold with Michael, or been this moved by desire.

She knew that in having to stay in this marriage, she would not hate this life that she was not supposed to have.

She did not move until Hawkeswell stirred. Then she slipped off the bed, and put on her gown to return to her room. He woke enough to notice. He reached for her.

Bending over, she kissed him. "I think that it is time to return to London. I have learned almost all that I will ever learn here. But first I want to call on Lady Cleobury. I have been remiss in not doing so. Then we can go."

Chapter Twenty-one

L ord Cleobury's estate was the closest landholding to Oldbury owned by a peer to actually have a peer in residence much of the year. Most of the others were leased to farmers or to mines. As a result, Lord Cleobury occupied a position of considerable influence in the county of Staffordshire.

"He normally attends county assemblies of any size or significance. The arrival of him and Lady Cleobury is always anticipated with excitement," Mrs. Geraldson explained while they rode in the carriage past fields nearing harvest. "He takes his position in the county very seriously, and rightfully considers it his duty to keep an eye on local matters."

"I expect that he has a say in who becomes justice of the peace and coroner and such," Verity said.

"I do not believe that such a situation could be attained without his approval."

Mrs. Geraldson had inserted herself into this visit, announcing it would be a good opportunity to see her dear friend Lady Cleobury after some weeks apart. Colleen had then decided to come too. With protection such as this, along with the coachman and a groom, Hawkeswell had concluded that his own presence was not required.

Lord Cleobury displayed disappointment at that decision. He condescended to receive the ladies along with his wife when they arrived, only to look in vain for his fellow peer to enter the drawing room too.

"Most unfortunate," he muttered upon hearing Verity's excuse that Hawkeswell had decided to ride the county to get a sense of the mood abroad in it. "I could have explained matters to his satisfaction, and looked forward to doing it, so I might avoid going to town for sessions this autumn. Not to be, I fear. Not to be." He turned his balding, narrow head to his wife. "You will have to come too, my dear. I daren't leave you here with the rabble all around."

"I am told that you have made superior preparations for the rabble, sir," Verity said.

"I have at that, but it takes a man to command the wall, does it not? With my absence we will be vulnerable and I fear if this house falls, so does the whole county."

"Hawkeswell expressed an interest in your defenses."

"Did he, now? Pity he did not come, so he could take note of them himself. Surrey is not far from London, and he may need the same. If you will come with me, Lady Hawkeswell, I will show you that which is visible, and you can describe it to him as best you are able."

His wife did not move to join them. She engaged Mrs. Geraldson with a question, making it clear that she at least had seen his lines of defense often enough already. Mrs.

Geraldson and Colleen sat to visit while Lord Cleobury
escorted Verity out to the back terrace.

There had been no exaggeration about his preparations.
Four cannon of good size stood there, their long snouts
extending beyond the low terrace wall. A pile of balls
waited for the uprising.

Did Lord Cleobury intend to fire these cannon himself?
Or did he assume that his servants would fight to the death
to protect his privilege?

"Manchester is that way," he said meaningfully, point-
ing toward the woods.

"If the rabble march, would they not more likely take
the road?"

"They are more cunning than you suspect, Lady Hawkeswell. Far more cunning. I have mapped the most direct
route from Manchester to this house, and I assure you
they will come right through that woods and this garden."

She admired the cannon and complimented him on his
shrewdness. "This county is fortunate indeed to have you
here, sir. The rabble must get through you to pillage the
rest."

"You assume they are only to the north. I regret to say
they are all around us. Vigilance is required in every direction. A few more hangings are in order, I say, to remind
men of the rights of property."

"Has that been necessary? The London papers have not
reported such things out of Staffordshire."

"The London papers do not know everything. Rest assured that we do not allow seditious behavior here, and
are quick to deal with it."

*Do you make people disappear? Have there already been
some hangings, that the papers and people do not know*

about? She ached to ask the questions, and to perceive the true character beneath Lord Cleobury's avuncular demeanor and harmless-looking, thin person. Her heart thickened, because she feared that she knew the answers to both questions.

She looked at the balls. Iron, and well made. The cannon appeared familiar too. Cast in one piece, they had been bored out. "Did you have these made at my father's ironworks?"

"I did indeed. The army thinks the cannon made there are superior. I count myself lucky that it is mere miles away."

"My cousin counts himself lucky for your interest and patronage in turn, I am sure."

"We have similar interests, my dear Lady Hawkeswell, and that is the source of any condescension on my part. The leaders in a county must stick together these days, despite their different stations. I hope that I am not so particular about the natural social order that I deny a fellow man in need when he is bedeviled by criminals."

"You refer to the trouble at the ironworks last winter, when the yeomanry were called up. Your voice would have been helpful to that call, I am sure."

He smiled indulgently, and wiggled his eyebrows to convey mystery. "That and other trouble. I expect there will be more. Bertram Thompson knows what he faces. He saw it before most others, and is smart enough to dig out the roots before the poisonous vine grows. Have no worries for your cousin, my dear."

He returned her to the drawing room. She spent the next hour discussing the latest fashions in hats and bonnets, all the while hiding her aching sorrow.

She suspected that Lord Cleobury, Bertram, and the

other "leaders" of the county had two years ago dug out a root named Michael Bowman.

She was not sorry to leave. She had learned what she came to learn, about her father's legacy and, she feared, about Michael.

She sent Bertram and Nancy a very short note announcing her departure. Other than Mrs. Geraldson, there was only one person who required a real leave-taking, and Hawkeswell took her to Katy's cottage the afternoon prior to their journey.

He escorted her to the door this time, and greeted Katy before excusing himself. Once more Verity sat in the only good chair and Katy on the stool in the little room that never seemed to have enough light.

"I want you to come with me," Verity said. "When I leave here tomorrow morning, I want you in the carriage beside me. Hawkeswell has agreed to it. You can live in the country if you like. His housekeeper in Surrey is a kind woman and you will not be ill-treated or made to feel unwelcome."

Katy's eyes filled with tears but she smiled with joy. "You are still a little girl, aren't you? To be worrying about your Katy, and you a countess at that. I can't be coming, though. How will Michael find me, when he comes back?"

"He will ask at the works, and they will tell him how to find you." She gritted her teeth against the urge to weep. She was sure that Katy guessed Michael was dead, but did not want to give up hope. She leaned forward, and took Katy's hands in hers. "You can wait for his return in Surrey as well as here."

Katy's head bowed low, until her head covered their

hands. She stayed like that, and her attempts at composure were visible in her tensing back.

"This is my home, Verity. I have lived here my entire life. This cottage is poor and I've little left, but the people of my girlhood are still down the road, and my friends are in the church graveyard. I can't be going at my age, and living among strangers."

"I am not a stranger, Katy."

She looked up, and reached out to pat Verity's face. "No, you are not, but you will be, bit by bit, as time goes by. You are a countess now, and will be more of one every day. There is no wrong in it. It is a wonderful thing, and I'm so proud of you. But it can't help but change you, child. When you leave here tomorrow, Oldbury will not be your home any longer. I think that you already know that."

She did know it. It had not been the same here even during this visit. It had not been what she remembered, or what she had dreamed of.

They all looked at her differently too, and took care in their talk. Even Mr. Travis, for all his friendliness, never really forgot he spoke to a countess. Her dream of coming home had been a child's dream, of the innocent play and happy times before her father died. She could not reclaim that, however. Even if Hawkeswell had given her the freedom to be Verity Thompson again, she could never be *that* Verity Thompson.

It was her turn to be moved. She slid off her chair, to the floor beside Katy's legs. She laid her head on Katy's lap as she had so often as a child and an unhappy girl. Katy stroked her head with comforting caresses while the tears spilled silently.

Chapter Twenty-two

Hawkeswell opened the French doors and stepped onto the terrace. A good deal of commotion greeted him.

Three men dug toward the back of the garden. Deep footings had already been built at four corners of a rectangle, and they now swung picks and shovels at Verity's command to create trenches of some kind.

Daphne Joyes stood beside Verity holding one side of a large drawing while Celia held the other. Periodically Verity would point to the drawing, then to the ground, and instruct the men further.

Colleen also stood with them, watching. She noticed him and came back to the terrace.

"She is ruining the garden," she said. "No town house needs a conservatory of that size, and she has chosen a rather ugly design. Why, it will not even connect with the house."

"It is not intended to house a few palms and a lemon tree. I am sure the design suits her intentions."

"Could you not convince her that one greenhouse in Surrey is adequate? I fear she will become known as eccentric. And these women . . ." She made a helpless gesture toward the friends. "You really need to consider her future, Hawkeswell, and be more firm with her."

He was of a mind to tell Colleen to tend to her own garden, but he held his tongue. She had been helpful to Verity, and offered friendship when most other women offered only cruel gossip. If Colleen ever pressed that friendship too far, he assumed that Verity would create more distance.

Furthermore, helping Verity also gave Colleen a purpose, and an excuse to escape her mother in Surrey. She had opened her mother's London house immediately, and seemed to prefer town to country now. She had become a frequent caller here, and often was with Verity when he returned in the evening.

"I promised her a free hand with the gardens, Colleen. As for the ladies of The Rarest Blooms, she will never give up those friendships. If I forbade her to see them, she would do it anyway."

Colleen's dismay reflected her opinion of a wife so willful. "Perhaps you can instruct her not to dig in the dirt herself, at least? Or to wear other than those old dresses and that horrible bonnet?"

He thought Verity looked charming in that old dress and bonnet. "She will always dig herself, from time to time, so it may be best if she does it in old dresses."

Colleen frowned at him. "You are not helping matters, Grayson."

He laughed. "The truth is I am not inclined to be firm with her about too much, dear cousin. Speak to me in a year or two, when the first passion has perhaps passed."

She eyed him curiously. "I . . . I had no idea that the marriage suited you so well." She gazed out at Verity, who was upbraiding a man with a shovel. "I am happy for you, of course."

But not entirely happy; that was clear. They had a long, old bond, and the last few years, their mutual singularity had been a part of it. Colleen's had been born of grief, and his own of indifference, but it served as common ground. He practically heard her mind beside him, coming to terms with being alone in new ways henceforth.

She had probably assumed that Verity would be the dutiful if dull wife and he would be the husband who barely noticed he was married. Hell, he had thought so too. His admission that there was more was giving him as much pause as it gave his cousin.

Saying it evoked a lightness of spirit in him. Joy, he supposed it would be called. If Colleen were a man, a friend like Summerhays, he might submit to the urge to confide that this first passion was very intense, very magnificent. He might even admit that his wife occupied his thoughts a good deal of the day, and that he could not imagine embracing another woman now.

"Perhaps it is time, Colleen, for you to consider finding a new passion too. It has been some years since he died."

Her head snapped around so she could look at him.

"It is not too late to marry. With the right settlement, it is never too late. I can take care of that part now. You need only find a man who is worthy of you."

Her eyes sparkled with tears. Her mouth quivered. She

looked out to the garden again. "Perhaps you are right. I am grateful, as always, Hawkeswell, for your generosity on my behalf."

"It is what brothers are for, is it not?" he asked, teasing her with a reference to their playful fantasy of old.

He really thought that she would weep then. She stretched up and kissed his cheek, then entered the house.

"I only said that I do not care for her," Audrianna said. "She wants to be one of us, but she would never understand the Rule. She would never just accept, and not pry."

Verity examined a small myrtle plant. Her own little greenhouse in London was almost finished, and she had come out to The Rarest Blooms to select her first plants to populate it. "Colleen does not want to be one of us, I am quite certain."

"Of course not. She looks down on us," Celia said. "But Audrianna is correct. She pries plenty, like most women."

"Then she wants her friendship with you to replace ours," Audrianna said.

"I do not think that is correct either," Verity said. "She does not want to be my friend. She wants to be my sister, so that she continues to be *his* sister."

"Sisters have more authority than friends," Daphne said. "You would, of course, be the *younger* sister in her mind, I assume."

Verity laughed. How true. Colleen wanted to direct as well as help. "She is kind, and good-hearted. Sometimes she intrudes more than I like, with advice that does not suit me. Since I believe she will be in my family forever, I have chosen to be agreeable. I do not want to create strife

on matters that do not signify. I confess that more important things prey on my mind than Colleen's designs for me."

Daphne set a sprouting amaryllis on the table where
they were sorting out the plants that would be sent to London. "I am sorry to hear that anything preys on your mind,
Verity."

Daphne did not betray any concern, but Audrianna did
with her frown. Celia remained busy with shears, trimming brown leaves from a large rubber plant.

Outside in the garden, Katherine hoed the market garden.

Katherine had been accepted here. According to Daphne,
she fit in nicely, and accepted the Rule by which they
lived. But she had not been here when Verity lived here,
so Verity was glad that Katherine was not with them right
now.

"Do you remember that day when I showed you all
those paper cuttings in my chamber? The oddities that I
noticed about them?"

"Of course," Celia said. "Did you learn what you needed
to know while you were at your home?"

"I am afraid that I did, and I do not know what to
do with it now. When we were in Oldbury I learned that
Katy's son has been missing since right before my wedding, and has not been heard from or seen. Nor was there
any trial, or any knowledge by his friends of his arrest."

Her friends puzzled over the mystery. "And yet your
cousin claimed to have him," Celia said.

"Yes. I believe that was true. I think . . . I fear that he
was killed."

Celia put down her shears. Daphne lost interest in the
plants.

"By your cousin?" Celia asked.

"My cousin and others." She told them about Lord Cleobury, and his allusions to pulling out bad vines.

"That was hardly an admission. It sounds as if Lord Cleobury is half mad. Cannon on the terrace, no less," Celia said. "There is no body. Perhaps you are seeing plots where none existed. He may have only gone off to seek his fortune."

"It is true that I have no proof. I could be wrong, and sometimes, for a while, I convince myself that I am. There is no evidence, as you say. No cause to voice my suspicions to anyone, except three dear friends who can do nothing but let me finally speak of it. I know that I can do nothing, but it still preys on my mind."

"As well it might," Audrianna said. "Can you not tell Hawkeswell? He could at least find out for certain if there was an arrest back then, and a trial. A peer can normally learn what he wants to know from the government and courts. Perhaps it happened in a different county, for example."

"I dare not tell him. He is aware that I sought information about Michael—that is the young man's name—and as a result he believes Michael was more to me than he was."

"Ah," Celia said.

"What do you mean, *ah*?" Daphne asked.

"I mean she is correct. A young man disappears two years ago, and Verity runs away from her wedding soon after. Hawkeswell suspects a connection, of course. Any man would, especially if his wife starts looking for that young man as soon as she can."

"You, however, do not agree with Hawkeswell's suspicions, I trust," Daphne said.

"Of course not. I merely agree with her that she cannot now ask him to look for this Michael, or help her to learn his fate."

"I think that she can," Audrianna said. "I think he will do it if she asks."

Celia rolled her eyes. "Audrianna, just because Lord Sebastian is your slave, it does not mean that every man puts on chains of love with a marriage. Quite the opposite."

Daphne ignored their little argument. "Did he believe you when you denied that Michael was an old lover, Verity?"

Had he? She was not sure. "I think he mostly believed me, but he still wonders."

"Is your marriage contentious or harmonious at this point?"

"I would say that it is mostly harmonious. In certain ways." She felt her face warming. "We do not argue much, is what I mean. We have a right understanding about . . . certain things."

Celia giggled. "I take back my *ah*, if those certain things have you blushing so badly."

"Then you do not fear him?" Daphne asked.

"Not at all. I know that you saw his temper, but please believe me on this."

Daphne removed her gloves and apron. She looked out the window, to where Katherine worked. "I thank you for allowing me that one bit of prying. Audrianna reassured me, but I have been worried." She turned back. "Perhaps you should ask for his help in this, Verity. It would be good to know for certain if you can. If something was done outside the law, if men are killing other men, no

matter what their reasons, it should not be allowed to continue if it can be stopped."

Verity did not disagree. All the same, she did not think
speaking of Michael to Hawkeswell would increase the
harmony that Daphne mentioned.

"Let us call Katherine, and have some refreshment,"
Daphne said. "Audrianna, did you bring that new song
with you?"

"Have you written a new one?" Verity asked. "I did not
know."

"That is because Colleen has been there the last few
times I called on you," Audrianna said. "But Celia will
sing it, and all my friends will hear it together for the first
time now."

"Perhaps you should sing it yourself, at Castleford's
dinner party next Tuesday," Verity teased.

Celia's eyes widened. "You will be dining with Castleford?"

"As will Verity," Audrianna said. "Sebastian says the
dinner is specifically for her benefit."

Celia caught Daphne's eye. Daphne's eyebrows rose a
fraction. "Ah."

The next Tuesday, Verity prepared to attend Castleford's dinner.

"My nerves are a tangle," she confessed while her abi-
gail helped her step into the dinner dress. "Hawkeswell
says that I will acquit myself well enough, but having met
the Duke of Castleford, I worry that I am to be the dinner
joke, not the dinner guest."

The maid did not reply. Verity wished that Daphne were
here, and Celia. Daphne would say soothing things to build

up her confidence, and Celia would touch her hair and dress four times and make her look a hundred times better.

She peered in the looking glass. She forced a smile so the reflection would not appear so dolorous.

A movement behind her caught the light. Twenty little orbs dangled and glistened; then many more dropped into view as her maid presented the treasure. A necklace made up of strands of pearls hung in front of her, then rested on her bare skin while fingers clasped it at her nape.

The dinner dress had the same color as the pearls, and the necklace looked stunning above it. She ran her fingertips over the perfect surfaces of the little mounds.

After that night in Surrey she had not favored these pearls for a long while. *Blame it on the pearls,* he had said, so she did. She still could not see them without feeling a twinge of rebellion, and a bit of anger at how he had trapped her through her own weakness.

They stood for so much. This marriage and this home, and even this world. Now she would wear them to a duke's dinner party, and accept her place as the countess of an ancient title while sitting among the very best of society. She was not so stupid as to resent that, or discount the many benefits of the life she had now. She just wished she could still be the girl from Oldbury too.

When you leave tomorrow, Oldbury will no longer be your home, Katy had said. Katy had been right, but one's heart is the last part to accept an unwelcomed truth. Her heart still wanted to play by the stream, and eat Katy's bread, and laugh with Michael. She still wanted to have the power to keep Bertram from being too hard on those good people.

"You are so beautiful, Madam," her maid said. "The rosettes on the bodice are perfect."

She had worried about the small rosettes, like everything else about tonight. She sorted through the topics for conversation that she had collected in her head.

"I will go down now."

Hawkeswell assumed, on seeing Verity in that dress the color of pearls, that she would be the most beautiful woman at the dinner party. Upon their arrival at Castleford's house, he saw that he had been correct.

Her slightly stilted etiquette appeared proud instead of careful tonight. Since proud people surrounded her, her manner actually spoke well of her. Castleford had not lied when he said the very best in society would come. Verity had to hold her own through introductions to two other dukes, one of them royal, and none other than the Prince Regent himself.

Castleford appeared sober. The same could not be said for a few of the other guests. One, the Earl of Rawsley, decided that being in his cups allowed for a bit of fun during dinner.

"You are a most lovely woman, Lady Hawkeswell," Rawsley said, angling over the table to see Verity, who sat two persons down. "Your husband has done well for himself on two counts, then."

Conversation flowed around without stop, but Hawkeswell noticed that most of the guests nearby kept at least one ear on this new exchange.

"Thank you, Lord Rawsley. If my husband thinks he did well on even one count, I am flattered."

"A good fortune flatters every woman who has one," Rawsley said, chortling. He turned filmy eyes on those nearby and up the table, to make sure they appreciated his wit. "Mills, wasn't it? Cotton and such?"

"Iron," Verity said with nary a blush. "My father was an inventor and an industrialist, but he first and foremost was an ironworker."

The other very best people smiled indulgently, even apologetically. Not because they thought it just fine that her father had worked iron, but because one of their own was being an ass.

"Iron, you say. Forges and furnaces and such?" Rawsley speared Hawkeswell with a critical gaze. "Sounds dirty and unpleasant."

"Also dangerous," Hawkeswell offered. "It takes a brave man to go into a blast furnace."

"We could not have prevailed against Bony without those brave men," the Prince Regent said.

"True, true." Rawsley downed some claret that he did not need. "Still . . ." He glanced disdainfully at Hawkeswell again.

"I own iron mines," Castleford said. He angled forward just enough to express deep interest. The lock of hair falling near one brow made him appear dangerous all by itself.

Hawkeswell pictured Tristan at his looking glass, ensuring he presented the perfect image of a proper duke, then flipping that one strand out of place to announce that, of course, it was all a feint. The women near him could not take their eyes off that damned rakish lock of brown hair.

"Are you trying to say something insulting about that, Rawsley, but the wine has you too befuddled to address it well?" Castleford quizzed.

"I said nothing about mines, Castleford."

"You spoke of iron. I heard it clearly."

"I was not speaking to you at all. I was addressing Lady Hawkeswell."

"Are you saying that you were trying to insult a lady instead of me? Really, Rawsley."

Rawsley might have been blindfolded now, he was so confused. His young wife, however, was not. She sensed where this was going, and glared at her husband with some worry in her eyes. The very best might accept Castleford's invitation to dine, but the smart ones avoided drawing too much of his attention while they did so.

Rawsley, unfortunately, was not smart. Nor was he aware of his wife's growing ill ease.

"If a woman is the daughter of an ironmonger, there is no insult in mentioning that she is the daughter of an iron-monger," Rawsley said in a haughty, sarcastic tone hardly intended to appease. "As for those mines of yours, con-gratulations. Your family fortune must have tripled during the war due to them, and you never had to dirty your hands yourself."

Quite a bit of conversation ended then. Hawkeswell saw Castleford's lids lower in a way he recognized. He caught Summerhays's eye in warning. Verity, whose drills in etiquette did not include how to hide her surprise when the very best people misbehaved, gaped.

The Prince Regent called for more wine, then happily settled back to watch the show, apparently content that he had not erred in choosing this dinner party over the other invitations he received.

"Calling Lady Hawkeswell the daughter of an iron-monger was indeed no insult, since she proudly calls her-self one, and for good cause. However, you insinuated that

Hawkeswell is now engaged in trade, and a very dirty one at that. I doubt he cares for that," Castleford said. "Do you, Hawkeswell?"

In unity, all the eyes on Castleford now turned to Hawkeswell. He cursed under his breath.

"In all fairness, Castleford, I would rather be called a tradesman than a war profiteer."

"Yes," Castleford said, his voice caressing the word slowly. "I was getting to that next."

"Rawsley," his wife hissed across the table.

Her husband wavered, but chose bravado instead of retreat. "Do you deny that you profited nicely from those mines during the war?"

Summerhays sighed. It was audible because absolutely no one was speaking now.

"I would have to ask my factors. I doubt that we brought the ore out at a loss. That would be stupid, not patriotic. Did you give away the grain grown on your lands or the wool from your sheep during the war, Rawsley?"

Rawsley tried to puzzle out how he could now have to justify his use of his land.

"You did not only indicate that I made a profit, but that I somehow profited excessively, because of the war," Castleford said. "However, if you apologize to me, and to Hawkeswell and his good wife, we can continue our dinner without any challenges."

Rawsley blanched at the allusion to duels. He sputtered and flushed and, since he was in his cups, sought to limit the defeat. "I did not insult the lady at all, as I said."

"I am losing my patience," Castleford said. Which he was, and woe unto Rawsley if he did. "You sought to embarrass her, and through her Hawkeswell, and I will not have one of my oldest friends taunted thus at my own table. You only failed because Lady Hawkeswell is not a slave to nonsense and cannot be embarrassed by a background that she has no reason to regret."

Cornered now, every eye on him, the center of a scene that would be talked about for weeks, Rawsley twisted in the wind, fussing with consternation. Finally he muttered something that probably was an apology that blamed his misspeaking on the wine.

Castleford smiled, and turned to the Prince Regent with a question. Other conversations started buzzing. Hawkeswell assumed that everyone thought a better end to the drama would have been someone calling someone else out, but from the looks of things the company decided this had been an interesting entertainment equal to the duke's reputation.

When the ladies left the gentlemen, Castleford offered Rawsley the first cigar to soothe his pride. Summerhays lit his own and sidled over to Hawkeswell.

"It appears that your wife has found favor with the duke after all. Rawsley was up to no good, and I think that entire spectacle was intended to draw his fire."

"Perhaps it was. Although there is no reason for any favor. His call on her that day was very brief, and so mild and polite that I thought some friendly spirit had possessed him. He was sober too, so that made three days of abstinence in a row." He gazed down the chamber at Castleford, who was enjoying a lot of ribald laughing with the Prince Regent. "Damnation, maybe he is becoming responsible on us."

Summerhays laughed. "As falls Castleford, so falls the world?"

"It is enough to drive me to drink in his stead."

"Too late. You are domesticated now. And if I may say it, you have appeared none the worse for it."

"Marriage is easy enough for a man. The changes have all been hers."

Summerhays found that very amusing. "Of course."

"I am in no mood for your self-satisfied smugness. You will have to excuse me. I have a question for our host."

He left Summerhays and repositioned himself in a chair near Castleford. Eventually another man claimed the Prince Regent's attention, and Hawkeswell in turn claimed Castleford's.

"That was quite a performance."

Castleford puffed deeply on his cigar. "You can thank me anytime it is convenient."

"I should thank you?"

"Had I not created a scene, you would be meeting poor Rawsley at dawn in some meadow. He was on his way to insulting you in his besotted sense of wit. Since your wife was being dragged into it, you would not have let it pass."

No, he wouldn't have. "Lady Rawsley appeared extremely grateful that you did not call him out yourself."

"Lady Rawsley, I have found, is always extremely grateful. It is in her nature."

"Well, now I know why you were so generous. No point in killing a man if you can cuckold him."

"A duel could complicate things too."

Hawkeswell could see how it might. Castleford would not want Lady Rawsley *too* grateful. "About those mines of yours. Do you have many?"

"During the war, only one. It came with the estate. However, I have been buying more."

"Indeed? The demand for iron is much decreased the

last two years. The value of my wife's legacy is a shadow of its former self."

"It is true that the demand has radically decreased. That is how I buy the mines so cheaply."

"Are you expecting another war?"

"I am expecting the effects of war without a war. Hawkeswell, you are not a stupid man. Far from it. I think that you know that your family fortune was ruined by two things. One was your father's uncanny consistency in losing when he gambled. The other was your family's adherence to land alone as the source of income."

Hawkeswell knew the limits of landholding better than most. He did not need anyone's instruction on that.

Castleford bent his head closer. "Hold on to that ironworks, my friend. Keep it solvent even if you have to sell your soul. In ten years the demand for my mines' ore and your mill's furnaces will make our current fortunes appear small."

He reached for the port, and called to another friend, dropping the subject as quickly as he had started it.

Chapter Twenty-three

Thinking back over the evening on the way home, Verity hoped the dinner party a success. While the very best people might disapprove of her as a countess, or pity Hawkeswell for having had to stoop so low, they could nevertheless be generous and gracious to one's face at least, and keep the gossip for another time.

The night created a euphoria, which gave her confidence, which helped her to make a decision while her maid brushed out her hair.

She put on a new undressing gown that she had commissioned. Made of the thinnest lawn, so fine and soft that it flowed like silk, it depended on its exquisite white fabric rather than embellishments for its beauty. Colleen had thought it too plain, much as some people always think the flowers with single petals less beautiful than the fuller blooms.

She reached up to unclasp the pearls, but thought better of it. He liked when she wore them. He had commented on it this evening in the coach. He thought they enhanced her appearance. No, that was not what he had said at all. He had said that she enhanced the pearls' beauty, which was an odd way to put it.

She dismissed her maid, and gently rapped on the door to Hawkeswell's dressing room. Hawkeswell opened it, and through the door she saw Drummund departing the other way.

"I did not mean to intrude," she said. "If you are still with your valet, I will—"

"Come in. I have only to wash, and we can talk about the dinner if you like."

She sat in one of the chairs. He stripped off his shirt and turned to the basin that Drummund had already prepared. Using soap and rag, he began to wash.

The lamp's glow flattered him, and she admired his strong back, and the way he moved in completing this simple chore. Arousal purred in her, while her gaze lingered on his shoulders and the lean sculpting of his arms and torso.

"I do want to talk to you, but not about the dinner."

He reached for a towel and dried his face. He turned to her while he buffed the water off his chest and arms. "I am listening."

"I have a favor to ask. I want something from you."

"Somehow, from your expression, I do not think it is a new gown."

"No. Nothing material."

"Of course not. That would be too easy. I am not going to like this request, am I?"

What could she say? No, he would not. He already knew that. His question had not been necessary. His eyes had darkened the way they did when he was not pleased. His gaze had turned serious.

"I see that you are still wearing the pearls. That means I am really not going to like this." He laughed a little.

She stood and walked over to him. A few beads of water still glistened on his chest. She dotted her finger on them, lifting them one by one. "You said that they make you forget yourself."

"Actually, I said that the way they look above your naked breasts makes me forget myself." He took her hand, and laid her palm flat on his skin. "If you intend to ask for something that I will not like, you had better use all your feminine wiles, Verity."

"What if I do not have sufficient wiles?"

"You underestimate yourself."

She was not sure that she had sufficient wiles, unfortunately. Even at her boldest, she was not very bold.

She kissed his chest, at the spots where those drops of water had been. Then she stepped back. Her fingers worked the buttons on her undressing gown. The lovely white fabric parted, showing skin from neck to stomach. The edges fluttered at the sides of her breasts.

He made no move to embrace her. She realized he expected her to do the rest, not him. Stirring deeply now, tightening from her own touch, she eased the white cloth off her shoulders and let it fall in a soft drop until it pooled at her feet.

He lightly stroked along the curve of pearls, then in a lower arc on her chest.

"You wanted me to do that myself," she said.

"Yes. But leave the pearls on."

"Are you going to tell me what else you want me to do, or must I ponder it out myself?"

"If I tell you, you may feel obligated, in order to get what you want."

"I will do nothing under obligation. That is not my nature."

He smiled in agreement, while his fingertips skimmed lower, lower. "Then I will tell you and show you and you can choose which favor you will grant. And I will see if I can convince you to grant them all."

Her ultimate request had already faded in importance. The erotic expectations occupied her mind now, and the way he gazed at her body and those pearls, and that skimming touch, so luring and exciting.

She did not require any instruction in a few things. She could continue taking the initiative at the beginning at least. She moved closer and laid her hands high on his chest. She kissed the skin in front of her, then his neck, then his lips.

His hands cupped her bottom and pulled her close, hard against him so her breasts pressed his chest and his erection prodded her stomach while he claimed her mouth in a hard, thrilling kiss. Furious and hot, he tasted with mouth and tongue, then moved to her neck and pulse, her chest and breast, all the while holding her harder, his hands grasping her bottom, even as they caressed, his hardness hot against her until in her spinning excitement she wanted to feel him and release her hunger the same way he did.

She caressed down his back, and around the top of his trousers to the front. Finding the buttons, she worked at them until the fabric sagged. Impatient now, she pushed it down, then his small clothes, to free his nakedness too. She dropped to her knees and pushed lower yet, uncovering his legs.

He looked down at her, his expression severe and his eyes burning. His whole body was taut and so was hers. Taut and alive and sensitive. Already anticipation created a compelling, delicious pleasure of desire.

She helped get the trousers off his feet.

"You look so beautiful there. So erotic," he said, watching her. "Pale. Bejewelled. Ready."

Yes, ready. She stood, with some difficulty. Her body was interested in other things besides holding her upright.

His fingertips circled her neck from nape to throat, toying with pearls and skin. They followed the drop of the largest, central pearl to the top of her breasts, then teased in paths around the swells, closer and closer to her two hard nipples. The chant of urges and begs began in her head like it always did when she was ready. She had always been weak against the cravings he could make her feel.

"I must try another wile, I think," she said. "This one?" She closed her hand around his erection. His reaction tensed through him.

She circled the tip with her thumb, then used both her hands to caress. His own touch grew less gentle, and he rubbed her nipples until the sensation grew so intense he might have been rubbing the flesh hidden by her mound.

"What is it you want?" he asked.

"You, inside me soon," she said. It was getting harder to stand. Harder to breathe or speak.

"I meant what is the favor you want? The request?"

She glanced down at her hands. She must be better at this than she thought, if he was capitulating so early. "I expected to need a few more wiles." And it may be better if she did, no matter what he asked now.

He cupped her head in his hands and looked at her intensely. "There are things I want from you, and that I want to do to you, and I do not want you to agree because of such things. Whatever it is you are requesting, it is yours. There is no need to give me pleasure for that reason now."

"You do not even know what it is."

He nodded. She embraced him tightly, and kissed him hard. "I am fortunate indeed to have a husband whom pleasure makes so agreeable."

She received a savage kiss in response, and an embrace so encompassing that his arms surrounded her. One hand gently squeezed her bottom, then followed the line of her cleft suggestively, finally finding those sensitive lips. She almost cried with joy at the feeling, and after two subtle strokes madness started closing in.

"Touch me again," he muttered in her ear. "Caress me again."

She did, taking pleasure in the wildness she felt straining at his control. "Is this all you wanted me to do? It was already yours."

"Not all," he said between feral kisses.

"What, then?"

"Your mouth, if you are willing."

That made no sense, and yet she understood what he meant. "That sounds very scandalous."

"Some think it is. I have shocked you." He kissed her hard. "Pay it no mind. Come, off to bed with you." He lifted her in his arms, carried her into his chamber, and laid her on the bed.

She waited while he dimmed the lamp, watching his body in the deepening golden wash of light. His dark hair hung recklessly around his head now. He came back to the bed while she still pondered his request. She eyed the object of his fascination.

"Perhaps . . ." she said.

"Perhaps?"

"Is it something ladies do?"

He got into bed. "Not most, I don't think so. Some do."

"The kind that go to orgies and such?"

"Others too. Some. Think nothing of it. I should have waited five years if I mentioned it at all."

"I may have only found the suggestion very funny in five years. It may be the sort of idea that it is best to strike at while the iron is hot."

"That was my thought on it. However—"

"Here is why I hesitate, other than the oddness of the notion." She looked down at the object under discussion. "It just seems that it would make more sense, and be less odd, if I knew it tasted good."

He covered his eyes with his hand and laughed. "I really can't help you there. I do not know."

She gave his erection a poke. "Do you have any wine in this apartment?"

He uncovered his eyes, startled and encouraged. "I have port."

"I like port."

He was gone at once, and soon returned with a glass and a decanter of port. He poured her some. She sipped it, and gestured to the bed. He lay down again.

She dribbled the port down his chest and loins, and made sure a goodly amount covered the area she wanted. Some of it dripped down his sides to stain the sheets.

"Oh, dear. Drummund will be furious."

"Drummund be damned." He reached to grab her.

She slapped his arms away. "Don't move. I don't want all that port on me, and it might ruin the pearls. Just lie there and hope I do not do this wrong or lose my nerve."

He placed his hands behind his head. "Do your worst. I will survive."

She thought him very brave. She rose up on her hands and knees and lowered her head to lick the wine off his chest. A good deal covered his flat nipples, and he seemed to like that part. Her tongue flicked and flicked down the rivulet of dark liquid, to his abdomen, tense now, so very tense. When she arrived at his erection, it seemed a natural thing to just flick more. She tasted, and tasted again, and Hawkeswell muttered a curse of euphoria.

H e was doomed.
   That thought entered Hawkeswell's head while he lay in weightless contentment with Verity in his arms.

Doomed. He did not give a damn right now, but even the blissful aftermath of the finest climax that he had experienced in memory could not keep the truth at bay forever.

He took some satisfaction that he had in no way coerced her to experiment tonight. He had promised her anything she wanted before she agreed.

Only now, anything could be . . . anything.

Worse, she was aware, he was certain, that she had just discovered a great secret to getting whatever she ever wanted, again and again, for as long as she lived.

He could not shake the notion that he had just ceded some critical ground in a battle that he was not even sure he was fighting.

She was wide-awake, but content in her own way. Not the most important way, however. Not the way he needed her content. He would take care of that soon, when he had recovered. Already his body was finding the notion appealing.

He fingered the strands of pearls, and admired their soft glow above her lovely breasts.

"What is the favor? The request?"

She bit her lower lip, and thoughtfully watched his fingers from beneath her lowered lids. "I will not hold you to your promise. It was not freely given."

"I was in no way tricked, and do not need any excuses. Now, what is it?"

"I need your help in something. As a lord, you know people and can obtain answers that I cannot. I need you to help me learn what became of Katy's son."

"Michael."

"Yes."

"You want me to find Michael."

He did not get truly angry, but his mood sharpened and the bliss died. Of course she would want to know what had happened, he told himself. It meant nothing. This Michael was no rival.

Another voice from deep within, from his soul, reminded him that she had been born for Michael or a man like him, and that she had never really wanted the Earl of Hawkeswell.

The odd part, the hardest part and even the most surprising part, was just how sad that other voice felt as it acknowledged the truth behind all the pleasure, no matter how glorious it may be in passing.

A good deal of anger emerged with that admission. More than he expected. It carried pain within its resentment. He looked at the pearls threading through his fingertips, and the snow white of her skin, and her delicate profile, and in his weakness of the moment he could not ignore the source of his reaction.

Little Verity Thompson, the ironworker's daughter, had stolen his heart, and he was condemned to love her in vain.

Doomed. Far worse than he had imagined.

"Good news or bad—I just want to know what became of him. Even if the truth is that he is dead."

"And if he is not? What then? Will you also want me to obtain his freedom, or bring him back to Oldbury?" The anger wanted to roar now, in defiance of his weakness. It wanted to block out the thick sorrow weighing like lead in his chest.

She turned on her side and looked at his face. "I am sorry I asked it. But it's not just a matter of Michael. . . . I believe others may have suffered the same fate." She told him an odd theory about Bertram and Cleobury and others, maybe even Albrighton, making men disappear. When she was finished, she kissed him. "I have no proof, of course. I know it's unfair to ask this of you."

Yet she had. She had trusted that he was better than he was.

He arranged the pearls, so they were high on her neck. He reached past her to the table that held the glass of port. "I am thinking that I should do for you as you did for me."

She frowned as the liquid dripped on her breasts. Her gaze followed the path he made down her body, and reflected growing surprise. She appeared relieved when he stopped at the top of her mound. He set the glass back on the table.

He swirled his tongue through the port on her breast. "Lie as I did, and just take it."

She set her hands behind her head. The position arched her back so her breasts rose high.

"Spread your legs," he said. She obeyed, completing the erotic image he had in his mind.

He gave her pleasure with his mouth and tongue, but he gave himself as much at least. Little anger remained in him now, just a small vestige that imbued the pounding desire with a ruthless edge. He tasted slowly, savoring skin and wine and scent and her cries. He worked his way down, as she had, determined to have what she had agreed was his, especially since he never would possess all that he wanted.

She startled when he did not stop where the wine ended, but instead kissed her mound. "But you did not—"

"I did not want to ruin it." He caressed high between her thighs gently so that the pleasure would defeat her shock. "I promise you will like it." He lured with his hand as well as his words, using sensation to overcome her misgivings.

She rocked against his hand and closed her eyes. Instinctively, almost imperceptibly, she parted her legs more. He positioned himself so the musk surrounded him.

The devil entered him then. He brought her along slowly, teasing her until she groaned. He maddened her until she cried out again and again, and finally begged for more. For relief. For him.

She came hard, thrashing, screaming. That strained his own control. Howling with a chaos of hungers both physical and darker, he rolled off the bed and pulled her to its edge and set her feet on the ground.

He turned her and bent her so her bottom rose in offering. She looked back at him, startled again despite the reveries of her release. He didn't give a damn about that now, only the unbearable effect her erotic position had on him. Teeth gritting, jaw tight, he pushed her back lower until she submitted the way he wanted her, with her arms and head on the bed and her bottom rounded and high, and her vulva visible, pink, and wet.

He caressed until she shivered with need, then entered her hard. He held her hips and thrust again and again until he released all angers and hungers in his body and soul.

Chapter Twenty-four

Hawkeswell rode his horse down the Strand, having spent two fruitless days looking for Michael Bowman.

He had passed many hours in clerks' offices looking at dusty books of records, only to find nothing. Michael had not been transported; that was clear. Nor sent to the hulks. Nor tried in an assize court. Nor, the best that he could tell, did Bowman stand at the Quarter sessions in Shropshire, Staffordshire, or Worchestershire, although those records were secondary, the complete ones being in the counties themselves.

It appeared, on the face of it, that the young man had simply taken off to seek his fortune elsewhere. It was an explanation that Hawkeswell would be happy to accept.

He remained lost in his thoughts as he neared the western end of The Strand. The appearance of another horse near his own flank jolted him alert.

Bertram Thompson paced his horse into place beside

him. Beaver hat high and blue coat crisp, Bertram took the place as though he had a right to be there.

"I need to talk to you, Hawkeswell. You have not replied to my letters."

"I have been ignoring your letters. I would think that my intention not to see you was clear, Thompson. Have you been following me all about town just to waylay me like this?"

"I had no choice. I have been approached by some gentlemen regarding the works. I am unable to reply to them until you consider their offer."

"There has been an offer for the works?" He had no choice but to stop his horse then, and move it to the side of the Strand.

Bertram followed, smugly satisfied that he had at least managed to make Hawkeswell pause in his tracks. "A very handsome offer."

"It is not for sale. I have the use of that property, and its income, but it is still owned by Verity. A judge would want assurance that she freely agreed to sell it before permitting such a thing. I am sure she would never so swear."

"The offer is not to purchase the works. It is to lease it."

Hawkeswell knew all about leasing land, but was out of his depths when it came to leasing a business. He did not intend to let Bertram know that.

"How much do they offer?"

"An average of the income from the last five years, minus fifteen percent. What with the variable demand for the iron now, and the decrease in orders overall, the security of this amount per annum has great appeal."

It certainly did. It would have more appeal if the five

years being averaged did not include the worst years in the works' history. Even so, only a fool would not give serious thought to an offer that removed the essential gamble inherent in any business off the table.

"How long is this lease?"

"Fifty years."

Fifty years of dependable income, unless the new managers were idiots, in which case they would go bankrupt and the lease would be broken. He could not deny the attraction of this offer, and Bertram's knowing smile said he saw as much.

"And you, Thompson? What will you do if this occurs?"

"I've other interests to pursue; don't you worry. I will not mind leaving that house and that hill and all that trouble. Should I be having them draw up the papers, so we can see just what the particulars are?"

Fifty years. He'd be dead by the time this lease ended. With the security of that income he could take care of his properties and responsibilities with an ease that would never be possible if he had to wait year by year to see what profits were made.

Of course, Verity would be horrified if he signed such papers. Furious. Her memories, her life, were anchored there, and such a lease would require she sever those ties in ways the current arrangement did not. He could never ask that of her. He did not even want to.

"There is little point in having them write the papers. We will not be leasing."

Bertram's disappointment expressed itself as an astonished sneer. "*No?* It is a most handsome offer."

"No."

"Let me explain in ways you might understand, milord.

Say you have farms leased to sheepherders. You get the rent no matter if the sheep live to be shorn or they die." He gestured broadly, to emphasize how obvious this was, and how he should not have to point it out. "The finances of the country are such that the works may not produce much wool, as it were. Better to let others take the risk on the sheep's health. It is the only prudent choice."

"You imply that I am either imprudent, or stupid. I merely have more faith in English industry than you do. As do the men who made you this oddly generous offer."

Bertram pulled his reins and pivoted his horse hard. "You know nothing of such things. I am doomed to be tied for life to an idiot."

"Idiot I may be, but I do not see the benefit of paying fifteen percent to obtain proper management. A good man costs far less. Mr. Travis and others spoke well of a young man named Michael. Better to have him back, to aid Mr. Travis so more special work for machines can be taken on."

"Damnation, will no one hear me when I say that he is gone? He will not be back. If you insist on putting any faith in that notion, we will all die poor."

He seemed very sure of that. Thompson knew that Michael's disappearance was permanent, Hawkeswell felt certain.

"I'll be having the papers drawn anyway and sent to you. I pray that you will seek counsel from men who are more familiar with such affairs and that they talk sense to you."

Thompson trotted away. Hawkeswell waited a few minutes, then aimed his own horse in the same direction.

Verity's cousin could encourage these men in their pursuit of the works all he wanted, but no lease would be signed. Verity deserved better, and Hawkeswell could not bear to see her sorrow and disillusion if he agreed to this.

Nor would he seek the counsel of men more familiar with business. He had already been advised on the matter, by a man who almost always won when he gambled, and whose wealth stood as testimony to his family's unfailing skill at amassing filthy lucre.

Do not lose control of that works. Such advice, given while Castleford was at least half-sober, could not be taken lightly.

"It has been some time since you have called on him privately, I gather," Summerhays said as he rode beside Hawkeswell.

"Yes. I also feel stupid making a morning call in the morning. He is sure to burn our ears for this."

"There is no choice. If we do not want to wait until Tuesday, we must come early, before he starts . . . doing whatever it is he chooses to do."

"Whoring, you mean."

"It is more likely that he was whoring last night. There may be women there."

"Oh, joy. I cannot wait."

"You are asking a favor, Hawkeswell. It won't do to be too particular."

"I am asking for his insights into the darker side of humanity, not a favor. What if he is not even awake yet? Hell, it isn't even ten o'clock."

"If he is not awake, we wait."

Hawkeswell stopped his horse. "*You* can wait. *I* do not wait. He may be Castleford, but I am Hawkeswell. My family counseled kings when his were nothing more than yeomen hoping to better themselves. Hawkeswell waits on royalty, and no one else. Certainly not parvenus like the house of St. Ives."

"My apologies. I meant to say, if he is not yet awake, you can leave and *come back on Tuesday.*"

They handed their horses to one of three periwigged grooms in front of Castleford's house. Hawkeswell gazed up the façade. "Look at this monstrosity. It is bigger than Somerset House, and Prussian from its foundations to its cornices. His grandfather knew no restraint. A trait that runs in the family."

"Rather like indebtedness runs in yours."

"Thank you, Summerhays, for the reminder that we all have our failings. You cannot know how that improves my humor."

A butler bedecked in livery and wig put them in a reception hall, took their cards, and departed. Hawkeswell cooled his heels, certain that Summerhays had erred badly in suggesting they come here to see if Tristan's besotted brain could see a way out of the logjam that had developed in trying to find Michael Bowman.

Not that he really wanted to find Bowman, damn it. If he ever did, Verity would probably weep with joy and throw herself into the young man's arms, and maybe even start an affair forthwith. Her father would bless the illicit union from the grave.

"What are you snarling at?" Summerhays asked.

"Fate. Passion. The stupidity of life."

The butler returned. The duke, they were informed, would receive them in his apartment.

Up the palatial staircase they trod. Into a huge sitting room, then through a dressing room of ridiculous size that sported more gold ormolu than was decent for a man. The butler escorted them right into the bedroom and left them standing beside the massive, silken-draped bed.

Propped up in it on at least twenty pillows, drinking coffee, still naked from the night's debauch under those sheets, lounged Castleford. Fortunately, no whores were currently with him.

"Good of you to agree to see us," Summerhays said.

"I almost didn't. I am exhausted. Be quick with it, will you, so I can get some sleep."

Hawkeswell peered down at that naked chest and mussed hair. "Do you expect us to stand here in front of your extreme and insulting dishabille like servants, watching you break your fast, *Your Grace*? Bloody hell, put on some clothes at least."

Castleford looked up lazily. He turned his gaze on Summerhays. "What is wrong with him, to get him all puffed up like he holds a bad wind that needs farting?"

"Fate. Passion. The stupidity of life."

Castleford drank some coffee. "In other words, he has fallen in love."

"Summerhays, please leave. I am going to strangle our old friend and do not want any witnesses."

"Stop being an ass, Hawkeswell. I think it is charming that you are in love with your errant little wife. It is unfashionable, but very touching." He set aside the tray, and gestured to some chairs. "Now, why have you disturbed me? It had better be an entertaining reason."

Forcing his annoyance to a low rumble, Hawkeswell grabbed a chair and set it near the damned bed. Summerhays did as well.

"We are wondering if you would turn your mind to nefarious calculations, which is a talent you on occasion exhibited in our distant past," Hawkeswell said. "Let us assume that men of consequence wanted someone gone. Disappeared and impossible to track. How might they do that?"

Castleford shrugged. "The easiest way is to kill him, of course. The problem with that is the danger of a body being found. More serious is your use of the word *men*. Plural. Murder is best done by one person, so there is no accomplice to sing later and get you hanged, or to blackmail you."

"Thought about this a bit already, have you?" Summerhays asked.

"In passing."

"And if, for the reasons you give, murder was not the chosen path?" Hawkeswell asked.

Castleford thought that over. "Ten years ago, I'd have him impressed and shipped to the West Indies. That might not work now. There are too many hands available with the war's end, and no need for a captain to take on the trouble."

"Since we are talking postwar, that is probably out."

"In that case, I would stick him on one of the hulks."

"There has been no arrest. No trial or conviction."

"Those ships are full of corruption of the body, soul, and law. The masters and gaolers can be bought. Imagine that you or I brought a boat alongside at night, and told the gaoler we had a convict with us and passed him up, along with a nice purse. Do you think he would be overly particular about the identity of the fellow, or why a peer had sailed him over without any papers?"

"If he were at all particular, it would be a disaster."

"Fine, be a coward. Then just switch your fellow with a real convict. If he protests he is not the real Tommy Thief, who will listen?"

Summerhays froze. Hawkeswell stared at Castleford, who blandly gazed back. "Can I strangle him now, Summerhays?"

Summerhays sighed. "Tristan, you have misunderstood. *We* are not going to make a man disappear."

"You said men of consequence. I just assumed—"

"We are looking for a man *others* may have caused to disappear."

"I see. That is more boring, but not without interest."

"I am relieved we have not become totally boring in not being criminals, but only somewhat," Hawkeswell said.

"I still say you should look to the hulks. It isn't as if anyone wants to know what really goes on there."

"He has a point," Summerhays said. "It may be worth a try. I can have a barrister go to the King's Bench and obtain a writ to allow us to search the hulks and—"

"Such tedious legalities," Castleford said with a groan of impatience. "Hawkeswell and I will just *do it*. None of these men will stand against an earl and a duke and ask for writs. You can come too, if you promise not to act too much like the member of the Commons that you are." He grinned with delight at Hawkeswell. "We must be sure to bring our swords."

Hawkeswell was dumbfounded by Castleford's assumption that he would join them. Summerhays was too, for a moment.

"Regrettably, Castleford, this cannot wait for next Tuesday," Summerhays said.

"He is correct," Hawkeswell agreed. "I must go two days hence, and trust your advice was wise. I will bring my sword as you suggest, however, and brandish it a bit in your honor."

"Two days hence?"

"Early morning."

"Eight, I think," Summerhays said. "No, actually, seven would be best." He stood. "You have been very helpful. We will leave now, so you can return to your sleep."

They almost made good their escape, but Castleford's voice caught them at the door.

"Seven will be a hellish time, but I expect you will need my yacht. I'll be damned if I am going to provide both the plan and the yacht and miss the fun. I will see you at the docks."

Chapter Twenty-five

Hawkeswell's mood remained surly the rest of the day and most of the next. He almost wrote to Summerhays and Castleford to call off the adventure at the hulks.

While his mind built excuses having to do with those tedious legalities Castleford hated, the thickness in his chest, so similar to what he felt when anticipating bad news, told the truth of it. No matter what Verity claimed, he did not believe that a reunion between her and this girlhood friend would be a small thing.

As his mood darkened, his imagination did too. He parsed through everything Verity had ever said about Oldbury, about Katy, about Bowman, and even about her reasons for running away.

He saw his willingness to believe she had been so bold because of her anger at being hoodwinked, and concluded that he had been an optimistic, dimwitted fool. His initial suspicions were more likely, that she had run off to elope with another man. He remembered his certainty that Katy Bowman had assumed that as well.

Well, Verity could not do that now. That path was closed. And yet, her emotions could never be constrained by law. That was the heart of it, he admitted dismally the afternoon before visiting the hulks. Right now he could forget the suspicion most of the time, and know some joy with her. If he had proof that another man had her heart, he did not think that would continue.

He was accommodating that miserable notion, thoroughly distracted by it, when he almost walked past Summerhays in Brooks's without seeing him. Only the sound of his own name brought him out of his reverie to find his friend right by his side.

"Has someone died? You look like it," Summerhays said, kicking out a chair in welcome.

He sat, and refused the offer to call for some brandy. "I am thinking about the morning."

"I do not believe it is concern with the vague authority you will wield that distracts you."

"Hardly."

Summerhays scrutinized him long and hard. Then he smiled a smile that often tamed the world to his command. "Early in my marriage, you gave me some advice. Should I now return the favor?"

"Early in your marriage, I was ignorant of marriage. That was my only excuse for not being more considerate of your jealousy."

"And yet, for a marriage that was not a love match, it was good advice, was it not? That affairs were inevitable, and I would be an ass to expect otherwise."

"Yes, good advice. I am so damned wise I can't stand myself."

He stared at nothing while he found some small solace in that wisdom. It lessened the restless ill ease, but
that thickness remained, dull now, and preparing for the
worst.

"I suppose I won't kill him if I am right," he said.

"That is good of you. Her past with him does not signify now, and you have no way of knowing the future."

Except the past did signify, and would affect the future.
He was sure of it. What Verity chose to do with her body
was the least of it too.

The dullness pervaded him the rest of the day. That
night it made the pleasure he experienced poignant. He
made love to her slowly, carefully, and thoroughly, savoring each taste, urging her to find release after release in
a long series of ecstasies. Only at the end did fury at his
powerlessness join his gentler emotions.

He bent her legs high and braced himself above her
and watched the way he joined with her and how passion
transformed her face. With each thrust his head and body
and blood angrily chanted *mine*, as if this power alone
could brand her heart and soul.

He astonished her. She did not think he could anymore, but he managed to this night. The pleasure
began sweetly, like trickles into her blood and down her
body. The way he handled her, as if she were a precious
treasure, wrenched her heart.

He lured her, and seduced her so completely that when
he turned hard and commanding at the end, when his
body claimed and his eyes compelled and he demanded
submissions she did not understand, she had no defenses
left. In the aftermath she lay beneath him, raw and sore

and so full of everything about him that she could barely breathe.

She ached from the void when he rolled away.

"I will be gone when you wake," he said. "I must do something early tomorrow."

She thought such practicalities odd things to speak of now. The night called for other words. Soft words and promises. She had stepped off a precipice, into mystery and wonder, and his voice set her feet on solid ground again.

"And I will be gone when you return. I am meeting my friends out of town. Daphne has arranged for us to visit Mr. Banks at Kew, and tour the private gardens there."

"Why don't you stay a few days with your friends too," he said while he sat and reached for his robe. She had not realized he would leave her bed so soon. When he spoke of being gone when she woke, she thought he meant from her side.

"I would like that. I could bring them home to Cumberworth, then send the carriage back here."

"The Rarest Blooms, all together once more. You will enjoy it. I will see you in several days, then, if not before."

He kissed her, and that sad sweetness moved her again, beckoning her, as it had with his first touches tonight. It was in him, she realized, flowing to her on the kiss.

"You forgot your sword," Summerhays observed.

"I do not need a sword to impress a gaoler. Castleford may need one, but I do not." He gazed at the impressive yacht being prepared by a crew of ten. "We are only going downriver, not sailing to France."

"It is sure to impress the officers on the hulks. For Castleford's sake, that is."

"He has two minutes to get his sodden ass here, or I am taking that yacht without him." He was in no mood to delay this even that long. Having determined that he would allow maudlin emotions to cause him to do the right thing by Verity despite his own best interests, he did not want to contemplate his own insanity any longer.

"Here he comes." Summerhays squinted down the pier. "Damnation, he is not alone."

No, he was not. He strode forward merrily, a woman under either arm and a bottle of wine in one hand.

"They cannot come," Hawkeswell said as soon as Castleford was at the dock.

"Of course they can. It is my yacht. In you go, pretty doves." He handed them down to a crew member who swung each aboard with unseemly flourish. "They learned I was sailing this morning and wanted to come, and I so enjoy a woman's gratitude," he explained.

He appeared sober enough, but Hawkeswell pried the wine bottle out of his hand anyway.

Castleford allowed it. "You forgot your sword," he said, patting his own.

"It appears I did. Fortunately for you."

"Gentlemen, let us be off," Castleford announced to the crew. "We set sail for mystery and adventure. Get us under way. Unfurl the main sail, et cetera, et cetera."

The whores thought him witty and brilliant. He thought himself so too. Summerhays sighed and hopped on board. Hawkeswell followed with more misgivings than he liked.

"No point in the sail, my lord," a crew member said. "It is too calm, so it will have to be oars."

"It is a good thing there are ten of you, then." Castleford removed his sword, lounged on a divan set under a sun canopy, and beckoned the women to join him.

Summerhays positioned himself as far away from that divan as possible, and looked out to the river with an oddly stoical face.

Hawkeswell joined him. "You think he is going to swive those two right in front of us, don't you?"

"I think that he is annoyed we did not wait until Tuesday to do this, and will prove his right to go to hell on his own schedule, no matter what our plans. Expect an invitation to join in."

"I trust he will at least wait until we are on the way back. We don't want to pull up against a hulk full of convicts while the show is in progress. There could be a riot."

Summerhays glanced over his shoulder. "It appears that any hope for discretion and good sense is, as always, wasted on him."

Feminine giggles and squeals filled the air. Hawkeswell kept his gaze to the river, and contemplated the non-existent legality of barging onto a series of disgusting hulks, demanding the right to search for Michael Bowman.

Chapter Twenty-six

"I do not know why he needs this bloody entourage. He is an ironworker, probably a radical, and we found him on a damned hulk," Castleford said. "More to the point, I don't know why I am part of this bloody entourage."

"You fell asleep as soon as we left the Home Office. We could not wake you for all our trying, so here you are," Hawkeswell said.

Castleford scowled and looked out the window again. "Three coaches, all with escutcheons. We look like a damned royal wedding. Why did Summerhays bring Wittonbury's?"

"He is collecting his wife and slipping off to Essex for a while."

"And why are you in here with me, instead of in your own coach?"

"Because I much prefer your company to that of our new friend."

The explanation appeased Castleford. It made perfect sense to him that his company was preferable to just about anyone's. He yawned a few times, folded his arms, and got comfortable. "So why isn't Summerhays here too, instead of his own coach, also enjoying my company?"

"Because, Your Grace, when you sleep, you sprawl. You toss. You flail. You take up the space of three men. Summerhays could not move to his own carriage fast enough."

Hawkeswell assumed Castleford would now return to his nap, and sleep until the last sorry chapter in the current drama was finished. Instead he grinned.

"Sidmouth's expression was amusing when we hauled Thompson in by his cravat." He imitated the Home Secretary's bug-eyed, gape-mouthed reaction to their intrusion.

Summerhays had wanted to be more decorous. Hawkeswell just wanted to be done with it. Castleford had decided that Hawkeswell's indifference tilted the decision to his preference for storming the Home Office much as they had boarded that hulk.

They had pushed past clerks and junior ministers and ignored the objections of various functionaries. They strode into Sidmouth's office this morning, with a horrified Bertram Thompson hustled along between them.

Without ceremony Hawkeswell had told Sidmouth to sit and listen. Then, on command, Bertram, who had somehow come to believe that his only choices were either confess or die, had poured out a tale of vigilantism that was violent enough to chill an Englishman's soul.

"I was annoyed that Sidmouth mentioned having his suspicions confirmed," Castleford said. "That was pride and conceit speaking. He did not want to admit that we had discovered a plot that he missed."

Actually, Verity had discovered the plot. If not for her tenacity regarding the missing Michael Bowman, Cleobury and the others might have made men disappear forever.

"I believe Sidmouth had suspicions. I think he has a man there, trying to make sense of things. I met him. It is none other than Albrighton."

"Albrighton? I'll be damned. He is back?"

"Yes. Living a country squire's life up in Staffordshire."

"How boring. He must be ready to put a pistol to his head."

"My thoughts exactly. Hence my suspicion that he is Sidmouth's man there. But not an agent provocateur. His role as a magistrate would make that impossible. So, then, why else?"

"Well, he won't be needed now, thanks to me."

"You are taking all the credit, I see."

"As well I should. It was my idea to look on the hulks, my yacht that got us there, my valet who cleaned up Bowman, my coats he is now wearing, and my persuasion that convinced Thompson to talk."

All of that was true, in particular the last point. Hawkeswell was not present when that persuasion was exercised yesterday, but it had been very effective.

"What did you say to him? Or do to him?"

"It worked, did it not, whatever it was?"

Hawkeswell looked at him.

Castleford looked right back. "Better me than Albrighton, is my guess."

The coach turned. Hawkeswell recognized the lane leading to The Rarest Blooms. He ignored the way his heart lurched at the realization that they had arrived.

"What is this place?" Castleford asked when the three carriages stopped. He stuck his head to the window and gave the house and its front garden a good inspection.

Hawkeswell reached for the door latch. "My wife's friends live here. Lady Sebastian's too."

"Are the friends as lovely as your wife?"

Hawkeswell paused in opening the carriage door. "Do not even think of it. I am sure that I speak for Summerhays too. These women are all like sisters to each other, and he and I will surely pay for any bad behavior on your part."

"Bloody hell, I only asked if they are lovely."

"Go back to sleep."

He stepped out of the coach. Summerhays had already gone to the door. Hawkeswell waited near the back of his own coach until Audrianna came out. She and Summerhays walked over to him.

"Goodness, this must have been an impressive parade on the road," she said, taking in the three coaches. "Verity is up in her chamber, Hawkeswell. The others are in the greenhouse."

Summerhays handed her valise to his coachman. "Why don't you come to Essex for a few days too, Grayson?" he said.

"Yes, do. I think Verity enjoyed the coast and would not mind visiting again," Audrianna said.

Summerhays smiled sadly, then looked meaningfully at Hawkeswell. "Either there or in town, I will see you soon."

They took their leave and walked toward the carriage. "Is that Castleford's coach? Why is he here?" Audrianna asked. She gazed around, frowning. "Who is that in Hawkeswell's?"

Summerhays took her arm. "I will explain on the journey, darling." He handed her into the coach, looked Hawkeswell's way again, then climbed in with her.

Hawkeswell watched the carriage roll. Then he turned his attention to the house. He took a deep breath, gritted his teeth, and walked to the door of his carriage. He looked inside.

A golden-haired young man with green eyes full of intelligence and good humor looked back, with curiosity.

Anger wanted to invade Hawkeswell. He would not allow it. He could not. God knew he could use its shield right now, but Verity deserved better. He did not want her thinking that he acted out of pique or jealousy. He wanted no misunderstandings today.

He opened the carriage door. "Come with me."

It was the best sort of autumn day, when the sun shone and a crisp, cool breeze carried seasonal scents in the window. Verity sat on the window seat of her old chamber, looking out at the garden, and the yellow leaves flying by.

Last night they had all talked forever, it seemed, with the kind of deep, intimate sharing that only women could know. She had finally told them about Bertram, and the fear, and those whippings and beatings. She could speak of it with composure only because she had already released the worst of the anger and emotion when she told Hawkeswell.

Audrianna had wept, but she was the only one who did. Daphne had always suspected, it turned out. Celia too. And Katherine—well, Katherine had understood better than any of the others, hadn't she?

Speaking of those sad years had been freeing, just as it had with Hawkeswell. Also exhausting. She had slept so soundly that the whole household had begun their day before she woke.

She needed to dress soon. Summerhays was coming for Audrianna, and the carriage from Hanover Square would probably arrive for her too. She had enjoyed her three days here, but it was time to go home.

A quiet rap sounded on the door. That would be Katherine, most likely. Katherine had stayed close during this visit, and they had formed a strong friendship. Verity called for her to enter.

The door opened, but Katherine was not on the other side of it. Hawkeswell was.

She appeared beautiful sitting by the window. The breeze caught tiny strands of hair and raised them in a gossamer dark crown. The light gave her pale skin a dewy glow. He filled his mind with the image of her there, looking so fresh and unspoiled, her hair still down and her eyes bright with welcome.

She smiled and held out her hand and he went to her. He kissed her hand and love flooded him until he could hardly contain it.

"Aren't you going to kiss me properly?" she asked. "I have spent two nights dreaming of you and your kisses."

"Of course." He touched his lips to hers. His soul shook at the contact and warmth, and from the joy she inspired in him.

He took her face in his hands and kissed more thoroughly. He savored how she enlivened and aroused him, and also the evidence of her responses.

She touched his hand as it lay on her cheek. "I will dress quickly and we can be off."

He noticed then that she was in her undressing gown, covered by a simple shawl. It gave him pause, and he wondered if he should indeed let her dress first.

He laughed at himself, but not with any humor. There was

no point, was there? It would not matter at all in the end.

He looked in her blue eyes and allowed the deepest parts of his heart to love her for a long, poignant moment. Then he mastered his emotion.

"I have a surprise for you, Verity. A special gift. One that will put you in my debt forever."

"You do?" She smiled like an excited child.

He let that smile enrapture him, while he marveled at this woman once more. She could be so innocent one moment, and so dangerously formidable the next.

He memorized the joy with which she looked at him. He branded the moment on his soul, so he might possess it forever. Then he went to the door, opened it, and gestured.

A thin, wiry young man with golden blond hair and a crooked smile walked in.

Verity's eyes widened. Her mouth gaped. "Michael!" She jumped off the window seat.

Hawkeswell turned away, left, and closed the door without looking back.

He went down the stairs and out of the house. He passed his own coach and aimed for Castleford's. Tristan had better be asleep. He needed no one to see him now. He wanted no conversation.

Deciding not to risk it, he gestured for the coachman to make room, and climbed up alongside. He felt as if someone had punched him in the middle of his body until he was weakened and bruised and short of breath. He told the coachman to return to London.

The man snapped the ribbons. The cattle stepped in unison. Hawkeswell stared blindly at their flying manes, and worked hard not to picture the reunion taking place at The Rarest Blooms.

"You are an idiot, Hawkeswell."

The insult came through the small window between the coachman and the carriage interior.

"Yes, I am. Thank you for the reminder. Now, go to sleep again."

"I know what you are up to, and it is mad. It is clear how you feel about her."

Hawkeswell groaned. He could not believe he was going to have to suffer this. "Exactly. Which means your advice is worthless. This isn't one of your whores."

"All the more reason not to be an idiot."

"I am in no mood to have a disembodied voice hurling insults at my ass for an hour. I feel like thrashing someone, so you would be wise to get your nose away from that opening."

"Thrash *me*? Hell. Stop the carriage."

Of course the coachman obeyed. Castleford stepped out and gestured silently. The coachman set aside the ribbons, climbed down, and walked to the back of the carriage to stand there. Castleford climbed up, took the ribbons, and started the horses on their way.

Hawkeswell folded his arms and stared straight ahead. Castleford had the good sense to offer nothing more than an old friend's company all the way back to London.

Verity embraced Michael like the lost friend he had been. Hawkeswell was right. This was a special gift. The very best one.

She looked past Michael to tell him so. To thank him. He was gone, however.

"Come and sit with me. I want to look at you for hours. Where did he find you?" She pulled Michael to the window seat. He dragged along, laughing.

"They had me on a hulk. Can you believe it? I'm in Lord Cleobury's cellar one day, then on a wagon, then the next thing I know it is a different wagon and it is full of convicts going south. I kept tellin' them my name, that I wasn't the man they thought, but the bastards just assumed no mistakes are ever made."

"A hulk? I hear they are terrible places."

"Terrible enough. Men die all around you." His smile fell and his eyes blanked. He suddenly appeared much older than when he walked in the room.

"Still, you look well, Michael. Thin, but otherwise not too much the worse for it."

"They cleaned me up for you. That Duke Castle was stuck with me when the other two went off somewhere." He pointed to his hair. "Does that look like hair you see in Oldbury? His valet did it to me. I'm a damned fop, I am. I'll never live it down when they see me like this back home."

They laughed at the way it was dressed, and she admired the fine coat that the duke had put him in.

"You should see his house, Veri. A palace. It is the sort of place where you are afraid to breathe. And heaven forbid you should need to fart."

They laughed some more. Then the laughter died, and they just looked at each other. She could not stop smiling. At him. At herself. At the absurd idea that, not so long ago, she was convinced that it was her duty to marry this old friend.

"You are all grown-up now, aren't ya?" he said. "You've got yourself a fine husband too."

"He is fine. The finest. He is a good man."

"If he bothered to find me, I'd say he is the best. You should have seen the three of them, walking down into that pit like the filth would part for them at their word. The captain tried to balk but that Duke Castle just touched this sword he had and stared until the captain was half his normal size. Then your earl boomed out my name. Hell, I was on my feet in a second, and for all I knew they had come to hang me."

She could picture that and had to laugh again. "You have sent word to your mother, I hope."

"Wrote to her that first night. Sent it to Mr. Travis. He'll go read it to her."

She let her heart feel the full relief that Katy would know, and her own that this had all ended well.

Michael quirked that crooked smile of his. "So, this earl of yours—does he know?"

"He knows about my first kiss. I admitted only to that, but I think he wonders if there was more."

"Best we leave him wondering, then. He looks the sort to kill a man if he's of a mind to. Though if he let me see you alone while you are dressed like that, he can't be too worried."

"He probably thinks this modest after how he has seen me."

Michael gaped in mock shock and they dissolved into giggles.

"He would never kill you, Michael, but, yes, it may be best to leave him wondering if he must. It was long ago, and we were children, but men are not very particular about the details when they get jealous, I think."

"No, we are not at that." He stood. "We should be going now, so I'll leave you to get ready. There is a very fine carriage out there, waiting to take us home in style. I'll never see the likes of it again, so I plan to stop at every coaching inn on the way and eat my fill to make up for the last two years. You'll just have to wait while I do."

"The carriage is for you alone, Michael. Not for me."

"That is not what your lord said. He even put your baggage in it. Said you'd be wanting to make sure the ironworks is in good hands too. He said—"

She was out the door before he finished. She ran down the stairs and outside. Hawkeswell's coach and four stood there, the matched bay horses almost immobile in their dignity. She frantically looked down the lane for any sign of Hawkeswell himself.

She spied her baggage atop the coach. Not one but three portmanteaus. A desperate excitement gripped her. Michael came out of the house, flashed his crooked smile, and walked over to the carriage.

Confusion and astonishment overwhelmed her. She could not believe that Hawkeswell was allowing her to visit Oldbury again so soon, and on her own, and with Michael as her escort.

She heard the door again behind her. She swerved to see Katherine standing there.

"This is for you," she said, handing over a letter. "Lord Hawkeswell found me in the kitchen, and said to give it to you."

She stared at it, and the name on the front made her breath catch. *Miss Verity Thompson*. Fear, anticipation, dread, and grief all mixed together while she unfolded the paper.

My darling,

As you can see, we found Mr. Bowman. I will write later with a fuller account of his discovery, and the larger plot as well, but for now it is enough that Katy's son has also been resurrected.

Your cousin Bertram felt moved to admit his misuse of you and his coercion on the marriage, in writing no less, amid confessing his many other sins and naming his accomplices. With that evidence and my agreement, you will have your annulment quickly when you make the petition, I am convinced. It is only right that you should.

Your maid assures me that your favorite garments are in the baggage, as are your jewels. Your cousin and his wife will not be returning to that stone house on the hill, so it is yours again. I do not doubt that the good memories will return and the bad ones will leave once its chambers are filled with your smiles.

I do not give you back your life because I have tired of you, Verity. I do not want you to think that. Quite the opposite. I have discovered, however, that my love for you means that I want you to have the life that you believe you were supposed to have, even if it means that I will not have the wife I have come to treasure.

Mr. Bowman seems a fine young man. I like him much more than I want to. I am sure that he will see you safely to Oldbury and, in doing so, spare me a difficult farewell.

Your servant,
Hawkeswell

Chapter Twenty-seven

Hawkeswell entered the library at his London house, shed his coats, and untied his cravat. The night's entertainment would have diverted any normal man, but he had found it unable to distract him. Fortunately, Summerhays and Audrianna, who had returned from Essex, were good friends and pretended their guest was not being a bore.

He went to a cabinet where spirits were stored, and poured himself a brandy. As he walked back past the writing table, he glanced at the account books resting there. They could not be put off any longer, but nothing good waited in them. He had access to a fortune right now that would rectify everything. He could help himself. However, it really was not his to use.

No word of Verity's petition had come yet, but it was only a matter of time. She had been gone ten days now, and would have settled in.

One letter had come from her, posted while she was on

her way north. It had been short, grateful, and ambiguous as hell. He had memorized it, and some nights, like this one, during hours of pretending he listened to conversations at dinners or followed the actors on a stage, he contemplated it too much.

Dear Lord Hawkeswell,

(Was the address intended to acknowledge a new distance between them, or merely the drills having their way?)

You left before I could express my eternal gratitude for your finding my dear childhood friend. Now I again have the advantage of your generosity in arranging for me to visit Oldbury.

You are too good. Far better than you know or believe. And I love you for it.

Verity.

I love you for it. He closed his eyes and saw her at the window seat that last day.

Well, it was something, this declaration of love, whatever kind of love it might be. Bold and honest too. She could have written "and you have my profound affection for it."

He was pleased she had written that. Glad that she had admitted it too. It would not change things, but it was good to share the truth of it. He appreciated knowing he had not been a total fool who had seen and sensed only what he wanted, not what was actually there.

He fully expected duty to drive her, however, not whatever love she had for him. He could not blame her. Most of his own life had been dictated and formed by duty. It would be churlish to assume those responsibilities determined his choices, but should not do the same for her.

He left the accounts for tomorrow, and moved to a sofa that faced the fireplace's low flames. The night promised to be very chilled. He would have to remember to visit the greenhouse and light the fire pots before he retired.

One of the plants had died, despite the clumsy efforts of him and the gardener. Maybe they all would before winter ended. He hoped not. He enjoyed going there, when he returned from sessions. All hell was letting loose in Parliament, and he found himself drawn to that glass house with its green plants. The echo of Verity's spirit still dwelled there, and he could indulge in a quiet nostalgia.

A booklet lay on the sofa, and he picked it up. It was a pocket map that he had used to judge her progress north. He opened it now to the page that showed the region around Oldbury.

He heard a servant enter the library through the door behind him. She had come to give the fire more fuel. He turned his head, to tell her not to bother, that he would be retiring soon.

His heart rose to his throat. No servant stood there.

Verity set down her reticule and parasol, and untied her bonnet's ribbons. She set that aside too, then fingered the closings of her spencer.

He stood and just watched her, wondering why she was here, hoping but not daring to hope at the same time.

Smiling, she walked over to him. She stood on her toes and gave him one of those bird pecks on his cheek. "You appear much as Mr. Travis did when I walked into his building that day at the works," she said. "It is truly I, Hawkeswell. I am not a ghost."

No, she was not.

She opened the spencer and pulled it off. Its absence revealed the skin of her lower neck and chest, and the many satin orbs encircling her in resplendent strands. She was wearing the pearls.

He pulled her into an embrace and kissed her hard. Too hard. Too desperately, but all his relief and gratitude was in the kiss and he could not have been gentler if he tried.

A commotion interrupted. Steps and voices on the stairs. Verity looked behind, over her shoulder. "Those would be my portmanteaus being carried up."

"You have returned to me for good, then? You have come back?"

"Yes, Grayson. I have come back. I have come home."

Verity wrapped the shawl snugly. She snuggled under Hawkeswell's embracing arm while they sat on the sofa in the library.

"You did not stay in Oldbury long," he said. "With the travel both ways, it could not have been more than four days."

"I stayed long enough to order my cousin's property packed away. Long enough to banish the bad memories from my father's house, as you advised. Also long enough to learn that Mr. Albrighton has arrested four men for being in league with my cousin. Cleobury, of course, was beyond his reach. I assume the House of Lords will try him soon enough."

She had also stayed long enough to be very sure she did not want to stay forever.

She had needed to see how that life would be before she rejected it. Michael had not been a factor at all. As soon as he walked into her chamber at The Rarest Blooms, she had known that there could not ever be a marriage between them, not even a practical one.

She could have embraced all the rest, though. She knew that she could when she walked through that house, and met with Mr. Travis. The problem, however, was that if she were Verity Thompson again, she could not be Hawkeswell's wife and lover.

She had concluded almost immediately that she could not live without him. If she tried, there would be no joy, no contentment, no passion. Since she would always love him, and never love another man, there could also be no other marriage, even if she were free.

"The House of Lords will deal with Cleobury," Hawkeswell said. "The evidence is damning."

"Mr. Albrighton found two bodies. The ones who disappeared onto the hulks were fortunate. The later ones were not." She looked up at him. "Michael told me to thank you for harrowing hell for him. He was very moved that you would bother, and thought it very noble of you."

"I did not do it to be noble."

She stretched up and kissed his cheek, then feathered her fingers on his lips. "No, you did it for me, because it mattered to me, even though you wondered why it mattered. I also know why you left us alone together, Grayson. A man must have to care for a woman a great deal to turn his back and not see, not know, when he wonders."

"Care enough to be a damned fool, you mean."

"You missed nothing that day except the joy of two old friends meeting, and a woman explaining that her husband is the finest of men and that she is very happy in her marriage."

He moved his head so he could look down at her up-turned face. "Did you really say that?"

"I did. I would have told him about the pleasure you give me, but I thought that inappropriate. I confess that I implied that you often see me naked."

He laughed. "You are a shocking woman."

"I did not tell him some things that I wanted, though. Not then, and not on our journey north. Not because they were not fit for his ears. I did not tell him because I should not speak of them to anyone before you. I want to tell others, though. My friends here, and yours. Michael and Katy. Everyone who will listen."

"What things were those?"

She kissed him again. "I want to say that I am in love with my earl, that he gives me much more than care and pleasure. That he moves my soul and awakens my heart and makes me smile. Won't our friends find that amusing, Hawkeswell? I ran away from a marriage and fought to be free, and now I am grateful that you are stuck with me."

He did not laugh. He did not even smile. He turned his body so he could look at her directly. She could see his surprise then.

"I am not good with these kinds of words, Verity. Not when it matters."

"I expect not. However, you are eloquent with your actions, Hawkeswell. Offering Verity Thompson her life back was the most loving act that I can imagine. I want you to know that you are not a damned fool. You are all that I want, and I am proud to be your countess."

He lifted her hand and held it to a long kiss, then moved the kiss to her mouth.

"I had accepted that I would love you in vain, Verity.

That although you reconciled to the marriage, your heart would always be rebellious, and you would always regret your life not being the way you thought it was supposed to be. So you have made me the happiest of men with your words."

He embraced her closely and they shared a special kiss, one poignant and heartfelt. She savored it, and felt a breeze of freedom blowing away the remnants of old hurts and resentments and questions in her heart.

She nestled in his arms, her head on his chest, in a sweet silence. It was, she decided, a timeless moment that she would make sure she remembered forever.

They may have stayed like that an hour or only a few minutes. She did not know. The intensity of the emotion did not lessen, but she accommodated it so she did not fear it disappearing if she moved.

"I suppose we will have to find someone to replace Bertram," she said.

"I expect so."

"Mr. Travis could do most of it, I am sure. Contract the work and such."

"He would not have time to work the lathes, then. He could not machine the bits."

The topic drifted away into the night. She let it go. Another day it could be found again.

"I'm told that a young man named Michael Bowman has the skill for replacing Travis in machining those bits, if we decide we trust him with that secret," he said. "Perhaps he could take over some of Travis's duties, and Travis could do most of Bertram's. If there are major decisions, he can leave them to us."

"It is one solution."

"A solution that you favor, I think."

"It would mean visiting Oldbury at least several times a year, to see how things are going there."

"I do not think that would be too inconvenient."

She tightened her embrace. Love flowed until her heart ached. He was giving her back her home yet again. She would be a steward of her father's legacy, the way it had been intended.

She had not realized that once it took root, love could grow and propagate, even after you thought it already filled you. But it did now, as they sat in front of the fire. She felt her love deepening and branching then and there, and it moved her profoundly.

"Hawkeswell, do you think the servants are well gone, above and below?"

"I expect so. Why do you ask?"

"I thought it would be better if they are, if I have wicked things in mind."

He laughed. "Please tell me that you do."

"Oh, yes, my love. I have spent hours in dreams about all the wicked things we do. Things I could never imagine wanting with any other man." She knelt on the sofa and kissed him aggressively, and let her fantasies have their way.

He lifted her skirt high and she climbed on his lap, facing him. "This is perfect," she said. "It is just as I pictured in one dream. Only I woke up before—well, before I wanted to." She parted her shawl and worked the buttons of her pelisse dress. "Isn't it convenient that this dress opens in the front?"

"Even more convenient that you have nothing on beneath it. It is no wonder that I love you. You were plotting this from when you woke."

"I was hopeful." She parted the dress as much as she

could, so her breasts were exposed to his gaze. "Touch me. Touch me the way I dreamed. Touch me and tell me that you love me, and I will tell you too. We will say it again and again today and forever, because love makes the pleasure so joyful and perfect."

"I love you, Verity. You make me joyful because you are perfect."

He told her he loved her again while his palms caressed her breasts and thighs. He told her again between deep kisses full of need and barely restrained fury. He told her right after he entered her, while relief and contentment drenched her and desire began its wonderful climb to freedom and madness.

She wrapped her arms around his neck. He grasped her hips and moved in her. Sensations intensified, and within them tiny shivers foreshadowed the ecstasy to come.

"This is so exquisite," she muttered into the crook of his neck between muffled cries. "You fill all of me, in every possible way. My senses and my heart and my body. You fill me completely, Hawkeswell."

She knew, as their fevered pleasure swept them away and their joy merged and the knowing deepened, she knew that this was how it was supposed to be.

Coming soon from *New York Times* bestselling author
MADELINE HUNTER

Celia comes into her own and discovers what it is like to be . . .

Sinful in Satin

Look for it in Fall 2010

Dangerous in Diamonds

There is only one man who could shake Daphne's composure.

Look for it in Spring 2011

The final two books in her ravishing quartet.

And don't miss the first novel in
Madeline Hunter's stunning quartet.
Read on for an excerpt from Audrianna's story . . .

Ravishing in Red

Now available from Jove Books

Chapter One

An independent woman is a woman unprotected. Audrianna had never understood her cousin Daphne's first
lesson to her as well as she did today.

An independent woman was also a woman of dubious
respectability.

Her entry into the Two Swords Coaching Inn outside
Brighton garnered more attention than any proper young
woman would like. Eyes examined her from head to toe.
Several men watched her solitary path across the public
room with bold interest, the likes of which she had never
been subjected to before.

The assumptions implied by all those stares darkened
her mood even more. She had embarked on this journey
full of righteous determination. The shining sun and un-
seasonably mild temperature for late January seemed designed by Providence to favor her great mission.

Providence had proven fickle. An hour out of London
the wind, rain, and increasing cold had begun, making her

deeply regret taking a seat on the coach's roof. Now she was drenched from hours of frigid rain, and more than a little vexed.

She gathered her poise and sought out the innkeeper. She asked for a chamber for the night. He eyed her long and hard, then looked around for the man who had lost her.

"Is your husband dealing with the stable?"

"No. I am alone."

The white, crepe skin of his aging face creased into a scowl. His mouth pursed in five different ways while he examined her again.

"I've a small chamber that you can have, but it overlooks the stable yard." His reluctant tone made it clear that he accommodated her against his better judgment.

An independent woman also gets the worst room at the inn, it seemed. "It will do, if it is dry and warm."

"Come with me, then."

He brought her to a room at the back of the second level. He built up the fire a little, but not much. She noted that there was not enough fuel to make it much warmer and also last through the night.

"I'll be needing the first night's fee in advance."

Audrianna swallowed her sense of insult. She dug into her reticule for three shillings. It would more than cover the chamber for one night, but she pressed it all into the man's hand.

"If someone arrives asking questions about Mr. Kelmsley, send that person up here but say nothing of my presence or anything else about me."

Her request made him frown more, but the coins in his hand kept him mute. He left with the shillings and she assumed she had struck a bargain. She only hoped that the fruits of this mission would be worth the cost to her reputation.

She noted the money left in her reticule. By morning she expected most of it to be spent. She would only be gone from London two days, but this journey would deplete the savings that she had accumulated from all those music lessons. She would endure months of clumsy scales and whining girls to replace it.

She plucked a scrap of paper from her reticule. She held the paper to the light of the fire even though she knew its words by heart. *The domino requests that Mr. Kelmsley meet him at the two swords in Brighton two nights hence, to discuss a matter of mutual benefit.*

It had been sheer luck that she even knew this advertisement had been placed in *The Times*. If her friend Lizzie did not comb through all such notices, in every paper and scandal sheet available, it might have escaped Audrianna's attention.

The surname was not spelled correctly, but she was sure the Mr. Kelmsley mentioned here was her father, Horatio Kelmsleigh. Clearly, whoever wanted to meet him did not know he was dead.

Images of her father invaded her mind. Her heart thickened and her eyes burned the way they always did whenever the memories overwhelmed her.

She saw him playing with her in the garden, and taking the blame when Mama scolded about her dirty shoes. She called up a distant, hazy memory of him, probably her oldest one. He was in his army uniform, so it was from before he sold his commission when Sarah was born, and took a position in the office of the Board of Ordnance, which oversaw the production of munitions during the war.

Mostly, however, she kept seeing his sad, troubled face during those last months, when he became the object of so much scorn.

She tucked the notice away. It had reminded her why she was here. Nothing else, not the rain or the stares or the rudeness, really mattered. Hopefully she was right in thinking this Domino possessed information that would have helped Papa clear his name.

She removed her blue mantle and the gray pelisse underneath and hung them on wall pegs to dry. She took off her bonnet and shook off the rain. Then she moved the chamber's one lamp to a table beside the door, and the one wooden chair to the shadows in the facing corner, beyond the hearth. If she sat there, she would immediately be able to see whoever entered, but that person would not see her very well at all at first.

She set her valise on the chair and opened it. The rest of Daphne's first lesson recited in her mind. *An independent woman is a woman unprotected, so she must learn to protect herself.*

Reaching in, she removed the pistol that she had buried beneath her spare garments.

L ord Sebastian Summerhays handed his mount to a drenched stable boy. The lad got in the long line waiting attendance by the grooms of the Two Swords.

Sebastian entered the inn's public room. A cross section of humanity huddled there beneath its open-beamed ceiling. The rain had forced riders to take refuge, and coaches had been delayed. Women and children filled most of the chairs and benches, and men arrayed themselves around the perimeter, taking turns near the fire to dry off.

That was where Sebastian stationed himself while the worst of the weather dripped off his riding coat. The odor of damp wool and unwashed bodies filled the air. A few servants did their best to salvage some silk hats and crepe bonnets, while others served expensive, unappetizing food. Sebastian cast a practiced eye on the sea of faces, looking for one that appeared suspicious, foreign, or at least as curious as himself.

The advertisement's use of a code name both annoyed and intrigued him. It would make this mission more difficult, but it also implied that secrets were involved. The notice itself, addressed to Kelmsley, indicated the writer did not know the man had been dead almost a year now.

That in turn suggested the Domino was not from London, or perhaps not even from England. Since the name was not spelled correctly, Sebastian trusted that the Domino was not a good friend or close associate of Horatio Kelmsleigh. Hopefully, the Domino did not even know what Kelmsleigh looked like.

Kelmsleigh's suicide had been unfortunate on many counts, one of which was the way it offered too easy an explanation for a mystery that Sebastian was sure had many more facets. Tonight he hoped to learn if he was correct.

"What ho, Summerhays. I did not expect to find you taking refuge along with me in this sorry way station."

The greeting near Sebastian's ear jerked him out of his search of the room. Grayson, Earl of Hawkeswell, beamed alongside him with a near empty tumbler of hot wine in hand. A smile of delight stretched beneath his blue eyes and artfully clipped black hair.

"A cloudburst caught me five miles back," Sebastian said. Hawkeswell was an old friend, and had been a close companion in his wilder days. Sebastian would normally be delighted to have his company to pass what promised to be a miserable night, but the reason for being here made

Hawkeswell an inconvenient discovery. "Are you on your way up to London, or coming down?"

"I am returning. I met with an estate agent in Brighton this morning."

"You are selling the property, then?"

"I have no choice."

Sebastian communicated his sympathy. Hawkeswell's finances had been bad since he inherited the title, and most of the unentailed property was gone. An attempt to rectify the problem through marriage had gone sadly awry when his wealthy bride went missing on her wedding day.

Hawkeswell looked around their environs. "No baggage? I trust you did not leave it on your horse. Anything of value will be stolen by morning."

Sebastian laughed lightly, and noncommittally. He had no baggage because he planned to be riding back to London tonight, and the weather and dark be damned.

"Do you have a chamber above? Is your baggage there? I asked for one, but the innkeeper has hired them all out, he says. Even my title did me no good. But if you have one, we can go smoke and drink and escape the stench down here."

"I do not have a chamber, I am sorry."

Hawkeswell's eyebrows rose above knowing eyes. "Not taking shelter at all, are you? And not heading for Brighton either, I'll wager. You are here to meet a woman. No, do not say a word. I understand the need for your elaborate dodges these days. All but the marquess now, aren't you? Can't be lifting skirts wherever and whenever anymore." He put his finger to his lips, mocking the need for discretion.

It was as good an explanation as any, so Sebastian let it stand. He remained friendly and attentive while he completed his scrutiny of all those faces. None struck him as more apt to be the Domino than any other.

Hawkeswell appeared likely to hang on all night. Sebastian needed to shake him, and decided Hawkeswell's own theory would have to do.

"You will have to excuse me. I need to speak to the innkeeper about the person I came here to meet."

He made good his escape. He found the proprietor dispensing ale to a wiry fellow with a low-brimmed brown hat.

"Was there anyone here asking about Mr. Kelmsley, or inviting inquiries about that name?"

The innkeeper peered at him, then went back to taking his customer's money. "Above, in the back, last door. The guest there would be the one you want, and I'll not be wanting to know why."

Sebastian aimed for the stairs. He wished Hawkeswell had been correct. Waiting out the weather on a feather bed, dry and cozy with some feminine warmth in his arms, would be a pleasant recompense for the miserable ride down here and the one waiting at mission's end. Instead he was stuck with duty and obligation, and a long conversation with someone known as the Domino.

Audrianna huddled beneath her shawl in the shadows. The low fire could not fight the damp chill in this chamber. That was not the only reason she shivered, however.

Her vigil was depleting the renewed resolve that she had summoned by reading that notice again. She had begun to see this plan from a different perspective, that of her entire life up until the last seven months.

From that viewpoint, her behavior today was utterly mad and inexcusably reckless.

Mama would certainly say so. Papa would have agreed. Roger would be appalled if he knew too. Proper young ladies did not ride alone on public coaches to public inns, and wait in dark chambers for unknown men to join them.

This expedition had begun to feel like a bizarre dream. She forced her nerves under control and demanded that her mind regain some of its determination.

She was here because no one else would be. The world had buried her father's good name with his body. His death had been proof enough that he was guilty of the accusations against him. Everyone assumed that remorse, not deep melancholy, had caused him to kill himself.

The whole family still wore his shame. Mama mourned the loss of friends even while she valiantly defended his memory. Even Uncle Rupert had ceased to write when the scandal broke, in an attempt to wash himself of stain by association. And Roger—well, his undying love could not surmount the scandal either.

She tried to maintain a semblance of indifference about that, but deep sorrow squeezed her heart at the thought of Roger. Eventually that would no longer happen, she trusted. At least she could take some small comfort in the knowledge that she would never be so disillusioned again. With the bad turn life had taken, no other man would ever propose.

She had told her mother that she would live with her cousin Daphne in order to mitigate the financial burdens caused by Papa's death, when the family was reduced to the income from Mama's small trust. In truth she had wanted to escape an old life stuck in the doldrums, and build a new one where she would find contentment within her changed expectations.

The crowd below created a soft din that reached her

ears. Up here on the second level all was quiet except for an occasional door closing. The silence provoked more ill ease. There were other travelers in those chambers, though. If this "Domino" attempted anything untoward, and she screamed, she trusted that aid would arrive quickly.

She pulled the shawl higher to ward off another chill. Beneath its woolen warmth, she closed her hand around Daphne's pistol. She had brought it to give her courage and so Daphne would not scold later that she had been unprotected.

Unfortunately, its weight in her hand only made her shiver again.

Sebastian pressed the latch. To his surprise it yielded. He eased open the door to the chamber.

A lamp just inside flashed its light up at him. The strong glow made the rest of the room a sea of darkness. He stepped inside so he could escape the harsh illumination. His eyes slowly adjusted.

A low blaze in the fireplace created its own sharp chiaroscuros. However, much like in paintings that exploited a similar effect, the dark began to come alive with forms and shapes the longer he gazed.

The head of the draped bed that faced the fire emerged, to join its foot that the flames bathed. Pegs on the wall beside the door showed hanging fabric. The corners of the chamber finally revealed their contents. A writing table. The hulk of a wardrobe.

A soft collection of shapes in another corner took form too, beyond the light of the fire. They gathered into something he recognized. A woman.

Her presence made him pause. He had thought the

Domino was a man. He could be forgiven that mistake, he supposed, but it had been an unfounded assumption.

The discovery that the Domino was only a woman immediately raised his spirits. He would learn what he needed to know quickly, and make short work of this meeting.

He smiled a smile that had charmed many women in his day. He walked toward the fireplace.

"Please stay there," she said. "I must insist that you do."

Insist, must she? That made him smile more. She had a young voice. Not girlish, though. Her appearance became more distinct as he focused on her.

Dark hair. Perhaps that interesting color where red shoots through the brown, like a chestnut horse's hue. Hard to judge her age, but he guessed middle twenties. Her face looked pretty, but in this light most women would be attractive. A dark shawl draped her lap and chest. Her dress appeared to be either gray or lavender, and was fairly plain from what he could see.

"I was only going to warm myself by the fire," he said. "The ride here drowned me."

Her head tipped back while she considered his explanation. "The fire then, but no closer."

He shed his riding coat. She visibly startled.

"So I can hang it to dry, if you do not mind," he explained.

She nodded.

He set it on one of the pegs. Accustomed now to the room's lighting, he could tell that the other garments there were a woman's mantle and pelisse. He took position at the fire and pretended to concentrate on its comfort, but he watched her out of the corner of his eye.

He smiled at her again while he turned his back to the warmth. She fidgeted under that shawl.

"I should warn you that I have a pistol." Her voice shook with anxiety.

"Rest assured that you will not need it."

She did not appear convinced. Green eyes, he thought. They expressed determination and some fear. The latter was a good sign. It indicated she was not stupid, and a bit of fear would be useful.

"I expected a man," he said.

"Mr. Kelmsleigh was not available, so I am here instead. I assume that you want compensation for your information, and I am prepared to pay if the sum is reasonable."

He masked his stunned reaction. She thought *he* was the Domino. Which meant she was not, of course.

He had never believed that the bad gunpowder that reached the front had been a matter of mere negligence on Kelmsleigh's part, although such negligence was bad enough to ruin a man. Instead he suspected conspiracy and fraud, and he doubted Kelmsleigh had devised and controlled the scheme. All the same, he had never expected to learn that any women were involved. Now this accomplice indicated at least one had been.

Only who the hell was she? Her identity might provide a link to the others involved in that plot.

She watched him cautiously. He could see her fear better now. She was not what he expected, but he guessed he was a surprise to her as well.

He had come here to pass himself off as Kelmsleigh. Instead someone else had read that advertisement and had come to buy information too.

He changed plans. He could not be Kelmsleigh anymore. But he could be the Domino.

Chapter Two

Oh, goodness. Oh, heavens.

This day was definitely not unfolding the way she had pictured.

She had not expected the Domino to be a gentleman. She had certainly not expected a tall, handsome, young gentleman with such a winning smile.

She was not sure what she had anticipated instead. She only knew that it was not this.

He seemed not at all concerned by her presence instead of her father's, or by her declaration of having a pistol. His manner remained amiable while he warmed himself in front of the fire. He kept flashing those brief, stunning smiles of reassurance.

They did not reassure her at all. Instead he struck her as very dangerous.

That could be due to the way the fire's light turned him into a collection of hard angles, or the way his eyes appeared much more intense and alert than his demeanor required.

It could be the result of his wealth, evidenced in the cut and make of that dark gray riding coat he had removed, and the quality of the high boots and snug doeskin that encased his legs. Even his dark hair was expensive, with the short, wispy, flyaway cut that damp and wind enhanced rather than ruined.

His appearance was the least of it, however. She could not ignore the way the atmosphere in the room had altered with his arrival, as if he gave off tiny, invisible lightning bolts of power.

"Sir, I think that we should get on with the purpose of this meeting."

"With the weather, there is no hurry. Neither one of us is going anywhere soon."

She wished that she had not allowed him to come so close. He stood no more than six feet away and towered above her. She could not ignore his size, or the way he made her feel small and vulnerable and at a bigger disadvantage than was fair.

"I would still like to finish this in good time."

One of those smiles half-formed, a private one that reflected some thought in his head. "Who are you?" he asked.

"Does it matter?"

"It may matter a great deal. For all I know, you thought I wanted to meet a different Kelmsleigh, and you will leave here with facts that you should not have. That could cause an innocent, unsuspecting man grief."

"I should say that is unlikely." Her voice sounded sharp to her own ears. He spoke as if his information would not be good news. "However, since you fear making revelations to a disinterested party, I will identify the Kelmsleigh who interests me. He was employed by the Board of Ordnance. I am hoping that your information relates to his position there."

His smile proved less amiable this time. A tad predatory, if truth be told. It could be the harsh light, of course, but—to her dismay, he stepped toward her with his attention fixed on her face.

"I insist that you stay where you are." She hated the way her demand came out a fearful bleat.

He continued toward her.

She jumped to her feet. The shawl fell to the ground. She did not aim the pistol but she gripped it soundly. "Do not come any closer. I do know how to fire this."

He halted an arm's span away. Close enough that she could see that his eyes were dark. Very dark. Close enough that if she did fire, she could not miss. He ignored the pistol and instead studied her face.

"Who are you?" he asked again.

"You call yourself something as silly as the Domino, and you demand that I reveal my name? My identity is no more important than yours."

"What is your part in all of this? Are you an accomplice? A lover? Perhaps you are a relative of one of the soldiers who died? I would not want this meeting to start a vendetta."

His gaze all but skewered her and his scrutiny unsettled her in the oddest way. For all his suspicions he kept flashing that vague, appealing smile that offered . . . friendship and . . . excitement and . . . things that she should not even be thinking about at this moment. He had the kind of face that made women silly, and it annoyed her that she was proving more susceptible than this situation should ever allow.

She raised the pistol just enough, so it did not point down but instead out from her hip. He glanced at the weapon, then his gaze was all for her face again. Only now he looked like a man who had been challenged but knew he would win the contest.

"What information do you have?" she demanded.

"How much money do you have?"

"Enough."

"How much do you think is enough?"

"I am not so stupid as to bargain against myself. Name your price."

"And if you don't have it?" He nodded to the pistol. "Do you think to force me to reveal everything, no matter what?"

Suddenly he was even closer. His body stood an inch from the pistol's barrel, and only a few more from her. She looked up at him in surprise.

Her breath caught. He appeared very dangerous now, in ways that had nothing to do with pistols . . .